TRUE MOXIE

SYLVIA BOURGEOIS

Coastwerks Press
Vancouver

––––––––––––––––––––––––––––

True Moxie is a work of fiction, but deals with many real issues including bullying, injury, and death. For more content warnings, please go to https://sylviabourgeois.com/content-warnings/

––––––––––––––––––––––––––––

Chapter 1

The day starts in the usual way — wet and windy. Rain drums on the roof and gurgles in the downspouts. I lie still, cozy under my down duvet, straining to hear the clatter of breakfast dishes downstairs. But other than the racket outside, the house is silent. Then, as the fog of sleep lifts, I remember. The raw hollow of my mum's absence envelops me. Every morning, it stops my heart and takes my breath away, like plunging into an icy lake. Even now, over six months later.

I swing my legs off the bed and onto the soft carpet before the memories hold me under the covers. Grabbing my robe, I walk across the hall to shower, then pull on a pair of faded jeans, a t-shirt, and a hoodie. Downstairs, I flip on the lights and start a pot of coffee. As the brew percolates, I open the almost empty fridge. A stick of butter on a plate. A liter of whole milk. Four eggs. A crisper full of red apples. And a two-four of lager.

After sniffing the milk, I dump the last of the granola into a bowl. Someone needs to get groceries today, but there's no movement from upstairs. A glance at the clock spurs me to hurry, packing a lunch between bites. I stack my dishes in the sink with yesterday's and pour a travel mug of caffeine. Out in the mudroom, I cram the brown paper bag next to a folder of blank university applications. I'm jerking the zipper of my backpack closed when footsteps shuffle down the stairs.

"There's coffee." I force a bright tone and look up at my dad. He's paused on the last tread, a four-day stubble and dark eye circles match his gloomy expression. "Will you go shopping? We're out of everything." I shrug on my jacket, willing him to respond. Eventually, he nods silently. On his way to the kitchen, he stops to gaze into the living room; a room we haven't entered since The Last Day. The slump in his posture tells me he won't make it to the store today.

The door slams behind me and I step out into the downpour, avoiding murky puddles in the rough gravel driveway. He needs to get his shit together. It's been long enough. If he's still in ghost mode when we start work next week, it won't go well. My throat tightens as I hurry along the faded center line. The rain blows in sheets up the asphalt road and the backs of my jeans are drenched by the time I reach the bus stop.

When the yellow school bus lurches to a halt in front of the leaning shelter, I bound up the stairs and nod at Nancy, the driver. She pulls the door shut behind me, the rowdy interior reeking of musty, wet children.

"Hey, Raptor Claw!" Robbie, a little shit in Grade 7, yells at me from the back row. The chatter on the bus suspends, waiting for my reaction. But I ignore them all and silently slide into my spot above the wheel well. I've endured twelve years of bus ride dread, but since The Worst Day, this stuff feels farther away. Big problems block out petty problems. And Robbie's taunting is definitely a petty problem.

I slouch low, my knees riding up the seat back in front of me. My hood shields my temple from the cold, fogged-up window. I rub a slow circle in the condensation, bigger and bigger, and watch the bright green salal bushes roll by outside.

At even spacing, gravel driveways interrupt the overgrown brush, giving glimpses of our neighbors' homes. I know part of everyone's story. The double-wide where I babysit on Friday nights, the parents just weeks from divorce. The giant log house where the twins and my used-to-be best friend Nora celebrate their parent's anniversary with the fervor of those deprived of birthday parties and Christmas. The sad house where Old Man Henry walks his big chocolate lab by driving beside it in a rusty maroon Oldsmobile. The crazy house. The bunkhouse. The pink house. And in turn, people know my name, who my father is, and dozens of so-called facts about me.

The bus seat creaks as I shift, the wet cotton of my jeans sticking to both the black plastic and my hamstrings. A screech from the backseat makes me turn. Robbie is holding his cupped hands high, declaring he has 'a ginormous daddy longlegs' today. He threatens to dump the spider onto the sisters sitting in front of him. The girls shriek in fear, spilling toward the window and out into the aisle. I lean my head against the glass, my pulse pounding, hating that we all just stay out of things.

The crowd snickers as the girls beg Robbie to stop. He cackles again, and it snaps the last thread of patience in me. Enough. I push by the other kids, holding onto the seat backs as I stumble to the back of the bus and stand over Robbie.

"Heeeey!" He protests as I squish his hands together, staring into his flinty eyes above flaring nostrils. "You cooow! No faaaair!" Robbie whines as he opens his empty palms, revealing his bluff about the spider. I push him firmly into his seat and nod at the sisters, surprising myself. Getting involved means Robbie will focus on me tomorrow. And the next day. But it actually feels good — sticking up for the girls. Somebody needs to. Nancy peers into her rearview and shouts, "Stay in your seats, puh-leaze!"

The bus speeds up as we pass the gas station and merge onto the two-lane highway. The arcing beats of the telephone lines flash by against a backdrop of second-growth. When we've rattled past precisely fifty-three wooden power poles — yes, I've counted them piles of times — the bus turns off the highway into town. Asphalt rumble strips and a 'Children Playing' sign remind drivers to slow down as the first houses come into view. Next to the police station, the bus takes another jerky right. Today both Mounties are parked below the flagpole, where the red maple leaf flaps wildly above the cruisers in the pouring rain.

As we near our first stop at the elementary school, the bus bounces over a speed bump. The little kids grab their lunch boxes and backpacks, their chatter and rustling reaching a crescendo. They jostle off the bus, scattering across the concrete schoolyard. I don't react when Robbie gives me the finger from the aisle, hoping I can handle whatever revenge the little punk is planning for me. My head knocks against the glass as the bus cuts the corner beside the sports field, where a wide ditch surrounds the turf.

I grin to myself, recalling the hours I used to spend in those ditches hunting frog eggs in my little red gumboots. The ditch was always deep with slimy green muck. During recess and lunch, I would push aside the reed grass with a stick, searching for gelatinous sacs of eggs. I'd keep the slimy masses in a Mason jar outside the back door of my classroom. After school, I would carefully carry my live treasures home. My mum would sigh, but smile gently and find a shady spot on the deck where I could watch the little gel balls grow from egg to tadpole to frog.

I drop my chin to my chest. Every memory of my mother still aches so, so much. Why is it the more you try *not* to think about something, the more those images cycle through your thoughts? My mum's brown wavy hair. Her gray-blue eyes, just like mine. Her mischievous smile and chipped front tooth. Comfortable shoes. Elastic-waist cotton pants. The striped wool sweater she knit herself.

My mother had been background music. Someone who washed my sheets, cooked our dinners, did the shopping, and asked me how my day was. Ever there, but not... not really notable. With that background music now suddenly gone, I'm realizing how much my mother touched every heartbeat of our lives.

I pull the worn sleeve of my gray hoodie over my knuckles, over the scar where my pinkie and ring finger should be, and wipe away a tear. Damn! With the little kids gone, the bus is quieter as it pulls back onto the main street. Across the aisle, Josh, one of the double-wide twins, swiftly moves his gaze to the window when I look over. I know from his sister Nora, my now ex-best friend, he has a crush on me. Or at least he *did* six months ago. Even if he saw my tears, it's unlikely he'll blab.

I can't get used to these waves of memories. They run shivers down my spine, stab me in the stomach and make my heart beat all wacky. The thoughts come from nowhere. Like yesterday, I was walking along the sidewalk to the library, when suddenly, my feet froze. My ribs clamped onto my insides as my brain flashed back to last year, when my mum was teasing me about something between the bookshelves. Will these vivid bursts of time traveling ever stop? Then again, do I want the memories to end? I'm already forgetting parts of her, details fading.

We ramble down the hill, past the Rotary park no one uses. At the high school, the bus parks in the roundabout, near a totem pole. Nancy opens the doors with a mechanical clunk and twists in her seat to watch us file off onto the half-moon stairs which lead to the front entrance. In a few short weeks, as is the town tradition, our graduation class will arrange itself on these steps for our last school photo together. By now most of the girls have gone down-island to buy their grad dresses, at one of the big wedding boutiques. The boys have it easier. A shop from down-island came to measure them for suit rentals. They only needed to pick a style and match their cummerbund to their dates' dress color.

I have a lot of sewing left to do on my grad dress. My mum had been an excellent seamstress, and we bought the pattern over a year ago. It was perfect for me. A simple A-line dress with a scoop neck and absolutely no lace or ruffles or frills. Then, two days after picking out the dress pattern, my mum got The Diagnosis. She wanted to start the dress, but lacked the energy. So my dad drove me to the fabric store, where I had really tried to make all the decisions myself. Should I get blue, my favorite color? Or green, which my mother said looked best with my face? And which type of fabric? The choices had bewildered me.

Surprisingly, my dad had stepped in to help. Back when we all still had hope, he had been his take-charge self. After waiting in the truck for over an hour, he came into the fabric store where he found me baffled. First, he asked about the fabric type. We knew my mum would want a natural fiber and together we had eventually decided on a thick brushed silk.

"It... you know... flows real nice." My dad had observed the fabric. "If you ever twirl... or whatever."

We had chuckled at this thought. I am not a twirler. Under the harsh fluorescent lights, we had draped a few different jewel tones of the silk across my chest, finally agreeing the emerald green color suited me best.

It's only four weeks until grad now, so my dress will need to be ready. And I still don't have shoes. Anyway, graduation is totally overblown. Most girls have looked forward to it for years. But not me.

Time spent with people we don't really like to celebrate something that isn't much of an accomplishment! All their fuss about dresses and shoes, hairdos and manicures, is hard for me to understand.

I slide into the bus aisle ahead of Josh and smile at Nancy as I step out into the downpour. With my pack over one shoulder, I take the stairs two at a time. I head up the ramp to my locker, shaking the rain from my blond hair, willing today to be a little easier.

Grade 12's get the best lockers, near the central ramp that connects the upper east and the lower west wing of the school. Amid the chatter of the hallway, I twirl the dial to enter my locker combination, shielding my hand from curious stares with my body. A crowd of hockey players lunges down the hall in their athletic jackets, shoving each other and narrating a step-by-step replay of a 'beauty goal, man!'. A couple in ripped jeans walks by, hand in hand, dragging with them the acrid scent of the smoking area. Cheap perfume mingles with the stale smoke as a clique of popular girls saunters down the ramp behind me. Their furtive glances and loud whispers used to fill me with uncertainty. Since The Worst Day, their opinions mean nothing to me. "Only twenty-two more days," I whisper to myself. "You'll make it. Only twenty-two more days."

I know my schedule without looking. Calculus and physics before lunch, then art and gym. I also have a session with Ms. Wells, the school counselor, over the lunch hour. Ugh. What a waste of my break. She's nice enough. As far as adults go, Ms. Wells is a favorite. But she won't understand how things have changed. Not at all.

Calculus and physics flash by. I love these classes. There is something so comforting about equations. One correct answer. No personal opinions. No gray areas. Just right or wrong. In physics, I sit alone now, near the back. Nora slides into a desk up front, as far from our usual seats as possible, avoiding my gaze. People can be so disappointing. The rhythmic focus of the calculations leaves me calm and in control. The memory waves of my mum never hit me while I'm doing math. When the bell shrills, I pack my books, file into the flow of students in the hall, and weave my way back to my locker, still talking to no one.

I pull my lunch and the folder of applications from my backpack. In the brown paper bag are the same three things I now eat every day: peanut butter and raspberry jam on wholewheat store-bought bread, cut diagonally and wrapped in plastic; a big red Fuji apple and two Oreo cookies. I unwrap half the sandwich and put the rest back on the top shelf, then slam the locker shut and stride down the ramp toward the school office and tiny counseling room.

Ms. Wells looks up when I tap on the open door. "Come in, Maia. Come in!" she says, motioning me to sit in the padded chair across from her desk. "How are you today?" She shuffles through a pile of folders.

"I'm fine," I respond. "Fine." The office is bright and tidy, and Ms. Wells has a couple of healthy plants behind her on the ledge below the windows. Outside in the courtyard, the rain is still pounding.

On the office walls, Ms. Wells has the typical inspirational counselor posters. Over the past six months, since the school and my dad decided I should see her every week, I've seen the whole rotation. This week, near her desk, above a cluttered bulletin board, hangs one of an enormous mountain with the quote "Tough times never last, but tough people do". On the wall, an orange sun setting over a rocky beach proclaims "Believe & Succeed". And alongside it, another poster shows a close-up of a drop falling into calm water making circular rings, with the quote "Attitude is a little thing that affects everything".

"Good God," I think, "does this shit work on anyone?" Ms. Wells hands me an application and I consider my name, typed into the first line. Maia Müller. No one else in this town has an umlaut in their name. And hardly anyone has parents whose English is their second language. My parents had only been a bit older than me when they left Europe for a farm in Quebec. They had moved west through Canadian mining towns, reaching for higher-paying jobs and more comfortable living conditions. When they ended up here, on the northern tip of this west coast island, the place stuck. For some reason.

Finally, Ms. Wells gets started. First, she congratulates me on my grades. Straight A's. Again. Still. Whatever. Next Ms. Wells moves to the fast-approaching deadlines for university applications. She's seen none of my forms. Nor have I asked any teachers to write recommendation letters — Ms. Wells has inquired. What exactly is my plan?

I think about this. Going to post-secondary school has always been the plan. I don't know what I want to do with my life. Not precisely. But I was going to finish high school, work the summer and then head to school in September. My mum had been the one who encouraged me to look at all the options. She believed I should love my career... and love to learn about it. But it's hard to imagine... picking a direction and committing to a single type of work *forever* is totally overwhelming. How do you *know*?

Anyway, my plans to leave for school are gone now. My dad made that clear. He will not be funding my post-secondary education. No money for my school. End of story. Instead, he needs me to work with him for a year. And although he hasn't said it out loud, I sense he wants me to take the business over from him and make it my own.

"I'm here to help, Maia." Ms. Wells interrupts my thoughts. "How can we get these applications out the door?"

I'm not sure how to answer. Telling Ms. Wells about my dad's current position regarding university will kick off a series of unpleasant conversations. Ms. Wells had been a friend of my mum's. And she's still a family friend and neighbor. When my parents needed to travel down-island for my mum's endless treatments, Ms. Wells would feed me dinner in her bright little kitchen. If she finds out now that my dad is not supporting my education, Ms. Wells will be pissed. And when Ms. Wells is pissed, she isn't quiet about it. So it's really better to avoid telling her the whole truth.

"Could you help get one teacher to draft a reference letter?" Pretending to apply to universities will cause the least amount of upset right now.

"Of course!" The corners of her brown eyes crinkle under her glasses as she flips some pages and makes a note in her daily planner. "Let me get Mr. Buckley to write one for you." Her eyes shift back to me and she grins. "He's your best bet out of all the math & science teachers. The rest of them, well, let's just say they're better with numbers than letters. Plus, your physics mark is spectacular. Yes, I think Mr. Buckley is a splendid choice for a reference letter!" Ms. Wells beams at her own cleverness.

She pulls out an application from my file, then scans through the pages.

"So. What's your topic for extracurricular activities? Your guiding work?" she asks.

Four years ago, when my dad lost his forestry job, my parents started a kayak wilderness guiding company. It was my mum's idea — something she had dreamed about for years. And together they built a decent business. It doesn't pay what my dad made out in the bush, especially since the weather up here limits the tourist season to the summer months. During school vacations, I would join them, doing the daily setup, cooking, and other chores on the trips. My parents had worked together, sharing their reverence for nature with clients, and it made them happy. For a short while, at least.

"Yes. Where they ask about 'an experience that taught me something about myself and the world.' I can talk about meeting new people... and about guiding work, I guess."

"I agree. And you should touch on your love of nature. Universities love that stuff." She nods, flipping to the next page.

"Yeah. That should work." I consider how to weave all those points into an essay.

Working as a guide is fun. I keep to myself at school, but with visitors from faraway places, I'm pretty open. Their lives fascinate me. Most clients are from big cities, used to viewing the landscape through glass from inside climate-controlled spaces. They come on these adventure trips to experience the raw beauty of the area, always excited to discover wildlife up close. It's normal to see wolves and bears, deer and elk, seals and otters, orcas and gray whales. These creatures are gorgeous and fascinating. But I enjoy our clients' reactions to the wilderness as much as I love the nature itself. The unspoiled vastness up here impresses these strangers. We can go for days without seeing another human. Some of our clients love the isolation, while others are totally unprepared for it. "Wait. What? No cell service? You're kidding!" they'll ask incredulously, stunned their newest gadget doesn't work everywhere.

"And what about this next question?" Ms. Wells asks. "'Explain how you responded to a problem and/or an unfamiliar situation. What did you do, what was the outcome, and what did you learn from the experience?'" Her eyes soften as she reads from the application. "Have you considered writing about your mum?".

I ponder those days: The Diagnosis, The Summer of Hell, The Worst Day, and The Last Day. Could I write about them? Sure. But will I write about them? No. Definitely not.

"I dunno," I say. "It's not really anyone's business, you know?"

"I don't disagree, Maia, but you can honor Maxi by writing about her. She'd be very proud of you." Ms. Wells yanks a Kleenex from the box on her desk, lifts her glasses, and wipes her eyes as she remembers her friend.

"I'll think about it."

"Can I ask, Maia, is there something else going on? You're less excited about going to school than you were during the fall. What's up?"

"I'm not really sure I want to go in September," I lie. "I think my dad would be really lonely if I leave. And he needs me to help on the guiding trips. Our season starts Thursday." I'm looking forward to skipping school, but I'm also apprehensive about this first trip back. My dad is doing better. Last week, he got the boat in the water, then ran up the coast to check on the trails and restock our supply cache. But when he starts the day in a trance like this morning, I worry it's too soon for him to work.

"Oh, Maia! I really hope you decide to go. You are so smart... so capable!" Ms. Wells folds her hands on the desk. "This year has been hard... terribly hard... for you... and Lars. None of this is fair." I can't argue and stare down at the carpet. "Getting back to work will help your dad. And you." She might be right. And if I keep saving my pay and tips, maybe —

"How are you and Nora, by the way?" I shake my head. There is no me and Nora. Not anymore. "I'm sorry, Maia," Ms. Wells says.

"Friendships can be hard. And moving away from your parents…" Her voice falters as she corrects herself. "… your dad… and the life you've always known takes a lot. It takes courage. And belief things *will* work out," Ms. Wells says. "And I know it's even harder to take those first steps… to leave when you don't have full support from home."

I feel the heat rising in my face. Does she know my dad's stance? This talk needs to stop.

"I'll finish the applications, Ms. Wells. I promise. And I'll send them in. That's all I can say for sure right now, okay?"

The rest of the counseling session flies by. Together, we brainstorm ideas for my essays. I even find the courage to mention the technical school program I researched the other night. Ms. Wells seems skeptical because someone with my grades "really belongs in university". But she also promises to check out the program outline.

When the bell rings, ending the lunch hour, I leave Ms. Wells' office, hope rekindling. Something I haven't felt in months. I was looking forward to going to school, and talking about it reminded me. I walk back to my locker, excited to give the applications my full effort. If I work all summer and get a couple of scholarships, I might have enough money to make it to Christmas break. It would be a start. Now I just need to get my dad on track. I have no idea how to help him, but I'm going to try. Harder. I have to.

CHAPTER 2

Full sun, blue skies, and calm waters. A rare day, almost making me forget we're one of the rainiest towns in our province. From the F350 back seat, I drag a bright yellow dry pack. After heaving it onto my shoulder, I hoist the gray and white cooler with both hands. As I head to the dock, I wonder if our clients will be on time.

I know little about them. They're a family of three, the Baldwins, from the big city. The mother's name is Anna, the father is Carl and their eighteen-year-old son is called Jack. They booked the first four-day trip of the season. It's what our brochure calls a 'combo trip'. A boat run up the coast, drop-off at the south trailhead with the kayaks, two days of kayaking, and a two-day hike over to the north trailhead, where we'll get picked up by a van shuttle.

Early June is always a crapshoot with the weather. It can be beautiful. And it can be torrential. The forecast for the next few days is unsettled. I'm hoping the rains hold off, so I can ease back into this adventure work. I've missed being out on the ocean and in the forest. But the work is physical and often uncomfortable. Shitting in the woods isn't for everyone, and I hope this first group isn't too high-maintenance.

My eyes crinkle as I think of Margo, a bleached blond, who came with her new husband, Jeff, last year. He was prepared — over prepared — with outdoor tools and technical clothing and an encyclope-dic knowledge of our flora. Margo, on the other hand, wore knee-high leather boots with a wedge heel, insisting they were great for walking in. My dad took one look at her footwear and refused her access to the boat. Margo got dragged to the general store, where the unsmiling owner found a pair of proper hiking boots and some plastic clogs that fit. She wrinkled her nose at her comfortable, but unfashionable feet, the entire trip.

Margo had needed help with everything. I checked her tent for insects, cleared the spider webs before she squatted and threaded her manicured fingers into her pack straps so she wouldn't break a nail. High-Maintenance Margo. But the extra effort had been worth it when we got Jeff's tip. I still wonder how anyone can pride themselves on being helpless, the way Margo did. People can be strange.

I drop the cooler to the dock and step onto the swim fin of the twenty-six-foot aluminum boat, glancing down at *Moxie* painted on the transom. When my dad bought the boat from a bankrupt logging contractor, it was named *Ruby Tuesday*. Ruby, the guy's ex-wife, still lived in town and we felt awkward keeping the name.

Deciding on the new name for the boat was easy. Before I was born, when my parents first moved to town, a neighbor commented how well mum's name matched her personality. With my dad's accent, the neighbor heard 'moxie' when my dad called her Maxi. Once dad looked up the definition of moxie, it became an instant nickname. And my mum had lived up to her nickname — always bold and gritty.

To rename the boat, my mum had been adamant about conducting a proper name purging and renaming ceremony — anything less was bad luck. So, to avoid the wrath of the gods, we had first removed every physical trace of the old boat's name. *Ruby Tuesday* was scrubbed from the transom, life ring, bow, ship logs and floating key chain. Then my mum wrote *Ruby Tuesday* on a metal garden tag with a water-soluble marker. According to legend, the name of every vessel is recorded in the 'Ledger of the Deep', and known personally to the sea gods. To expunge the name *Ruby Tuesday* from the gods' ledger, my mum stood on the bow, grinning with a twinkle in her eye, and recited the timeless declaration:

> "Oh, mighty and great ruler of the seas and oceans, to whom all ships and we who venture upon your vast domain are required to pay homage, implore you in your graciousness to expunge for all time from your records and recollection the name *Ruby Tuesday* which has ceased to be an entity in your kingdom. As proof thereof, we submit this ingot bearing her name to be corrupted through your powers and forever be purged from the sea."

Then she dropped the tag into the ocean and poured a bottle of Champagne overboard, from East to West, saying,

> "In grateful acknowledgment of your munificence and dispensation, we offer these libations to your majesty and your court."

Apparently, this gets the sea gods drunk, so they forget the old boat's name.

She had continued the renaming ceremony with mischievous formality. First, we appeased the sea gods by pouring another bottle of Champagne into the ocean from West to East, introducing the *Moxie* to their ledger. Then we appeased the four wind god brothers by facing each of their four compass directions. She poured a generous amount of Champagne into a flute and flicked it overboard in each direction while addressing the gods by name.

I smile at the memory. The ceremony had been ridiculous. And fun. As we had toasted the renamed *Moxie* and taken sips of bubbly, my dad had grumbled about wasting three bottles of Champagne. Mum smiled playfully, stood on tip-toe, and kissed his scowl away, saying, "You'll thank me when this boat has a long, lucky lifetime."

The boat is a converted crew boat, seating ten. I drop the bag of food from my shoulder onto the colorful pile of supplies already on board. Then I lug the cooler full of perishables onto the deck. Later, we'll divide the food between the kayaks for the first leg of our trip. By the time we get to the hike, we'll carry freeze-dried meals to keep the weight down. Besides the food, there are five orange dry packs, one per adventurer, on the pile. Each pack holds a sleeping bag, mat, and tent. The guests will add their belongings to these bags when they arrive.

A car door slams in the parking lot and a short, plump woman opens a silver Range Rover's hatch. She's talking to a dark-haired young man. Her movements are quick and excited. He leans in, listening, then helps with the bags. I wait for the father to get out of the vehicle, which would confirm my hunch these are the Baldwins. But no one else appears. Well. Now what?

I re-stack the bags, buying time and hoping my dad gets back, so I can avoid the whole greeting ceremony. Right on cue, my dad's voice calls out from across the gravel lot. He towers over Anna as he shakes her hand and then Jack's. They're too far away to make out words, but Anna says something to my dad. He looks down at the dock, then turns back to Anna and nods once. He motions in the general direction of the boat with his head and he picks up two of their bags, walking toward me. When he doesn't slow down or look back, Anna glances over at Jack. They shrug, then Jack grabs the last bag from the Range Rover and they both stride to catch up. My dad is a man of few words.

With the gear stacked on the deck, I climb up on the narrow ledge beside the cabin to the roof rack, holding four fiberglass touring kayaks. I check the ropes on each one, stalling, so I'm away from the guests for the introductions. In the past few months, I've learned a few tricks to avoid handshakes.

Their footsteps thump on the dock's wooden planks and I sneak a look at Jack from behind a kayak. Maroon hoodie, dark gray jeans, brand new skater shoes, and a frayed ball cap. He's tall, almost six feet, and athletic. He looks bored and unhappy. That could make this trip difficult. The worst clients are those who are high-maintenance or don't want to be here.

"This is us." My dad drops the bags and looks up at me on the roof. "This is my daughter, Maia. She's our cook, nature expert, and all-around helper. Maia, this is Anna. And Jack." He gestures at each of us. It's been weeks since I've heard him say so many words at one time. Maybe this trip can be the start of getting back to normal... our new normal.

I smile tightly and give them a quick wave. "Nice to meet you both." Jack's dark eyes catch mine for an instant and my throat closes. Nope, he does not want to be here.

Anna's wearing runners, khaki nylon pants, a pink fleece, and a white ball cap with her brown ponytail threaded through the back closure. Clearly, she read through our brochure and followed our directions that warn against wearing cotton. Anna has a smile that hits every part of her face. I'm going to like this lady. One bright spot on this trip so far.

Jack is another story. He now avoids my gaze, standing off to the side, fiddling with an iPod connected to the cord of his earbuds. He either hasn't read the brochure or, more likely, didn't listen to Anna's rules about clothing. Everything he's wearing is cotton. In our Conservation and Outdoor Recreation course we were reminded daily that "cotton kills" because it absorbs more water than other fabrics and loses its ability to insulate when wet. I groan inwardly — having people who won't follow directions makes a trip so much harder.

But you're getting paid for this, I remind myself. And you get to miss school to be here. These people don't need to be your friends. Just smile, be helpful and go the extra mile for the guests like mum taught you. Then maybe, just maybe, there will be a gratuity in it for you at the end of the week. Judging by their vehicle, this family can afford to tip us!

Once the kayak check is finished, I climb back down onto the deck. "Where's Mr. Baldwin?" I glance toward the parking lot again.

"As it turns out, Carl won't be joining us." An odd expression crosses Anna's face. "He got tied up at work and was going to join us this morning. But he's..." Her eyebrows knit together in a flash of pain. "... He's still tied up." Anna glances toward Jack. He looks back at her without saying a word. Something's off, but I can't tell what. Doesn't matter. Not my business.

"Four is a good number," my dad says. "Pass me the extra pack, Maia." I pick one of the guest packs and pass it to him. "We'll still bring all the food," he says. "Don't want hangry teens."

I give Anna and Jack each their dry pack and instruct them to move their clothes into them. The dry packs are a rugged waterproof fabric with a water-resistant roll-top closure. Useful when we have water on all sides of us. Anna is pretty minimalist for a city girl. She lays her bathroom kit on the deck as she folds her belongings into the pack. It's a clear zip-top bag with travel-sized toothpaste, dry shampoo, sunscreen, and soap; a toothbrush, and Tylenol. Impressively light.

Jack stuffs a new-looking pair of hiking boots into his dry pack, then adds his socks, underwear, T-shirts, one pair of pants, and a clear bag of bath supplies with even less in it than Anna's. Jack finishes first and I turn so I'm able to grab the pack from him with my left hand.

When Anna is also ready, my dad waves her over and says, "Let's take the extra bags up. Then we'll go." Together they walk to the vehicles, Anna chattering and my dad answering in short syllables.

Jack stands on the dock, studying me with a look of... what? Curiosity, maybe? "Come on board," I motion him over. I have to talk to him at some point.

"Huh?" he says, taking out an earbud.

"Come on board," I repeat. He nods and steps onto the side rail. But as he jumps, his foot gets tangled in the dock line. Jack is flying toward me, about to take a face-plant on the gritty deck. I grab for his arm with both hands. My help slows Jack's fall, and only his other hand skids across the deck.

"Shit!" Jack says. I pull him upright and he glances at me, cheeks flushing. He smells of spice and coconut suntan lotion. Nice. Then his gaze drops to my right hand, still pulling on his arm. His eyes widen, taking in the gnarled scar and missing fingers. He pulls back and I spin away. I'm still not used to seeing people's shock. Most of the town has seen my injury by now. But strangers struggle with an appropriate reaction.

"Are you okay?" I ask, my back to Jack, watching Anna and my dad walk down the ramp. Her bright colors dazzle in the sunshine next to my dad's faded and grimy attire.

"Yeah," Jack says. But a sharp intake of his breath from behind me tells me otherwise.

"What happened?" Anna hops on board.

"I'm fine. I tripped," Jack says. My dad assesses Jack's minor wound and reads Anna's reaction from where he stands on the dock. I take an ice pack from the cooler, wrap a clean fish towel around it, and pass the whole thing to Anna.

"Thanks love." Anna examines Jack's hand. "You're fine." She closes Jack's palm around the towel-wrapped ice pack. "You'll be fine." My dad nods once, satisfied with her underreaction.

Chapter 3

We spend another ten minutes at the dock, running through the safety briefing we've presented dozens of times. Life jackets, life ring, flares. First aid kit, emergency beacon, self-inflating life raft. And the basics of how to use the VHF radio. Anna and Jack pay as much attention as I do to flight attendants when they do their safety dance. Which is fine. We've never needed this gear.

By the time we leave the harbor, the sun is high over the adjacent islands. The sky is a deep blue, fading to lighter hues near the horizon. The water reflects the sky, every piece of seaweed and driftwood easy to spot on the calm ocean.

Once past the harbor's breakwater, my dad powers up the 370 horsepower inboard Volvo, which growls to life. A faint whiff of diesel exhaust enters the rumbling cabin as the bow rises sharply. The boat levels as we reach planing speed and my dad steers wide of the shallows, marked by floating beds of kelp. Anna is sitting up front, next to him. She points to the ferry and my dad explains it services the small communities on two islands behind us. Moments later Anna squeals, smiling. I follow her gaze and see the black dome of a seal's head, its enormous eyes staring down our boat until it decides it's seen enough and dives under beside us.

A little farther on, Anna points to the lighthouse, with its classic color scheme in Canadian red and white. It's a combined lighthouse and fog alarm, built over one hundred years ago to keep shipping and fishing vessels safe. In this weather, it's a picturesque scene. The red roof stands out against the bleached driftwood and dark green forest beyond. On many other days, the deep blast of the foghorn is the only evidence of the building and the island it's built on. The fog around here is often maddeningly dense, making navigation for vessels without radar disorienting and nearly impossible.

Behind the two front bucket seats, the boat has two benches on each side of the aisle, all facing forward. Jack's sitting in the spot kitty-corner from me, still holding the ice pack. My back is against the outer wall of the boat, legs stretched out along the seat. From this position, I have an excellent view of Jack's profile. He's running a finger around the wheel on his iPod, ignoring the scenery and Anna's chatter. His eyelashes are an inch long and there's a bit of stubble along his jawline. My mum would have called him a handsome boy. Not much of a talker. But that's fine with me. I often have to spend this entire two-hour boat ride answering questions from guests. And many of those conversations are challenging.

People from the city often have powerful feelings against so many of the activities that feed the families in our small town. These guests come with opinions on salmon fishing and logging and gravel pits, based on bogus information they've seen on TV. They assume since we run a guiding outfit, we're a family of tree-huggers. We are not. I mean, our family takes care of nature. Obviously, our kayak trips "leave no trace". But we also understand harvesting resources from nature is the cost of humans inhabiting this planet. So we minimize our footprint and communicate to our guests that the logger, fisher, and miner stereotypes differ from the real people doing those jobs right here in this town.

Take Eva's dad, Matti, for instance. He's a thick Finnish fisherman, with blue eyes and messy blond hair. Tough, but also the nicest man, always helping neighbors. Last year, after the windstorm, he spent four days cleaning up fallen trees from everyone's yards. And a couple of years ago, I saw him put an armload of salmon into the deep freeze in Charlie's garage after Charlie broke his leg and couldn't work. Matti never looks for credit for any of his generosity.

My dad's buddies, who all still work in the forest, aren't the tree-killing nature-destroying lumberjacks portrayed in environmental propaganda. They love and protect the places they work in, so they can enjoy those same places when they go out to hunt and hike and snowmobile. They're true conservationists.

It's so strange that city people want to wipe their asses with toilet paper, but vilify anyone who cuts down a tree to make their toilet paper. The resources which go into everything they buy at a big box store need to come from somewhere. But these facts are easy to ignore. It's weird how people don't think things through. They're just too far away to see the complete cycle. It's a debate that gets my dad pretty hot. He knows he needs to watch how much he says around our guests. My mum was much more diplomatic. Today, I'm thankful Anna and Jack aren't debating the merits of small-town living. It's an easy way to lose a tip, sharing your actual opinions.

We travel in contented silence for a long while. The steady drone of the engine and the rhythm of the boat relaxes me. The sunshine beaming through the windows warms me up. A small flock of petrels flies low over the water with short, stiff wing beats. Islands dot the ocean — endless shapes of jagged black rock below the high tide line, covered in contorted trees above. My dad points to a couple of bald eagles, perched high in a fir tree. Their white feathered heads move, scanning the water with keen eyes, searching for a salmon dinner.

My dad's broad shoulders are clad in a thick grey base layer. His shaggy brown hair is longer than usual, and he hasn't shaved in a week. He sits erect, one large hand on the wheel, laced leather boots on the captain's step, peering out over the bow rail for obstacles. He turns sharply now, avoiding a log, his thick fingers gripping the wheel. As a little girl, I would place my palms on his, amazed at their size and ruggedness. His cracked fingernails are the size of quarters, and countless scars record run-ins with lawn mowers and band saws. My mum would lift his big mitt to her lips, laughing at how grimy his hands always looked, even after he showered. A long working life stained his fingerprints black. I wonder if this run up the coast is reminding him of my mum, too. Everywhere I look, there are memories of her. I shake my head, vowing to focus on what is. Not what was.

Gulls and ducks dot the surface of the ocean, diving under as our boat invades their fishing grounds. Jack's now grinning at something on his iPod. Nice. Stunning landscape all around and he's focused on a tiny digital screen.

We're halfway to the trailhead when the outline of a whale's tail sinks below the ocean surface out the far window. My training kicks in, and I point to where the whale went under. Anna looks at me wide-eyed, while Jack ignores everyone.

"There! A humpback," I track its underwater speed and direction. "It should come up again… right around… there!" I point just as the giant whale rolls across the surface. Mist sprays from its blowhole before it arches and dives back under again with a wave of its enormous tail.

"Holy moly!" Anna says with a grin, "Those things are huge! Jack, did you see that?" Anna asks, nudging his shoulder. But Jack pushes her hand away with a glare.

"Over forty tons and sixty feet long." I ignore Jack's grumpiness. "And all they eat is plankton and little tiny fish! They are so awesome. Do you know they can't tell we're up here? Dolphins have echolocation, so they can sense when there's a boat above them. But these giant whales, they have no idea we're up here." Anna's jaw drops. I grin and say, "Yeah. Don't think about that fact too much." We scan the surface for a long while, but the humpback doesn't come up again.

When we're nearing the trailhead bay, I pass Anna and Jack each a laminated map. It shows our planned route and we'll tuck these cards under the elastic cords on the front of our kayaks. We've found our guests like to track their progress. Jack folds the card and stuffs it into his back pocket without speaking, but I show Anna where we'll be anchoring. It's a sheltered spot, which isn't necessary today, since the water's flat as a mirror. But on windier days, anchoring in the cove makes it easier to get the kayaks off the roof and safely loaded with our supplies and our guests. Once the kayaks are packed, we'll paddle along the coast to a sandy beach to make camp.

Tonight I'll cook smoked salmon linguine. Most guests love it and it's simple to make. I'll boil ocean water to cook the pasta. In the cast iron pan, I'll melt some cream cheese, thin it with water and add the little container of capers and fresh chopped dill I prepped yesterday. Dump in a vacuum pack of smoked Chinook from last season and, boom, oceanfront dining at its best! I love the reaction I get to my cooking, but honestly, it's mostly the fresh air and exercise that makes things taste so good. My parents use a German saying, "Hunger ist der beste Koch" which translates to "hunger is the best chef". And it's true.

Anna flips over the route map where I've added a collage of my mum's wildlife photos. Anna studies the pictures and smiles widely. "Are we going to see all of these animals?"

"Probably not. You're only here four days," I say, "but we took all those photos, so there's definitely a chance to see each one."

"Lars... Maia... you live in a pretty special part of the world." Anna shakes her head like she can't quite believe it.

"We do." My dad's voice is soft as he speaks his first words in over an hour. I know he's thinking of mum now. Every piece of scenery is a stark reminder of how things used to be. I don't think the others notice, but I can tell when he's thinking of her by the way his expression blanks out.

While Anna praises the beauty of this landscape, it can also be treacherous. The weather should be predictable, but up here fog, wind, and rain can show up with little warning. Even those with decades of experience reading the land and sea get caught. And this is a remote part of the world to have trouble in.

"Wow. It's like we're in a cloud." A few minutes later, Anna leans forward, gazing outside as the boat slows, her lips pursed. The morning fog bank hasn't burned off up here. Visibility has reduced gradually and now we can barely see twenty feet ahead of us.

My dad lifts his ball cap and scratches the top of his head, then slows the throttle to an idle. He peers intently over the bow, then back at the radar, navigating by sight now impossible. Where the wipers aren't clearing the windshield, thick mist builds up on the glass until it's opaque. I look over his shoulder, where the radar shows the shore contours, but no other boats dot the screen.

"The bay is just up ahead there, where we'll anchor the boat." I point to our left, forcing brightness into my tone.

It's always nicer to kayak when the visibility is good. Hopefully, the sun wins the battle over the fog today.

We glide slowly into the bay. My dad monitors the depth sounder until we're in just twenty feet of water. He punches reverse until the boat almost stops, then hits the controls to lower the anchor. The chain clanks as it drops over the bow roller, then splashes into the water, unwinding the gold and white anchor rope. The fish-finder's sonar tracks the anchor's descent in a colorful angled line. When the screen shows it hit bottom, the rope slackens. My dad counts out another fifty feet, making sure there's enough scope for safe anchorage. Then he kills the engine and we're plunged into a thick quiet. The waves lap against the hull as we drift toward the bay's north shore. Although the sky is a bright white, the fog bank in the bay is thick, muffling the sounds around us even more.

"Tell the story, Maia." My dad stares toward the tidal flats, barely visible through the haze. I shoot him a startled glance, remembering how well my mum told this tale every time we waited for the anchor to set. I hadn't considered how this part of the tour would go; who would now tell this story? After a long hesitation, I'm finally able to begin.

"This bay has quite a history." Anna watches me, unaware of the turmoil this task is causing me. "Indigenous peoples have been at home here for centuries. The rest of the world became aware of this area in the late 1700s. Explorers came by ship, looking for resources to make their voyage sponsors rich. Ships came from Spain and Russia, Britain, and America. And those captains *did* find treasures here." My dad focuses out into the fog, but the slight eye crinkle and upturn of his mouth spur me on. He's pleased.

"By the early 1800s contact between the white traders and the indigenous peoples here was common. Both sides wanted the other's offering. Sea otter pelts fetched high prices in China." I'm getting into the story now. Anna flinches, and I'm sure she's imagining the slaughter of those charismatic little marine mammals. "The indigenous villages saw great wealth from this trading. For a time, anyway. In the 1830s the Hudson's Bay Company even had a trading post here. But inevitably, the fur trade brought a lot of bad to the indigenous people. They died of new diseases they weren't immune to. And white settlers introduced alcohol, guns, and culture that quickly changed traditions... traditions that had existed here for millennia."

"In 1894, some pioneers settled right there." I point up the bay. "Four men built a small cabin. They arrived late in the season and expected more settlers to join them in the spring. But that winter, after a heavy rainstorm, a rockslide pushed the men's cabin about a hundred feet into this bay." I look to my right, where I imagine they ended up. "Three men survived the rockslide with minor cuts and bruises, but the fourth man's leg was trapped under logs. He was stuck out in the water here, alive, but freezing." I glance from Anna, whose eyes are wide, to Jack, who's pretending not to listen. "They hoped the rising tide would shift the logs and free the man. But it didn't. The water kept rising, and he would have drowned. So this guy convinced his buddies to amputate his leg with an ax." Anna looks horrified and now I'm sure Jack is listening because his eyebrows raise in surprise.

"His buddies do the deed and he survives the amputation." I cringe, imagining their task. "But the guy dies anyway... from exposure and blood loss... the next afternoon."

"That poor man," Anna says, shaking her head. "Can you imagine how much that would've hurt?"

Without thinking, I rub the scarred stumps on my right hand. I don't have to imagine how much it hurt. I know. Across the aisle, my dad's rugged features tighten. The boat is awkwardly silent. Then we feel a slight thud as the anchor sets in the ocean floor and the rope pulls taut against the boat. The rising tide slowly pulls the bow around until the sounder shows us pointing due west.

"Anyway," I say brightly, "the rest of the history here is less terrible. There was a general store and a fish cannery in the 1900s. And more recently a logging operation. People haven't lived here in fifty years."

"It's hard to believe anyone *ever* lived here," Anna says. "It's so pristine."

"True," I say, "the pilings along the shore, tangled in blackberry vines, are all that's left. Nature takes back her hold pretty quick around here."

"Let's unload," my dad says now. That's my cue to climb onto the roof and untie the kayaks, so I scoot off the bench and slide open the door. Out on the deck, I stop short, my lungs filling with the acrid stench of smoke.

CHAPTER 4

"Something's wrong!" I say, "Dad! Do you smell that?" He pushes past me and lifts the large, square cover over the inboard motor. Smoke billows out and on the far left, orange flames flicker.

"Shit! Maia, fire extinguisher!" my dad barks, propping the hatch open. I grab the red thirty-pound extinguisher from the bracket in the corner. My dad yanks the pin, aiming the nozzle. Back and forth, back and forth, sending fine yellow powder down into the engine compartment.

I glance over my shoulder, where Jack and Anna are standing, wide-eyed. Although I think the fire's under control, my safety training kicks in again. "Put on your life jackets. Do you remember how to do that?" Anna nods and pulls the self-inflating PFDs from the cuddy we had shown them during the safety briefing. Maybe she had been paying attention.

Back outside, I'm horrified to see the fire spreading. Bright orange and yellow flames lick up out of the engine compartment, well above the deck level now. Thick black smoke curls across the deck and up into the dense fog. My dad has abandoned the empty extinguisher and is crouching on the back swim fin to fill a five-gallon bucket with seawater, dumping it onto the flaming engine. There's a loud 'whoosh' as the heat turns ocean into steam, but the fire keeps growing.

"Get them out on the bow. Now!" His eyes bulge and sweat beads on his upper lip. "And move the gear." He leans down to fill the bucket again. Anna and Jack hear the commands, too. Anna jumps down the two steps into the berth and unlocks the escape hatch. She definitely paid attention to the safety briefing. Good for her. Jack, however, stands motionless, holding his precious electronics in one fist, stunned by the chaos.

I hand the first of the dry packs to Jack behind me. "Let's go! Take this! Move!" He's still frozen. Come on, buddy! Show a little self-preservation. Finally, Jack snaps out of his daze. He takes the pack and tosses it down to Anna, who drags it onto the sleeping berth and then crams it up through the hatch onto the outside bow deck.

When I try to grab the next pack, I get a lungful of smoky steam and start coughing uncontrollably. Still choking, I close my eyes and hold my breath, pulling another pack inside. Inhaling the cleaner air from inside the cabin, I reach outside again. I peer across the deck to my dad, but black smoke hides the other end of the boat. Before I can retrieve the next bag, the heat makes me yank my hand back. The fire cracks and snaps and I smell singed hair.

"Dad!... Dad, where are you?" I shout into the smoke and heat, but I can't see him. I can't see anything. The billowing smoke and heat push me inside, and I abandon the rest of our supplies. It's too hot to get them. "Dad, where are you?!" I scream louder now, my heartbeat thrashing in my ears and black spots crossing my vision. I take a step toward the fire once more. I need to find him. Need to help him. But the inferno forces me back again.

"We need to get upfront, Maia!" Anna is shouting from the berth. "Now! Get up here!" I glance over my shoulder as Jack's legs disappear up through the hatch. Anna climbs out of the berth toward me, grabbing my arm. "He'll be okay. We can't help from here." She looks down into the fiery engine pit. I try to pull away from her, but she grabs my face between both her hands. "We need to get off this boat, Maia. Now!" Her eyes flash. "He'll be okay. He'll be okay." She drops her hands from my face and looks over my shoulder into the smoke. "We need to get out." Snatching my hand, she drags me toward the bow. I snatch two more life jackets on my way by the captain's seat. Jack is already outside and when Anna stands on the sleeping bunk, Jack grabs her and lifts her up onto the deck by her armpits. I follow Anna, stick my head up out of the hatch, and let Jack haul me up, too.

The scene from the bow is terrifying. Orange flames create a bright halo in the fog bank, topped by a growing plume of black smoke. The jerky movements of my dad's silhouette on the stern are faintly visible in the haze. It looks like he's still trying to put out the fire, bending, then dumping water. Clipping my life jacket, I survey the disaster.

"I want the kayaks off! We need them." I won't be able to launch them in the normal way. From up here, I'll shove them off the rack, sideways, and hope they land right side up. I scramble up onto the roof and reach over to untie the ropes at the back of the boat. Jack catches on to what I'm doing and starts untying the ropes near the front. Just as he steps toward the windshield, I feel a surge in the fire. Not exactly an explosion, but a rushing rumble of ignition I feel through the metal roof. Jack peers down through the windshield into the cabin we just left, his mouth falling open as he freezes.

"Come down!" His voice is shrill when he shakes himself back into action. I just need another minute up here, I think, ignoring Jack, grappling to untie the next kayak.

"Get down! Now!" Anna's hoarse voice joins Jack's. The metal under me warms, and I glance over my shoulder as a cloud of black smoke pushes out the bow hatch behind them. They're both waving me off the roof, so I scoot back down over the edge where Jack grabs my waist, easing me down. On the other side of the windshield, swirling orange flames engulf the cabin.

"Shit!" I suppress the panic rushing into my gut. It won't be possible to get the kayaks down. "Shit!" We have one option left. "The life raft!" I jump over to the port rail, where I release the straps on the rectangular cradle. The white plastic case drops into the ocean and I grab the deployment rope, acutely aware I've never done this before. But when we bought the raft, my mum had made us all watch the instructional DVD about a dozen times. Why didn't I review it this season? But I remember what to do. I keep tearing on the rope. Fifty feet of line comes out of the container before it locks up. Jack and Anna are watching impatiently, casting fearful glances over their shoulders at the fireball inside.

"Now a good yank... and it should inflate," I yell over the rushing rumbles of the fire. I give the rope a hard jerk, and just like in the video, the case cracks open and the orange life raft emerges. There's a new sound now, a hissing, as the carbon dioxide cylinder inflates and unfolds the raft. It's done in less than a minute. Now there's a floating orange hexagon attached to the rope in my hand.

The life raft's peaked canopy reaches the bow of the boat. We spin the raft until the oval access opening is directly below us. Jack throws the two packs we salvaged and the extra life jacket down into it. With few words and no actual planning, Anna climbs over the rail, ready to drop into the raft. I grip the rope and Jack lies on his stomach to grab a handle on the canopy.

"Go!" Jack tells Anna, who's touching the edge of the raft with her foot. She lets go and lands with a thud, the raft floating away from us with her impact.

"You go next. Gimme the rope," Jack says. I look at him in protest, hauling the raft back into place. I'm the guide. He's the customer. I should go last. "I'm taller," he says. "I'll reach the raft with my feet when I hang. It's safer if I go last." His logic makes sense. And there's no time to argue. I hop over the rail, hanging from both hands and feeling for the raft edge with my toes.

"Okay?" I yell down at Anna.

"All clear," Anna says, "Drop in." I tumble into the wobbly raft. When I flop over, Jack's legs are already dangling through the access. He was right. He's able to touch the floor of the raft while holding onto the boat. Anna snags his life jacket, so he falls into the raft and not out when he lets go.

"Drop!" Anna says. We're toppled in all directions as the raft bends and rocks under us. I untangle myself from the others and sit up. Anna stares blankly out the access hatch, clutching the spare life jacket tight to her chest. Was it really moments ago that we were talking about a hundred-year-old rockslide?

CHAPTER 5

"Have you found the paddles?" I grope the raft floor behind me, knowing there are supplies somewhere. "And the line cutter?"

The raft is about seven feet across, an almost round hexagon. A thin, silver insulated pad covers the floor. Two inflated tubes, stacked on top of each other, shape the sides. The roof canopy peaks in the middle, where there's about five feet of headroom.

Anna pulls something from underneath her. "These?" She hands over a canvas case. Inside, I find two short-handled paddles and a floating knife.

"Cut us free of the boat." I hand the knife to Jack, who already has his head out the access opening. When he's cut the rope, I sheathe the knife and hand it back to Anna. Then I scramble beside Jack, giving him a paddle. "We've gotta get to the back of the boat and find my dad." I paddle. Jack joins in, making us spin around. We struggle to move the circular raft forward instead of rotating it. With Anna's calm suggestions, we finally start working together, steering the raft toward the stern.

We float slowly along the burning boat. Debris from the fire drops into the water beside us, so we paddle farther away, to protect the raft from damage. We're twenty feet from the flames, but the heat still rips at our faces and arms. I wipe a clammy palm on my pant leg, my white-knuckle grip on the paddle slipping. My stomach is rock hard, and it feels like a month has passed since I've seen my dad. Where is he? He can't possibly still be on the boat. There's a blast that makes me flinch, as breaking glass tinkles, then splashes into the ocean. Jack lifts a single eyebrow as the flames from the cabin lick up through the shattered windows to the kayaks on the roof. We're finally nearing the stern of the boat. Behind the kicker motor, the swim deck is empty. Where is he!?

"Dad! Dad!" I scream shrilly, paddling frantically. The aft door stands open. Nothing but flames and heat and acrid smoke. "Where is he?" I blink rapidly at Jack. A vein pulses hard against a tendon in his neck. His lips are a tight line, brows furrowed. Jack just sets his shoulders and keeps paddling. Bile rises in my throat and my stomach clenches. This can't be. I can't lose my dad too. I glance over my shoulder at Anna. She's found the lookout sleeve in the canopy and has her head out the backside of the raft. Just then, Anna shouts.

"There! Behind us... turn! Turn us around." She pulls her head back inside. "I see him! He's in the water."

My heart beats wildly. Jack and I turn the raft in the direction Anna points. When the raft spins, I get my first glimpse of him floating on his back, maybe fifteen feet away. "Dad!" I scream. Thank goodness.

"Here... Maia...." My name comes out as a moan, barely audible. And he doesn't move toward us. He doesn't move at all. Just floats, staring up into the fog.

We maneuver the raft beside him. He remains motionless, blinking slowly, and my heart races. "We need to get him out of the water," I say. "This cold will give him hypothermia." Anna pushes me aside so she can get a better look. "I'm a nurse." She firmly takes charge. "Let me see."

Jack grabs the shoulder of my dad's grey wool shirt. It's scorched all over and my dad moans as Anna talks to him softly. "Where are you hurt, Lars?"

"Burnt... my hands... arms... couldn't stop it... tried to stop it." His voice cracks, a hoarse whisper.

"It's okay. We're all okay. Let's get you onto this raft." She turns to Jack and me. "We're going to haul him in, okay? Don't touch his hands or arms." To my dad, Anna says, "These two are going to grab your shoulders, okay? We're going to drag you. If you can kick your feet, that will help. It's going to hurt, Lars. I'm sorry." Facing Jack and me, Anna continues. "Okay, the faster we do this, the better. Do not listen to him if he wants us to stop. He needs to get out of the water. Now. Okay?" We both nod and kneel side by side at the opening.

We lean out of the raft and grab my dad under his shoulders. "Ready? One, two, three!" Jack says. We pull, hard. My dad has never verbalized pain, and his grunting screams are horrible. The agonizing rescue takes forever. My dad is a solid man. 200 pounds of muscle. Getting him up and over the inflated rail of the raft takes all of my physical strength. Forcing myself to keep going despite his moaning cries takes all my inner strength. But finally, all four of us are inside. Wet and panting.

My dad sprawls on his back, across the center of the raft. Anna has propped his head up on a dry pack. She's kneeling beside him. I can't make out her words, but hear that comforting croon used on babies. And injured men, evidently. Jack and I sit back against the sides of the raft on either side of my dad's feet, panting. "Are you okay?" I ask Jack, looking him over. With Anna caring for my dad, it's kind of my job to check on our next weakest link.

"I'm not hurt, if that's what you mean," Jack says. "But I don't think any of us are okay. Do you?" I shake my head. No. We are far from okay.

"Lars says to get to shore. To the trailhead. Maia, do you know what he means?" Anna looks up at us, biting her lip.

I nod. I know exactly what my dad means. A white-lettered provincial park sign marks the trailhead halfway along the north shore of the bay. This trailhead is only accessible by boat, so the sign faces the ocean. The problem is, I have no idea where we are right now. The fog is still hiding all landmarks. We're floating in grayness. Dark gray ocean, gray fog, light gray sky. A murky mess. I think for a minute.

"Spin us around so I can see the boat," I say to Jack. It's still burning, the flames lower now. The windows are gone and the stanchions on one side have collapsed, so the roof sits black and crooked. The kayaks are a gooey mess, like melted crayons. I picture the depth sounder screen when we anchored. "See the position of the boat? Like, if you imagine a line from the anchor rope to the back of the boat? It's pointing west. We need to go north. So... if we paddle perpendicular to that line. That way," I say, pointing. Jack pulls the laminated trip map from the back pocket of his jeans.

"Show me where we are," he says. I point out roughly where we anchored the boat, and where I think we are now.

"And this is the trailhead. See the star on the map."

"We don't want to end up out here, though," Jack says, pointing toward the open ocean to the east on the map.

"I know," I say quietly, "but the tide is rising. It'll keep pushing us toward the head of the bay, not out into the open water. And I'm pretty sure about our direction compared to the boat. We don't have much else to go by." I look out into the dense, featureless haze, thicker and darker than it was even minutes ago. Back inside, Anna has found a first aid kit, included with the life raft. With the scissors, she's cutting what's left of my dad's shirt from cuff to shoulder. He has his eyes closed, teeth gritted, trying not to flinch. Anna pulls open the charred remains of the shirt. A sheet of skin peels away with the sleeve to reveal a shiny red, white, and black mess of flesh on dad's forearm and hand. The sickening scent of barbecue and burnt hair fills the life raft. I clamp my eyes shut and my throat burns. Holy shit. Shit. When I finally open my eyes, Jack is staring at me.

"Let's get at it," he says. And we paddle in what we hope is the right direction.

Jack and I fall into a rhythm, paddling the raft slowly across the flat, calm waters of the bay. "It feels like we're dragging something," Jack says.

"We kinda are," I say, "there's big water ballast pockets on the bottom of these rafts. It's so the raft is stable if you're out in big swells."

"Makes sense," Jack says. But it sure doesn't make for easy paddling, I think, glancing behind us. Anna is carefully wrapping bandages around my dad's arms, ignoring his mumbled protests. "Look! Over there. Is that the shore?" Jack asks.

The outline of land emerges from the fog, and I try to assess our position again. We spin back toward the low flickering silhouette of *Moxie*. But from here, with most of her submerged, it's hard to tell whether we should follow the shore to the left or right to connect with the trailhead.

As I consider our options, a raven lifts off from a treetop, gliding out of the fog toward us. It flies low to the water, coming so close we can see the shine of its brown eye as a shrill caw escapes its bent beak. The big black bird then yanks its wingtips up, banking to our right, as if beckoning us to follow. "Maybe he's telling us something," I say with a shrug, hoping the shore is in this direction.

"There!" I shout, after another fifteen minutes of steady paddling. "That's where we want to get to." I point toward the familiar white dogwood flower on the provincial park sign. The shoreline here is a series of jagged, black rocks, covered in sharp barnacles and slippery, puffy mitten-shaped pods of rockweed. It's not a friendly place to land an inflatable craft. We paddle closer to shore, keeping an eye on our depth. My arms feel like rubber and Jack must be tired too. But he hasn't complained. That's something.

Jack points to a gap between two tall rock outcrops, "Maybe in there? It looks wide enough to get through. And the shore isn't too steep." He's right. The rest of the shoreline doesn't really have a beach. Everywhere else the rocks tower straight up from the water, where the dense brush starts.

"Good spot." I agree. We carefully maneuver the raft toward shore. Anna sticks herself out the lookout sleeve again. We carefully guide the raft by paddling and pushing off the rocky outcrops. At last, we feel the floor scrape against the rocky beach beneath us.

Jack gets out first, stepping into the frigid calf-deep water without hesitation. He stops me before I jump out and says, "Let me carry you to shore. No point in all of us getting soaked." I pause, then nod. He lifts me easily, his biceps pushing against my back and hamstrings, as I put my arms around his neck. I hop out of his arms as soon as we get to dry land, my stomach quivering. Jack hands me the raft rope and sloshes back to it. He and Anna discuss something, then there are a few quick grunts from my dad. Jack and Anna gently shift him. First, his boots appear, then his legs hang out over the edge of the raft. Jack takes hold of the shirt on his chest, while Anna pushes him from behind. They get him to an awkward sitting position, with my dad holding his now-bandaged forearms out in front of him, zombie style.

"Do you think you can rock yourself upright?" Jack asks, "I'll make sure you don't fall forward. And careful. These rocks are slippery as hell." My dad nods once. It takes a couple of tries, but he eventually rolls himself up to standing. Jack puts an arm around his waist and helps him hobble over the slippery ocean floor, to the rocky beach beside me. My dad takes a step toward me, then stops, eyebrows drawn. We haven't talked since I smelled smoke on the boat deck, which feels like a lifetime ago.

"How's my girl?" His voice is low, ragged, and hoarse.

"I'm fine." I wrap my arms around his thick, wet chest, hiding my sudden tears. He can't hug me back, but he leans his frozen cheek down into my hair and whispers, "You did good out there, girl. Real good." I savor the musky scent of him, suddenly realizing we haven't touched since The Last Day. Too long. Then I take a big, settling breath and pull away, knowing he expects me to suck it up.

Jack carries Anna to shore, then returns to the raft. I survey the terrain, trying to figure out exactly where we are, while Jack brings the supplies and finally the life raft itself to shore.

"The trailhead is that way." I've been here many times and hoist a dry pack over my shoulders. "I'll go find a good route." Anna helps my dad sit down on a log. He's shivering uncontrollably and needs a fire right away. Jack has pulled his iPod out of his pocket, rubbing it clean with the cuff of his hoodie. Seriously?

"I'll come with you," Jack says, stuffing the device back into his pocket and grabbing the other pack. I let him follow me without responding. We scramble over slippery rocks, driftwood logs and finally punch through the thick salal brush to find the path. It's not far, but it'll be a tough route for my dad to climb without using his hands. Once on the path, the walk to the rustic campsite is steep. I know the spot, although we rarely stay here. Our typical itinerary has us kayak to a beautiful sandy beach up the coast for our first night. But, today is far from typical and our new plan is unclear. Getting all of us warm and dry is job number one.

"We need to start a fire," I say to Jack, pointing at the fire pit. "Could you collect some driftwood while I go get the others?" Jack just stares at me for a moment, his face unreadable, then nods.

"Sure. No problem. Let me get right to work." Jack grumbles and throws down his pack. "I can't believe the mess you guys got us into." None of the replies that pop into my mind should be said out loud. So I just walk back to the beach, fuming.

"It's not far," I say to Anna and my dad, "but there are a few spots where we'll need to help you," I say firmly, looking at my dad. He grunts a non-committal response.

"He's not an easy patient, is he?" Anna says.

"You have no idea." I wonder how she'd handle his past few months. My dad grunts again as he stands up. We pick our way up to the path slowly and he accepts our help, just to make sure he doesn't lose his balance.

When we reach the campsite, Jack has stacked a few pieces of drift-wood beside the fire pit. I look down the beach trail, expecting to see him returning with another armful of twisted sticks. Instead, Jack's sitting on a log with his back to us, his earbuds in, flicking the muck off his formerly pristine shoes. City kid.

Chapter 6

"Let's see which packs we ended up with." I decide to ignore Jack's selfish position on the beach. Opening the first bag, I hope it's not one of the guests'. My dad and I carry a bunch of extra supplies, including things like the big tarp, parachute cord, water bottles, packets of freeze-dried food, toilet paper, and, most critical right now, a waterproof lighter. The first pack turns out to be Anna's. Damn. I cross my fingers and open the other one. It's my dad's. Nice. Our first bit of good luck today, I think, digging to the bottom for the lighter. Before I do anything else, I'll start the fire.

I pull my silver Swiss Army knife from my pocket and work on the fire. I kneel, bracing a chunk of cedar driftwood against the rock fire ring. Slowly, I shave off thin strips until I have a good handful in a pile. The sharp, woodsy scent makes me think of my dad's sawmill. I shudder, looking down at my right hand. Gripping a knife is more difficult now, without my last two fingers. It's doable, just different. After rotating the cedar chunk, I carve another series of strips, this time cutting only part way. The wood ends up with crescents of kindling attached to it — my favorite fire-starting trick.

Behind me, Anna digs through my dad's pack for dry clothes. My dad sits hunched on a stump beside her, shivering and pale, his forearms resting gingerly on his thighs. Piling the cedar shavings inside the pit, I click the lighter at the base of the stack. Flames lick up and I lay the kindling with the crescents over the flames, careful not to crush my tiny fire. I watch the progress, then lay more small sticks on the fire, always leaving plenty of air gaps. Adding larger pieces, the flames soon take hold for good. The warmth of this fire already feels comforting, in stark contrast to the terrifying blaze of the boat.

"There." I wipe my hands on my pants, glancing at my dad. "This should warm you up." Jack sits with his back to us, on the beach, listening to music. Fine. I'd rather have his negativity far away from me. These two are guests and I have a lot to do. If he's happy sitting on a log, fine with me.

I walk back over to Anna and my dad, eyeing the packs. Without the kayaks or our boat, we'll probably have to sleep here tonight. "I should pitch the tents," I say.

"No," my dad says, "You need to walk to the —"

"No way," I say. "No way am I leaving you!" I lift my chin, my fingernails digging into my palms. I'm not sure what the plan should be, but leaving my injured dad with a couple of city slickers is not it. Absolutely not.

" — beach. You need to go... you can flag down a fishing boat. Tonight." His nostrils flare and his face reddens.

"I won't leave you!" I shake my head and stomp over to the tent area. No matter what we decide, my dad's not going anywhere. He'll be more comfortable lying down in a tent. So I let the routine of setting up camp absorb me.

There are four tent pads surrounding the fire pit. The spots are level and soft with spruce and hemlock needles. I start with the tent from dad's pack. Once it's set up, I get the tent from Anna's pack and set it up opposite the first. I wonder what the sleeping arrangements tonight will be. Every combination I come up with is awkward.

I add more wood to the fire and watch my dad and Anna. They've been talking quietly while I set up camp. I pretended not to notice the animated discussion about getting my dad into dry underwear. They went behind the outhouse at one point. I'm guessing my dad allowed Anna to help him strip and redress because he's now dry. He's also taken off his soaked hiking boots and has on a pair of his colorful foam clogs.

"How are you doing? Does it hurt a lot?" I balance his hiking boots on the fire ring to dry.

"It's okay," he says. I wonder how true that is. Anna's brow furrows in concern. And fear. She inflates a sleeping mat and directs my dad to lie down under a sleeping bag in the first tent. He does as he's told. He must feel pretty bad to be bossed around like that.

"How are you, Maia?" Anna asks after helping my dad settle. "Are you hurt?" I shake my head no. Not injured. But not okay either, I think.

"Thanks for helping him," I say. "Are you okay?"

"I'm fine. Dry. Not hurt." Anna scans the campsite. "Where's Jack?"

"I'm not sure." I glance at where I last saw him. "If he's not in the outhouse, he must've gone farther down the beach."

"I'll go see what he's up to." Anna starts down the trail, tucking her hair under her ball cap.

Even though it's not raining right now, past trips have taught us we need to be ready for it. Rain can come on suddenly and hard, so we always set up the tarp when we make camp. Even if there're no clouds in sight. A tarp set up halfway over the fire will keep the heat near the tents. I peer up into the dense canopy of old-growth, searching for the right branches. First, I need two spots to tie up the ridgeline rope, each a few feet outside the fire pit. Once I imagine its position, I tie a small piece of bark onto the end of one rope so I can throw it over the first branch. It takes me a couple of shots, but I get the first rope in place. Then I do the same with the other end of it. With the rope slack on the ground, I position the tarp over the ridgeline rope and feed both ends through the tie-out points. Then I haul on the rope. As it tightens, the tarp raises off the ground, hanging like a bedsheet on a clothesline. I just have to secure the corners.

After twenty minutes and some adjusting, I have a pretty good shelter. One-half of the tarp stretches over the fire pit. It's high enough that most of the smoke finds its way out. The last two corners I've tied lower, so the tarp hangs almost vertically and close to the ground. This way, it will trap and reflect more heat from the fire.

Anna and Jack aren't back yet, so I check on my dad.

"The boat. Did you see?" he asks when I scoot under the tent fly. The sleeping bag is tucked around his pale face.

"She's gone... sunk. After we pulled you out." From the life raft, I had watched as the ocean covered the carefully painted black letters spelling out *Moxie*, then swallowed the hull to the roofline.

"What a mess."

"Yeah," I say. "Do you know when Rick's next charter is?" I ask, referring to our friend and water taxi captain.

"In five days. Ran into him... yesterday. On the dock. Not many bookings. Won't be up 'til Tuesday morning," says my dad. "You really need to walk out, Maia."

"I won't!" I say. "I can't just leave you here... what about the hand-held?" Referring to our VHF radio, I feel a heartbeat of hope.

"It was in the food pack."

"Shit," I say under my breath. The food pack didn't make it off the boat. So we wait for help. Definitely not the trip Jack and Anna signed up for.

Ten minutes later, Anna comes back up the trail, Jack following behind her. They both look tired, worried, and cold. I can relate.

"Jack's still wet," Anna says as she approaches the fire. "Can I check your dad's pack for some dry pants?"

"I'll do it," I say. Jack's skate shoes are soaked too, so I hand him one of my dad's boots, still drying on the fire ring. "Will these fit?" He takes off his shoe to reveal a muddy cotton sport sock. "Hold on." A shadow of concern follows me to the backpacks. Jack must be freezing.

I come back a moment later with a pair of my dad's gray wool work socks and khaki-colored nylon pants. The boots will be a good fit, but Jack leaves them by the fire while he changes.

Once Jack returns, he sits on a stump, warming his woolly feet on the rocks. Anna arranges herself cross-legged next to the door of my dad's tent.

"So what's the plan, Lars?" she asks. On my haunches beside the fire, I wonder how he'll reply.

"Not good," my dad says. "No boat, no kayaks, no radios. Some freeze-dried food." He mumbles, staring up at the tent ceiling. "The water taxi comes Tuesday. Five days. We can make it five days."

"I'll be honest," Anna says, hesitating. She glances at me, then turns to my dad. "I don't think you have five days. Not if you want to use your hands... and fingers... again." My stomach tightens, and I study the flames as Anna continues. "I've treated burn patients. Your burns are very, very serious. You need a hospital, sterile bandages, antibiotics," she says, her face softening. "Being out here for days is not an option for you. What else can we do to get help?" She looks at each of us, eyebrows raised. "Anyone? Ideas?"

"We could light a signal fire down on the point." Jack makes a quiet suggestion.

"Our burning boat was a huge signal fire. I don't think there's anyone around. Or they'd be here." I picture the lonely radar screen, where our boat had been the only moving blip.

"There are flares." Jack tries again. "In the lifeboat." My dad looks over, a tentative smile building.

"Flare gun? Or handhelds?" my dad asks.

"Just handhelds, I think, three of them."

"Better than nothin'." My dad shakes his head a bit. "Could signal if anyone cruises into the bay. A flare gun would've been better." He's mumbling, almost to himself. "Maybe could've signaled a float plane..." He's so pale. My palms are suddenly clammy. I imagine my dad without fingers. Without hands. I shudder and squeeze my eyes shut. As if closing my eyelids will stop the images flashing through my mind. I'm pretty sure Anna isn't even telling us the whole truth. There is something unreadable in her expression. A look I remember seeing on Maggie and the faces of other nurses who cared for my mum. Sympathy. Mixed with helplessness. "I'll get more wood." I stand abruptly and stride toward the beach, desperate to be alone.

I don't stop until I'm right down on the rocky point, the campsite no longer visible behind me. Sitting on a flat rock, I wrap my arms around my shins, chin resting on my knees. I'm so afraid for my dad. I take a deep breath, trying to calm the buzzing in my brain. The cool air smells of briny seaweed and the fog holds me in a dense white blanket, hiding all landmarks. The narrow section of ocean visible is still glassy, with only the softest waves gurgling against the rocky outcrop below me.

Without distractions, my mind flashes back to the boat. The rumbling heat of the fireball in the cabin. The thudding of my frenzied heartbeat as we searched for my dad. The warm rush of relief when we found him. Then more gut-churning terror as I recall his raw flesh and the stench of burnt meat and hair. I rock gently, back and forth, forehead on my knees. Haven't we had enough? Haven't we been through enough? I'm so done. So done with things I can't control.

A soft whooshing makes me peek to my right. It's the raven, showing off its impressive wingspan as it lands on the point.

"What are you doing here?" I ask the big black bird. It tilts its head, one dark eye looking my way, then gives a low croaking call, its throat hackles puffing. My mum's smile rushes at me through the fog. We had a moment like this a few years ago, watching crows and ravens down on the beach back home. She had shown me the differences between the two species until I could identify each. Their flight, landing, call, tail feathers, and beaks are all quite different if you know what to look for.

We'd gone on that beach walk to talk about a speech I had to give for school. I had been terrified. I still hate speaking in front of groups. But mum had been so sensible and encouraging. What was I actually afraid of? Looking silly? She had made me realize everyone felt the same. What could we do to make speaking to the class easier? Practice? So I practiced my speech. Alone, then on my parents. I recited that speech so many times, I believed the whole thing would go well.

And it did go well. I got off the bus and ran home that day, thrilled to tell my mum how it had gone. She had loaned me her gold bracelet that morning. My mum told me I was prepared, and the bracelet was just to remind me of all the work I'd done. And it *had* given me strength. The cool metal hidden under the sleeve of my hoodie had boosted my confidence.

My breath catches now, my body remembering my scrambled search for that bracelet on The Last Day. I had gone into my parents' room upstairs, a place I rarely entered. But that day I stepped into their sanctuary with purpose. I had been so sure finding the bracelet, having it, wearing it would help. It had been Grosmüti's, my mum's mum's, crafted of thin oval links. My dad wouldn't mind if I took it. He'd never liked jewelry and especially didn't like that bracelet. Or maybe it was my grandmother he didn't like.

Anyway, I had crept into their ensuite, to the small cedar box in the mirrored medicine cabinet where my mum had kept her sparse jewelry collection. I knew the contents by heart: a set of round gold stud earrings; a blond lock of hair, tied with a blue satin ribbon, from my first haircut; a baby tooth, which the tooth fairy had paid me a quarter for, in a tiny cotton pouch; and Grosmüti's gold bracelet.

But the bracelet hadn't been there. The earrings, tooth, and hair were there. But the bracelet had been missing. I needed that bracelet! Stunned, I tore apart the medicine cabinet, the bathroom drawers, and their bedside tables. Where could it be? I couldn't ask my dad. I didn't want to admit I'd been snooping through their stuff. And I've been scared to bring up anything related to my mum with him. That night, as I hugged my pillow, I felt foolish. Why was I putting so much value on a physical thing?

I had just wanted one thing of hers. Something joyful. Something that had nothing to do with pain or chemo or cancer or death. She had only worn that bracelet on special occasions. Events where my mum danced and laughed and cried happy tears. I still wonder what happened to it. And I still wish I had that bracelet.

Now, as the raven croaks again, I remember my mum's soft eyes twinkling at me the afternoon of my speech, her hands wrapped around the mug of tea we always shared when I got home.

"It feels good, doesn't it? Makes you happy when you get through something that scares you," she had said gently. "The best way out is always through, Maia. Remember that."

And suddenly I know what to do. Right now. I'm going to walk out. Walking out is something I *can* do. One thing I can control. Action that might bring help to my dad sooner. Anna will look after him better than I can while I'm gone. She's the nurse.

I jump to my feet, scaring the raven into flight. "Thanks, buddy!" I say as it glides across the water, disappearing into the fog. My mum's wise words release some tension from my chest as I stride toward camp. Where the rocky beach becomes a forest trail, a speck of color in the brush catches my attention. I step closer and recognize one of our laminated maps. Folded into a perfect paper airplane. Jack! It could only be him defacing mum's carefully curated work. Asshole, I think, stuffing the map into my back pocket.

Back at camp, I go to Anna and my dad, facing away from Jack. I can't handle him right now. "I'm going to walk out," I say. They look at me, unmoving. "I'll take the trail from here to the next beach. First thing in the morning. The salmon charters run right by that beach. I'll have a good chance of flagging one of them down. I'll take some flares." My dad nods, staring straight up with a loud exhale.

"How far is it?" Anna asks.

"Probably an eight-hour hike. It took me six late last summer. But it was way less muddy then." I need to do this. I've never been more sure of anything.

CHAPTER 7

Anna's hungry, so we'll eat before discussing our plan further. I pull two pouches of freeze-dried beef stew from my dad's pack. All we need is hot water, but our cooking supplies didn't make it. My brow furrows.

"Do you still have your coffee mug?" I ask Anna. I twist the black plastic top off of the mug she hands me, leaving just the stainless steel cup.

"It'll get sooty," I say, "but I think this will work."

There are three water bottles, each full of a liter of fresh water. I fill Anna's mug halfway and balance it between a couple of rocks right in the fire. "This will take a while to heat." I look up at Anna, who has been crouched next to my dad, murmuring. It's weird not having him out here and in charge. Anna sits on a log near me and watches the fire for a few minutes. Jack slides into his skater shoes like slippers, crushing the heel tab to shuffle toward the outhouse.

"You need to take that trail now." Anna breaks the silence. "I —" She stops, unsure how to continue. "Your dad's in bad shape. He sounds okay, but his body is going into shock. Without proper treatment, his burns will get infected. And out here, without antibiotics, an infection can..." Anna tosses a pine cone into the flames.

"Can what, Anna?" I know, but I need her to say it.

"An infection out here can be deadly, Maia." Anna looks at me gently. "I'm not sure Lars realizes how bad he is. And maybe that's good. I won't be able to do much for him. Getting to proper medical care is what he needs," she says. I know she's right and nod slowly. "I'll have Jack come with you. I can't let you go alone."

"I don't know." The last thing I want is to spend eight hours alone with Jack. "He won't want to do that. I don't think he likes us at all."

"Are you kidding?" Anna says. "Jack likes you fine. He's a bit stunned by you, I think. He hasn't spent time with girls who do real things. And I know he's acting like an idiot." Anna smirks, shrugging her shoulders. "All teenage boys act like idiots around girls they like."

"I don't... I mean... he's just not used to hiking like I am." I'm not buying her interpretation of Jack's attitude toward me. Not for a minute. "He'll have a hard time on this part of the trail. It's not a good idea."

"No argument. You can't go alone. And you have to go." As Jack returns and warms his hands over the fire, Anna says, "So Jack will go with you. Right, Jack?"

"What?"

"You'll hike with Maia to the next beach," Anna says to him. "She knows the way, and going together is safer." I pull the crumpled trail map from my back pocket, giving Jack a defiant glare. He twists away from my silent accusation, throwing a skeptical look back at Anna. From my crouched spot by the fire, I watch their wordless conversation.

"You'll be useful," Anna says, "and it'll make us grown-ups feel better knowing Maia's not alone out there." Jack returns Anna's encouraging smile with a long, doubtful stare. When he finally nods back at her, I get the feeling they've already talked about this option.

"Better than sittin' and waitin', I guess. So what's the plan exactly?" Jack asks. I stare down at the map and consider how to answer, as Anna crouches under the tent fly to check on my dad. I finally decide nothing good will come of speaking my mind. How mature of me.

"We're here," I say finally, pointing at the yellow star marking the trailhead. "Tomorrow morning, we'll follow this trail, up the hill here, across the upland marsh, and then back down to the first beach here." I point out the route on the creased map, still pissed at Jack. This will not be easy, but he's our guest and I'm a guide. My emotions are supposed to stay out of it.

I hear a grunt from the tent, where Anna has her hand on my dad's forehead. He groans again as he tries to shift his position. Anna says a few words I can't hear. My dad closes his eyes, turning his head away. She ducks out of the tent.

"You should leave right away. He's already running a fever." Anna's words are firm and somber this time.

"But we usually start this trek early in the day." It's a tough hike to add to the day we've already had. I gaze up at the dense fog. Even if we start right now, we've probably got less than eight hours of daylight. And we need time for packing and reorganizing our supplies before we can leave.

"He's getting worse fast," Anna says. "If there's a chance to flag a boat from that beach tonight, go now."

After a beat, I nod. "Let's get to work, then."

❧

We empty both packs and make three piles of gear: one for each of our 'to go' packs, and one for the supplies we'll leave. None of Jack's or my clothing has survived the boat fire, so Anna gives me a pair of her socks and underwear. "They're clean," she says, smiling.

On the first day of hiking, blisters are common. Jack wearing boots that aren't his own concerns me, but staying warm if we get wet is the next big challenge. Anna worries aloud that my dad will become hypothermic, so we split the warm layers evenly between our two groups. The two sets of rain gear will go with Jack and me, while Anna and my dad have the tarp and a tent.

Our freshwater supply is tiny for four people. This campsite has no water source, so we leave two bottles here and take one with us. Jack and I can refill from the river at the next beach.

With the coolers and food pack lost, the food supply is also pathetic. Not counting the two packets we're cooking now, we have ten pouches of freeze-dried meals: four beef stew and six Pad Thai chicken. Each group takes half, then we also divide the eight protein bars equally.

Next, we go through the miscellaneous supplies. The life raft stuff will stay here, but Jack and I take two handheld flares. I have my jackknife, so we leave Anna the other knife. There's a headlamp from my dad's pack, which we leave with Anna. Jack and I take the roll of toilet paper since there's a well-stocked outhouse right by this camp. I've already used some of the parachute cord to set up the tarp and cut off the unused portion now. I coil the rope around my hand and elbow, secure it into a neat loop, and toss it on the 'to go' pile.

"There's only one lighter." I nod toward the fire pit.

"You guys need to take the lighter. And the coffee mug," Anna says, "This fire's burning well, there's lots of wood. I'll just make damn sure I don't let it go out," she says. I nod. It's the right decision and I'm glad Anna sees it that way, too.

Finally, we dismantle the empty tent, put up less than an hour ago. I open the vent of the sleeping mat, rolling the stale air out of it. Jack and Anna fold the fly while I yank the tent pegs and put them in a small nylon pouch. The orange tent billows to the ground as I remove the last arching tent pole. Although he has his earbuds in, I notice Jack pays close attention to everything I do. Good. Together, we fold and roll the tent inside the fly, then stuff the whole works back into its carry bag.

"It's less heavy than usual. But this stuff will get us up and over to the next beach." I say this with more confidence than I feel. Jack is going to slow me down. I really hope he's up for this challenge.

In the fire, the water in the mug is steaming. I pull my sleeve over my hand and move it off the flames. "A thermal mug doesn't make the best cooking pan," I say, "but it's better than nothing at all." I tear the top from the first silver pouch, getting a whiff of beefy spice, before pouring in the warm water. I reseal the pouch with the zipper top, give it a shake and say to Anna, "Gourmet meal in fifteen minutes." Then I refill the coffee mug with water to make the second portion.

We don't have any cutlery, so while we wait for the beef stew to rehydrate, I choose a flat piece of driftwood and start whittling. Jack slumps on a log across from me, still listening to his music. He moves only to rotate my dad's boots occasionally, drying by the fire. Anna has her hand on my dad's forehead again.

"There." I've smoothed the wood, narrowed the top as a handle, and hollowed out the bottom, like a spoon. I don't wait for a response from Jack, just open the pouch of food. It's barely warm, but has re-hydrated nicely. "Here, you first." I hand Jack the spoon and pouch. Without removing his earbuds, he takes the food with a silent nod.

Anna joins us by the fire, and Jack passes her the pouch. "Here. Have some," Jack says. "It's actually pretty good." The first positive words out of him.

"How is he?" I ask Anna, as she takes another bite of stew.

"No better. Resting," she says, "I'll try to get some of this into him." She motions at the food bag in her hands. "You should go talk to him now. He wants to see you before you leave."

I scoot under the fly next to my dad. "Hey," I whisper. His eyes open and he looks up at me.

"I'm sorry... Maia," he whispers. "Sorry." The word comes out with an almost inaudible sigh as he slowly shakes his head. I remember the last time he said those words to me, our roles reversed. Then it was me lying in the hospital bed, my hand bandaged up to my elbow. After a moment, he asks, "What changed your mind?" His voice is clearer, head tilting. I suddenly decide to tell him the truth. We haven't talked about mum, not since The Last Day. But it's about time we did.

"I remembered something mum told me," I say, observing his expression, "when I was down on the beach just now." He doesn't ask what I remembered, just nods and closes his blue eyes. His features soften at her memory.

"She was full of good. Full of good advice. Good ideas," my dad says hoarsely. "If you have trouble, do what she would do." I nod, so glad he's finally verbalized a good memory of my precious mum. That's a huge step forward. "She did the right thing. We did the right thing. Never doubt that." His gruff statement surprises me and I close my eyes, hugging myself tightly, rocking a little, remembering it all.

When I finally find my voice, I say, "We're leaving you guys the tarp... and two bottles of water. And half the food." Turning to practicalities changes the subject. "I don't know about taking Jack, but I guess I have to," I say. "He won't be easy to lead."

"Maybe not. He's an indoor human." My dad grunts the last two words, our code for guests who don't do well out here. "You stay out of trouble with him," my dad says. An expression I don't recognize crosses his pale face. Tears suddenly block my vision, as memories of the last year swirl through my mind. I wipe my eyes, snuffling. We discuss what we'll do once we summon help, with no mention of what could go wrong. No point in listing the perils out loud. We both know. Out beyond the tent fly, Jack is loading his pack.

"I think it's time," I say, absently rubbing the knuckles where my fingers should be. "See you in a day… or two." I reach over, patting his thigh through the sleeping bag.

"You be careful, my girl," my dad says. "Be smart. Head in the game." He repeats one of mum's favorite phrases.

"Head in the game," I say, and smile. "And you listen to Anna. Don't be so stubborn." I glance out at her. "You're lucky she's a nurse. And a pretty nice person." I'm crawling out of the tent when my dad's voice makes me turn again.

"The supply cache. It's there if you need it. Use it." His words puzzle me. Jack and I aren't going anywhere near the cache. We're only going to the next beach. But there's no time to debate my dad's thinking. We need to get moving. Without looking back, I pack up the rest of my gear.

Chapter 8

With my pack over one shoulder, I wrestle into it and then bounce the load into a comfortable position. I grope behind me for the waist belt, buckle it, and cinch it over my hips.

"You ready?" I ask, clipping my chest strap. Anna brushes invisible debris from Jack's sleeve, then reaches her hands up on his shoulders.

"Be careful," she says. Anna pulls Jack down into a quick hug, which he returns, clearing his throat. She turns to me. "And you be careful, too." Jack and I both nod. Minimal fuss — I appreciate that in Anna.

"We'll see you tomorrow... or the next day," I say. Anna and I share a long look, wordlessly agreeing to take good care of each other's people. "Ready?" I ask again.

"Sure." Jack gives Anna a last smile and puts one earbud in. We start up the trail at a slow, steady pace. It's the middle of the day, but the path is gloomy. The forest canopy covers us entirely and the thick fog is so low the tree tops disappear into it. The trail steepens sharply after the first bend. I take a deep breath of the damp, sweet, cool air. I love being in the woods.

The sword ferns droop onto the path, their stems shining wet and heavy. We step over the twisted roots of cedar trees and up the natural steps of cat-tail moss-covered boulders. Invisible wisps of spider webs crisscross the path, and I bat them off my cheeks and eyelashes. I clear most of the gossamer threads by leading, but soon Jack feels the first silky cobweb. He flinches and sidesteps, brushing wildly at his face.

The salal brush on both sides of us is so thick, we can only see a few feet into it. If you go off the beaten track here, you're invisible after just a step or two. Now and then, the brush rustles or twigs snap beyond the trail. Each time, Jack freezes, scanning our surroundings wide-eyed. I don't comment, just wait until he's ready to continue. Our guests get less skittish as they spend more time out here. Forest sounds can intimidate — like spending a night in a creaky, unfamiliar house.

We walk without talking, taking in the wood's voices until we get to the first climb a half-hour later. I didn't see any point in warning Jack about it. I stop at the base of the cliff and Jack walks up beside me, pulling out his earbud.

"Damn." He cranes his neck. In front of us is fifty feet of near-vertical slope. A thick gray rope starts at our feet and disappears up into a fog-filled clearing at the top. Natural footholds of huge tree roots, fallen logs, and lichen-crusted rocks lead up into the grayness. "We're climbing that?"

"Yep," I say. "Just pretend it's a really steep set of stairs." I grab the rough rope and step onto the first tree root. "I'll go first. Always three points of contact," I instruct. "Two hands and a foot, or two feet and a hand. And never let go of the rope. Grab it as high up as you can reach before you take your next step. And Jack?" I pause until his eyes meet mine. "No earbuds."

"Do I follow you right away?" Jack ignores my jab, but tucks his earbuds away and turns his ball cap around so the brim covers his neck.

"No. Wait until I hit the top," I say. "The ground's unstable up there, so stand back. And watch out for falling rocks."

I start my climb, keenly aware of Jack's gaze on my butt. Focus. I really need to pay attention to every foot placement. Tripping on this cliff with a heavy pack on will hurt even if I don't fall all the way down.

And my right hand still doesn't give me a reliable grip. The hours of physio I've done have improved my strength and range of motion, but my hand will never function like it used to. It's amazing how much work your two smallest fingers do in normal activities like picking up a mug or holding a steak knife. Or gripping a thick rope like I'm doing now.

My climb is steady until I'm halfway. There's a heavy cedar bough that's fallen across the trail. The spays of branches with their flat, scale-like leaves poke out from the bough in all directions. It's too big to climb over, so we'll have to go under. I break off branches from the underside, creating an opening we can fit through. Keeping myself tight to the mossy slope, I shimmy under the bough. Something on my pack gets caught, so I have to backtrack once. But after a few minutes, I'm past this snag.

I peer down at Jack. "You gotta suck yourself close to the slope here... or your pack will get stuck, too."

"Got it."

Once I get over the crest, I call down to Jack. "Your turn. Take your time. Be sure of every step." I kneel beside the tree, which anchors the climbing rope, watching Jack start his ascent. He's awkward at first. It's an odd rhythm, climbing along a rope on such a steep slope. Plus, the pack puts your balance off. But he does well. I can see he's coordinated and in good shape. And I can see he's listening. He's not trying to show off by being super speedy. I relax a little.

When he's halfway, he disappears under the fallen cedar bough. The rope moves to the beat of his slow steps. First one hand, then his other, emerges from beneath the cedar, firmly gripping the rope as he climbs. When the top of his ball cap becomes visible, he looks skyward and gives me a quick thumbs-up. Then there's a loud crack, and Jack shouts in alarm. Rockfall clatters and Jack grunts as he slides away under the cedar bough.

I peer over the edge, my heart pounding. Jack's boots dig into a couple of boulders, just downslope of the cedar bough, with the rest of him still hidden behind the branches. The forest is quiet, except for the tinkling of falling stones. "Jack!" I say, "Jack, are you okay?"

The cedar rustles as he moves around under it. Jack grunts with exertion, then says, "Yeah... I'm fine... but I think I'm stuck." The bough jostles again. "I can't move up... or down," Jack says. "I snagged my pack on something. I can't see what."

"Are you still on the rope?" He's slid off to the right.

"No. And I can't reach it from here." There's more rustling and then, barely audible, Jack says, "Damn it!"

"I'm coming down." I drop my pack. "Don't move," I say. "Wait until I'm down there. You don't want to slide any further." I slowly rappel down toward Jack. I stay to the left, trying not to kick any rocks loose down on him.

When I reach the cedar, I duck my head under the bough to get a look at what's happened. Jack is sprawled flat against the slope, his face resting on a moss-covered tree root. A large branch has pulled his pack up over the back of his head. He's standing on his tiptoes on a couple of boulders, his hands gripping roots on the slope above him. The fallen bough has him pinned so tightly to the slope that he can't see where to take his next step.

"You okay?" I ask again. There's blood on his cheek and dirt smeared above his eyebrow.

"Yeah. I didn't fall far. I just don't know which way to move... so I don't make it worse."

"No worries. I see the problem." Gripping the climbing rope with both hands, I take two more careful steps toward him. "I'm going to break off that branch to free your pack." I give the climbing rope a whip, moving to the right and closer to Jack. With my left hand firmly gripping the rope, I can just reach the branch with my injured hand. After I unhook his pack from the broken limb, I plant my feet under the cedar bough and use the strength in my legs to lift it off Jack. His pack falls back into place, free of the snag.

"I can't get this rope any closer," I say. "So we need to get you over this way a bit more." I see what needs to happen to do this safely, and don't like it. But I bury my hesitation, stretching my injured hand toward Jack. "Grab my wrist. Then push yourself up so you can see where to step." Jack looks at my hand, hesitates, and raises his eyebrows at me. "It's okay," I say with a small smile. "You won't hurt me. That hand's just not very strong, so it's better if you hold on to my wrist." After a beat, Jack does as he's told. We both strain as he finds a better foothold for one foot and then the other. He holds onto my wrist until he's close enough to reach the rope with his other hand. Finally, we're both standing comfortably on bigger rocks, holding onto the rope with both hands, with me perched a few feet above him.

"That was exciting," I say. Jack is shaking his head, staring over at the branch. When he finally peers up at me, I give him a nod and a thumbs up, then I clamber back up to the top. I'm able to move more quickly without my pack, but after Jack's slip-up, I'm even more deliberate with each step. Rolling over the crest, I yell down for the second time today, "Your turn!"

This time, Jack ascends without issues. I move back from the top of the cliff as his flushed face comes into view.

"Well, that's the first one done," I say. Jack flops himself beside me onto the soft, mossy ground lying on his back.

"There's more of these cliffs?"

"Yeah. But this is the hardest." I say. Jack's long eyelashes brush his cheek above the bloody scratch as he blinks, looking up at the foggy tree line.

"Thanks for that, down there." He turns toward me, his voice soft. "You saved my ass." Jack's face holds none of the revulsion I'm used to seeing on kids' faces after they get a good view of my hand.

"You're bleeding," I say, pointing to his face.

"Just a flesh wound." Jack fingers his cheek. "Doesn't hurt."

"So then. You okay to keep going?"

"Sure," Jack says, hauling himself up and adjusting his earbuds. "Lead the way."

The trail continues to climb to the right. We come to the next cliff, shorter than the first, and we manage it with no problems. At the top, we sit for a brief break. About an hour and a half ago we left the trailhead, and we've already gained almost 400 meters in elevation.

"This section is the hardest part of the whole coastal trail." I pass Jack the water bottle. He takes a sip as I absently rub the knuckles of my right hand.

"Does it hurt?" he asks. I look down and jerk the sleeve of my hoodie over the scars.

"Not much," I say, without looking up.

"What happened?" I'm tired of that question. At school, most kids know the whole story. Or at least they think they do. Those who ask have a morbid curiosity that prompts smart-ass one-liners from me. Grizzly bear. Shark attack. That kind of thing. Usually, that shuts the person down and stops the conversation.

But Jack's question now feels sincere, so I meet his gaze. "I was running my dad's sawmill. And I made a mistake." Not the whole truth, but hopefully enough to satisfy Jack.

"You can run a sawmill?" he asks, eyes widening.

"Sure," I say, "It's not complicated. I mean, it's hard work. But operating it is easy."

"Sounds dangerous," Jack says, shaking his head. "My parents would never let me try something like that."

"Not dangerous at all!" Grinning, I shove my injured hand toward him. Jack freezes, his mouth hanging open, then bursts out laughing.

"Sorry!" He chokes out between laughs. "I wasn't thinking... I shouldn't have said that."

"It's fine." I wave off his apology, laughing with him. It feels good to share a joke with someone. I haven't laughed in a long time. A really long time. "It happened last fall," I say. "I'm getting used to it."

"Well, damn Maia. It sure doesn't slow you down." Jack kicks my boot with his, and a broad smile reaches his eyes as he shakes his head at me. Huh? Heat rises in my face and I turn away, puzzled by our exchange.

CHAPTER 9

"We should get moving." I change the subject, knowing the clock is ticking for my dad. I pull my pack over my shoulders. Jack follows my lead, then puts in a single earbud. The trail here opens up, the steep stand of giant old-growth giving way to a flat marshland. The trees are shorter and contorted, harsh conditions stunting their growth.

"How come the big trees don't grow up here?" Jack asks. We walk onto the first section of the boardwalk, and he seems eager to keep the conversation going.

"Something about the soil," I say. "I think it's acidic because of the poor drainage, maybe." Jack takes in the change in scenery. We follow the silver wood planks of the old boardwalk as it zig-zags through the upland bog. Down in the muskeg ground cover are curving waterways and small ponds. All the foliage up here is tiny. When I was little, it was easy to imagine that fairies lived in these places. I smile, still sensing the enchantment.

Only the steady thunk of our boots on the boardwalk breaks the silence. When Jack's steps suddenly stop, I glance back at him. What's he afraid of now, I wonder? He's looking ahead, to our right. I follow his gaze and realize Jack is staring in awe, not fear. Watching us motionless is a sandhill crane, a wisp of green foliage hanging from its long, thin, black beak. It's dark slate gray, with tan body feathers, which makes it blend into the surrounding fog. Its bright red crown and orange eyeball stand out, though. Without the clunking of our footsteps, we can hear a snoring purr coming from the bird's throat. It tilts its head and lifts a skinny leg. The wrinkled black skin pulls taut over its knobby knees as it steps away from us. Its neck straightens and bobs as it walks to the rhythm of its prancing gait.

Then suddenly, the huge bird lurches forward and in a single step takes flight. Its wings spread to an immense six feet across, pumping the damp air with a powerful whooshing flurry. The sound gets louder as the tree line forces the bird to circle toward us. I look straight up as it flies directly overhead in a graceful arc. Its long neck stretched out, wings flapping strongly, and clawed skinny feet trailing its heavy body. Jack's eyes are wide and his mouth hangs open, gazing after the bird until it disappears into the fog behind us.

"Wow!" Jack says. "I've never seen anything so huge, so close." His pure amazement thaws a bit more of my coldness toward him.

"I know, right?" I say. "I still don't get how those things can fly. They're so cool." I walk again, but continue in my guiding voice, "I'm not sure where its partner is. Do you know sandhill cranes mate for life?" I turn to look at Jack as he says something unintelligible behind me. "What?" I ask, not clear if he meant for me to hear.

"Nothing." Jack shakes his head and stares off into the distance. Then he sighs and looks up. "I just wish people had the same decency as those birds. To mate for life, I mean," he says. I wonder if he expects a response. When Jack stays silent, I decide to leave it. We need to get going. I give him a smile and start walking again.

After a moment, I hear Jack's footsteps match pace with mine.

Crossing the upland bog will take us another couple of hours. Some of the trail is boardwalks, and the rest is directly on the soggy marshland. We soon encounter the first muddy section. We don't talk much and I wonder how Jack's viewing this whole adventure. I should distract my guest from the discomforts of the hike, so I teach Jack our family's mud rating scale.

"It's a scale of one to ten," I say. "One is like a really dry mud. Like stuff you can easily stand on, just wet enough that you leave nice footprints. Then two is a bit wetter. Five is something like bird poop. Eight is self-leveling and ten is swimmable." I chuckle at the mental image of breast-stroking through the muck.

"So... this stuff here... is like a four, maybe?" Jack asks. "Chocolate frosting?"

I smile over at him and say, "I think you've cracked the Müller family mud rating code." Jack grins back and steps carefully over a puddle. But he miscalculates the consistency of the ground. With one step, the mud buries his right knee. Unable to stop his forward momentum, his left foot ends up beside his right. Suddenly, he's a foot shorter than me. Jack windmills his arms around wildly, struggling not to face-plant into the mud. I watch helplessly, trying to suppress a giggle.

"Well damn," Jack says, staying upright. "I'd call this mud a goose-shit five. Wouldn't you?"

"I would totally agree." I respond formally, playing along, but it's hard not to laugh. "So... do you want to know the tricks for extracting yourself from deep mud?" I ask, falling into my guide voice again.

"I think I got this." Jack tries to lift his knee and wiggle his foot out of the muck. His movements sink him deeper and he struggles to keep his balance. "Damn," Jack says again.

"Toss me your pack. Before you turtle." I'm conscious of the time we're wasting.

"Turtle?"

"It's when your pack pulls you over backward. And you can't get up. Like a turtle flipped onto its shell."

"Not happening. I got this." But with every motion, he sinks further. I wait a few more minutes, taking off my pack on solid ground. When Jack's worked himself down so far that the mud's over his knees, I step in more firmly.

"Jack, you're making things worse," I say. "Toss me your pack." Jack looks down at himself, then up at me.

"Fine." With jerky movements, he unbuckles, still struggling to keep his balance. Once the pack is off, he tosses it to me.

"Good," I say. "Now try to take a small step backward." Jack tries to lift first one foot, then the other, but the thick mud holds him in place. "Wait a sec," I say, and disappear behind him into the brush. A few minutes later, I hand him two smooth, sturdy branches. "Hold them like ski poles."

Jack takes the sticks and tests their strength before leaning his full weight on them. Slowly, he wiggles one boot out of the muck. It releases with a satisfying slurp, and Jack manages a small step backward. The ground behind him is more stable, and once he's wiggled his other foot out, I'm able to reach his elbow. With my help and the walking sticks, Jack works more rigorously to lift his feet. Two more steps and he's on solid ground.

"Wow. Hard work." He flops down beside his pack, panting. The bottom half of the khaki nylon pants he's borrowed from my dad are a shiny dark brown. He scrapes the mud off with a stick. "Ugh." He wrinkles his nose. "Smells a bit like goose-shit five, too." The mud hole's surface is already level again. Pieces of moss float on the thin layer of murky water on top, imitating much firmer ground. Nature's hiker trap, I think.

"Here, let me help," I say. It takes another ten minutes to scrape most of the muck from his legs and pants. We don't even talk about a change of clothes — we don't have one. And we're not wasting any drinking water to get Jack any cleaner. "Probably best to let the rest dry and flake off as we go," I say. "How does it feel?"

"Gross and sticky," he says with a shrug. "But I'll be fine." To my surprise, Jack wraps his earbuds around his iPod, tucking the whole works into his pocket. He might be warming up to this wilderness.

⚘

We buckle our packs and each take a walking stick. With them, we can test the depth of any future mud traps. As we start down the trail again, we're interrupted by a loud goose-like honk. It's the sandhill crane, flying over us in the direction we came from.

"I wonder if that's our crane's mate?" I carefully pick my way around the mud Jack just got out of. Then, to distract him from his most recent misstep, I ask, "So who were you talking about back there? Who didn't mate for life?"

I keep walking, my back to Jack as he trudges behind me. He's quiet for a time, then says, "You know how my dad bailed on this trip?"

"Yeah."

"Well, I'm pretty sure he's seeing someone at his work," Jack says. "Actually, I *know* he's messing around on my mum." I stop and stare at him, shocked by his flat monotone.

"That really sucks," I say. He's hunched over, staring down at his hands. I'm touched he's sharing this with me. Guests often open up to us on these trips. Just not usually this soon. "Are you sure?" I picture Anna's kind face. She's so nice! Jack nods his head and shoves past me, still talking.

"I was downtown, thrifting with my friends. A couple of weeks ago. A Friday. We didn't have school. And I saw him. He parked up the block from where we were. And I watched him open the car door. For this woman. This young woman. In a skirt and high heels. Pretty." Jack shares the memory in clipped sentences. "He put his arm around her. Guided her into a restaurant." Then Jack lurches to a stop, startled, taking half a step back.

I suppress a smile as a squirrel darts out of the brush and across the path in front of us. Jack looks ready to flee, but it's nothing to be afraid of. The little squirrel freezes, mid-trail, when it realizes it's not alone. It looks up at us with huge black eyes, its head cocked to one side, then sits back on its brownish-red haunches. It brings its tiny front paws to its mouth, turning a piece of pine cone and nibbling at it furiously. Then it pops the whole thing into a bulging cheek, holds its bushy tail high, and takes a few more sprints up the path. Freezing again, it stares back at us once more, then scurries up a tree.

"I'm really sorry, Jack," I say. "Does your mum know?" Jack walks ahead of me again, shaking his head.

"No... I don't think she knows. She might suspect. But it's not like she'd talk to me about it," Jack says. "And I haven't told anyone. Not until now, anyway. He's such... an... ass... hole!" Jack hits the ground hard with his walking stick, shouting each syllable as he stomps up the path.

From above us, the squirrel chatters loudly, sounding equally pissed. "That little guy agrees with you! And so do I," I say. Jack cracks just a hint of a smile as he looks up at the noisy critter.

CHAPTER 10

Stunted conifers loom from the fog as we plod along the boardwalk. We approach a damaged section, where three planks have rotted away. I steady myself with the walking stick, then step carefully onto the timber structure below before hopping back up to the boardwalk on the other side.

Jack makes his crossing, copying me. Landing beside me, he winces in pain. "What's wrong?" I grab his forearm as he pushes past me. "Hey... you're hurting," I say.

"It's nothing," Jack says. "These boots are rubbing a bit... that's all. It's nothing." He can't disguise his limp as he stomps away from me.

"It looks like it hurts, Jack." When I don't follow him, he finally stops. "We need to take a look... see what we can do," I say. Blistered feet can make even the best of trips pretty dreadful. And this trip is nowhere near the best.

The boardwalk ends with two steps leading down onto the muskeg. I drop my pack and motion for Jack to sit. Perched on the top tread, he takes off his boots while I dig for the zipper bag of first aid supplies. We left a lot with Anna and my dad, but have bandages, tape, moleskin, ointment, and painkillers.

Jack wrings out my dad's socks, wet from his muddy adventure. Brown water drips into the bog below. "Gross." Jack looks up with a rueful smile. He crosses his foot over his knee, peering at the heel.

"No wonder you're limping." I inspect the angry, fluid-filled blister. Jack rubs his thumb over the dime-sized welt gingerly. His other foot is even worse. The blister has rubbed open, the skin ripped off, and the tender wound below raw and red. "Okay," I say. "Let's take care of these." I pull out my jackknife and say, "I'm going to cut pieces of moleskin to protect those sore spots."

I consider moving away, but then lay the moleskin on the wooden step. It's slow work, using my injured hand to carve four large circular patches. And somehow, I don't mind Jack watching as I cut another circle, a little bigger than his blisters, in the center of two of the patches.

I finally hold up the donut-shaped bandages proudly. Jack is observing me with a look that makes my tummy flutter. Heat rises through the back of my neck and cheeks. "Dry off your heels so this stuff will stick," I say, looking away. Jack rubs his feet with the sleeve of his hoodie and I pass him the antiseptic ointment. "Dab some on each heel. Then stick a donut piece around each one," I say. Jack winces as he smears the cream on. He twists, trying to position the moleskin. It would be faster and better if I help. We really need to move if we're going to make it to the beach before it gets dark.

"Will you let me do it?" I ask. Jack hesitates, then hands the patches to me. Our fingers touch with a spark and I inhale a waft of his crisp scent — the spice and coconut are now mixed with smoke. His hair flops forward as he peers at his heel, and I'm filled with an urge to push his bangs back. What the hell?! The skin on my finger still tingles where we touched, and a shiver runs through me as I focus on Jack's blisters again. I stick the circle of moleskin around each blister, then cover the sores with the full patches. "There." I press firmly on the soft brown fabric to secure the tacky side to Jack's skin. "Let me tape your ankle." I wrap two strips of the stretchy white first-aid tape all the way around his foot, so the moleskin can't come off. "How's that feel?"

"Weird," Jack says.

"Well, hopefully, it helps." Jack reaches for his grimy socks. "Wait. Don't we have another pair of socks?" I find a pair of Anna's wool socks and hand them over to Jack, who shakes his head.

"Those are yours."

"Don't be an idiot," I say. "My feet are dry. Put these on." I snatch the filthy socks from him and slide them under a strap on Jack's pack. Jack delicately slips his feet, now clad in Anna's purple socks, into my dad's wet boots. He ties his laces, then stomps.

"Good to go?" I ask.

"Good to go."

I peer up at him with genuine concern and say, "You gotta let me know if anything else hurts."

Jack nods, then says, "I know you're worried about getting there before dark. I just didn't want to slow us down."

"It's not your fault," I say. "They're not your boots. And this hike will take forever if your feet are messed up. So speak up if it gets worse. Deal?"

"Deal." Jack hops down off the step to stand beside me.

"And Jack," I say, "You're doing really well. This is a tough hike. I've had people refuse to continue way before this point. You're doing great." I smile, actually meaning it. Jack fiddles with the straps on his pack, but a grin creeps across his features as he turns aside. Nothing like a well-placed pep talk, my mum used to say.

We trudge away from the boardwalk, over more boggy muskeg. After traversing the muddy sections cautiously, we're enveloped by another stand of dank forest as the terrain changes again.

The foggy gloom hangs amongst the trees. Unlike the soft needle-matted trail under the old-growth trees, the path here is rough. Winding roots interlace the trail. We walk carefully, so we don't trip or roll an ankle. Along the dark brown, root-filled path, there's every shade of green. The light green scrub of sphagnum moss. The darker olive fronds of deer ferns. The bright green, leathery leaves of salal, with pink bell-shaped blossoms arranged on ruddy stems. And beside us, tall huckleberry bushes, with small fragile leaves, grow in patches. In a couple of months, the little red berries will be abundant in the rare spots where sunlight pushes through to the forest floor. I hope I'm back here when those perfect explosions of sweet tartness are ready to be picked.

"Psst." Jack signals from behind me. Now what, I wonder? We need to make up some time. We can't be stopping every five minutes.

Jack's got a finger to his lips and points into a small clearing. Off to our left, uphill a bit, is a black-tailed deer. She looks back at a fawn, lifting its small black hoofs higher than necessary with every step. The tiny creature isn't quite used to being up on its own legs. The mama deer peeks in our direction, where Jack and I are standing motionless, hardly daring to breathe. She decides we're not a threat and turns her attention back to her youngster. The fawn is a soft fluffy brown, speckled with white dots. Its ears are dark and its eyes are huge and shiny black. It turns back to its mother, snuggling underneath her to suckle hungrily. The mama deer leans down, licking and cleaning her charge with her long pink tongue.

There's a snap in the woods behind us somewhere. The adult deer immediately stands erect, her cupped ears twitching; her round black eyes scanning the terrain. She nudges the fawn off her teat and walks away from us. We watch, smiling at each other, as the cute little fawn tumbles along, its skinny legs out wide for balance.

"Very cute." Jack smiles as the deer moves out of sight. I grin back.

"That fawn must be almost brand new," I say. "I've never seen one so small. Lucky we're some of the first people along the trail this season — the animals aren't keeping their little ones away yet."

We continue along the trail, and I wonder how Jack would react if I told him we hunt and harvest a black-tail every fall. I smile to myself, recalling how hard we usually have to work to track those bucks. They never just show up on the trail when we're hunting. But there's no reason to share this with Jack and risk a debate. Instead, I pick up the pace — we need to get going.

"So, do your mum and dad get along?" Jack breaks the silence after a few moments, circling back to the conversation we started after Jack's mud bath.

"They used to." I swallow the tightness in my throat.

"Are they divorced?"

"No," I say. "My mum died last year."

"Oh... sorry." Then I hear him say, "Damn it," under his breath. I glance back. He looks so dejected that I feel sorry for him.

"It's okay." I hop over a puddle. "I mean, it sucks, and I hate what happened to her. But it is what it is. And I don't mind that you asked. You didn't know." And to my surprise, I really don't mind that he asked. Jack is just making conversation. He doesn't *mean* to bring up all the shitty things in my life. Although he *has* managed to talk about both my worst moments today.

"My parents used to run these guiding trips together." I lead at a good pace and keep talking, not because I want to tell Jack all this, but because he needs the distraction. "They got along good. Spending time together outside was about their favorite thing to do." I say. "All the stuff I know about the plants and animals I learned from being out here with them."

"You're lucky to have that," Jack says. Then he realizes he's stepped in it again. "I mean, you're lucky you are... were able to spend so much time with your parents." Jack tries to explain himself, but trails off. "My parents are always too busy doing their own things now."

"What do you mean?" I ask. From what I've seen of Jack and Anna, they're pretty close.

"It was better when I was little," Jack says. "My mum worked a regular shift as a nurse. My dad was a project manager or something, building stuff. They had more time back then. We'd drive all together to my hockey games. They'd run the clock, volunteer. It was great." Jack's voice trails off again.

"What changed?" I glance up at him as I lift a fallen branch off the trail.

"I dunno," Jack says. "I guess it was my dad's job, mostly. My mum stopped working when he got promoted to some development company... started working way more hours. And now when he's not at work, he's meeting clients for dinners and breakfasts and golf on the weekends. He's barely ever home," Jack says. "I mean, this trip was supposed to make up for a bunch of the things he promised to do with us. But here he goes again. Bailing. I should be used to it by now." Jack kicks the ground behind me as he grumbles.

"That really sucks."

"It does," he says. "At least your mum didn't choose to leave your life —" He cuts himself off, then adds quickly, "— not that it's the same thing."

"No. She didn't choose to leave my life. Not exactly, anyway." I remember those angry last days. After a few steps, Jack speaks again.

"What happened to her?"

"She had breast cancer," I say. "She fought for a long while. Then we thought she beat it. But it came back. It was fast. Awful." My voice cracks. I gaze straight ahead and then reach up to wipe away a couple of tears. Will it ever stop aching like this, I wonder?

Chapter 11

We stand close to the trunk of a fir tree, and I lean against the rugged bark as I dig for food. "How are you doing?" I ask.

"Okay."

"Really? 'Cause I'm sore and hungry and cold."

Jack looks up with a wry smile. "I would rather be anywhere else right now," he says. "Anywhere else!" He shakes his fist up at the murky sky, but there's still a twinkle in his dark eyes.

"It's another hour or so." I unwrap a protein bar and give Jack half. "I wonder how my dad's doing." Jack's features soften as he looks at me, waking the butterflies inside me again.

"I'm sure he's fine," Jack says. "Your dad is tough. He'll be fine." I nod back at him without comment, distracted and betrayed by my body's reaction to Jack. Does he feel it, too? Likely not, I decide, watching him finish his snack and take a last sip of water. When we step back out onto the trail, the familiar earthy scent of the damp forest calms me.

The path slopes downhill now, demanding less energy, but it's rugged and our progress is slow.

"So, are you graduating this year?" Maybe I can distract us from the miserableness of the walk.

"Yeah," Jack says, "You?"

"Yep. I'm in grade twelve, too. What are you doing next year?" I'm actually curious.

"Not totally sure." Jack is quiet for a few steps. "My dad wants me to take engineering. University somewhere."

"But you don't want to?"

"I dunno," Jack says, "I just can't picture surviving another four years of school. I don't really like school."

"But you're good at it? Good enough to get into engineering?"

"I guess so," Jack says. "I mean, I'm no genius, but if I pay attention in class and do the homework, I do fine. What about you?"

"I don't know," I say. "I don't know what I want, really. I just saw my school counselor the other day. She's all set on me applying for engineering, too."

"But you don't want to, either?"

"I think I'll send in the applications," I say. "But even if I get in somewhere, I can't go."

"Why not?" I don't answer Jack right away, and he stays quiet, too. We maneuver down a steep section, balancing on our walking sticks over a natural staircase created by the tree roots.

"My dad won't pay for it," I say eventually. "And I don't have enough money saved to go." Jack isn't from here. He'll never talk to anyone in town. No harm in being honest with him.

"Can't? Or won't pay for it?"

"Won't," I say. "He wants me to work with him for a couple seasons. Maybe that's the right thing to do."

"Plenty of kids go to university without their parents' money."

"Maybe," I say, "But most of them have their parents' support. I mean, even if they can't pay for school, at least they want their kids to go. My dad's just so *against* it."

"I don't get —" Jack's reply ends in a grunt. I twist around as Jack's feet kick out and he falls onto his pack. He bumps down a couple of big roots before lurching to a stop on his butt near my feet.

"You okay?" I offer him my left hand and haul him upright. Jack rubs his hip and arches his back.

"I'm good," he says. "What was — oh, gross!" A slimy mess of squished banana slug sticks to his boot, pine needles clinging to the mucus of its silvery guts. Jack recoils, scraping the gooey mess off on a rock while shaking his head and muttering. He glances at the golf ball-sized mass of entrails, then turns, making a choking noise in his throat.

I swallow a giggle as Jack finally looks over, disgusted. Without comment, I continue, but also adjust our pace so Jack doesn't have to rush to keep up. I forget he's not used to this kind of terrain. We don't need a twisted ankle. That would slow us down permanently.

"I don't exactly get why my dad's so anti-university." I pick my way down the next section of the trail. "He never went, and I know he used to fight with the more educated people at work," I say. "He's very practical. And really smart. But I think I was twelve before I realized that 'fuckin-engineer' was actually two words." I grin over my shoulder at Jack. "That's just how he always referred to them. Fuckin-engineers. Never just engineer," I laugh. "He's got what my mum used to call a 'healthy disrespect for academics'."

"You should go to school if you want to go. You'll find a way."

"Maybe. What do you want to do, if not engineering?" I shift the conversation away from my wacky family. Jack is quiet as the terrain gets even steeper and we plunk down a long set of wooden steps. At the bottom is a boardwalk. It crosses over a creek, rushing with foamy brown water, dangerously close to the underside of the planks. Somewhere upstream, heavy rain is falling.

As we get back onto the muddy trail, Jack finally answers, "Honestly, I think I wanna learn a trade. I'm not sure what, exactly. But the tech college near us came to our school. Set up booths in the gym, you know? There are a few courses I'd like. And the schooling is short. Like months, not years."

"I know. There's a building course I was looking at. Every class sounds fun. And it's only two years," I say. "But my counselor thinks it's a 'waste of my brains'. Which is actually pretty stupid." Anger tinges my voice. "Why shouldn't smart people go to trade school?" Jack shrugs his shoulders.

"Right? Teachers think everyone needs university. I don't think that's true," Jack says. We continue our downhill trek, the puddles and streams spawning dark brown mud on the trail.

"Are we there yet?" Jack asks. I stoop to re-tie a bootlace and flash him a quick smile.

"Not quite," I say. "But it's not too much further." We walk without talking for a long while. Birds, squirrels, and frogs serenade us along the trail, occasionally interrupting the muffled silence of the fog.

Finally, we're at the top of the last staircase above the beach. The ocean is close, filling my lungs with a tangy sea breeze. I hop down the steps ahead of Jack with a burst of energy. "Almost there!"

❧

At the bottom of the stairs, our view brightens as we leave the dark cover of the forest. Blocking our way to the beach is a crisscrossed mess of blow-downs. The wild winter storms have stacked entire trees up against the edge of the beach. We pick our way through the thick trunks, twisted roots, and poky branches of the debris. Sometimes we clamber over a log, sometimes we fit underneath.

Eventually, we stand side by side in the sand and pebbles, just above the green line of seaweed marking high tide. The dark ocean's edge stretches before us, sixty feet down the beach. My heart sinks as I take in the scene. "Shit," I breathe. In good weather, you can see the mainland mountains. Today, there's a wall of white and gray, so close I feel I can touch it. The fog is still thick, hugging the coastline and limiting our view to just a hundred feet offshore.

"What's the problem?" Jack's confused by the disappointment on my face. "We made it didn't we?"

"This fog," I say. "The charter fishing boats hug this shore on their run home. But with this fog, we won't see them. It's too thick. They go by too far offshore." I point to both ends of the beach, where reefs of jagged black rock disappear into the haze. "There's no way we'll see them. And no way they'll see us." Panic rises in me as I realize what I'm saying is true. "Shit!"

A stampede of fear hits me. I unbuckle my pack and drop it into the sand, hardly registering how good it feels to be free of its weight. I picture my dad lying in a tent down the coast on our right. His burnt hands will be painful now, the infection taking hold in his raw wounds. I walk away from Jack, my eyes unseeing as they fill with tears. Stupid fog. What the hell am I supposed to do next?

I trip on something solid and end up on my ass in the sand. I roll up to a sitting position and slam both fists into the ground. Then, wrapping my arms around my knees, I bury my head in the damp fabric of my khakis. Breathing in quick, heavy gulps, I try to calm my heart. We made good time and got here before dark. For nothing. The rushing in my head muffles the beach sounds. Then the sand on my left shifts as Jack sits down beside me.

"Hey." His voice is barely audible. "Hey. It'll be okay." He shifts his hips over close to mine and drapes an arm across my shoulders. I don't look up, but let him move me until my forehead rests against his chest. Through my panic, I feel a twinge of lightness as Jack pulls me closer. I've never had a boy hold me. He wraps his other arm in front of us and I feel his chin rest on my hair.

And so, with Jack shielding me from the world for a minute, I cry. Silent tears stream down my cheeks and my shoulders shudder. All of it runs through my mind. Dad. Pain. Mum. Ache. School. Lonely.

Jack just sits, holding me, rocking a little, and shushing at me. After a long while, my breathing slows and the tears turn off. I tilt my head so I can see Jack's face past the sides of my hood. "Sorry. I don't do this." I inhale deeply. "Cry, I mean. I don't cry. I'm really pretty tough."

Jack looks down at me, loosening his grip, but not letting me go. "You've got reasons," he says, "To be upset, I mean. A lot has happened in the last ten hours." Has it only been ten hours? It feels like half a lifetime.

Jack pulls the sleeve of his hoodie out onto his thumb. He reaches over, and with the soft gray jersey, wipes the tears from my face gently. He puts a hand on my cheek, then pulls back, looking at me with his big dark eyes. I smile meekly — no other response comes to me. He just nestles my head back on his chest. We sit, wrapped together, looking out into the thick, cold fog.

CHAPTER 12

I did *not* see *that* coming. Holy moly. Funny how the touch of a nice boy can make a bad day better. The unrelenting fog will make a rescue today impossible. This realization has cemented a cold lump in my gut. Despite that, I feel a small smile unfold across my face as I breathe in the wet, salty air. I'm not sure what to say to Jack. So I say nothing for a few more moments, pushing my panic and impatience aside. Because it feels nice. So very nice. To sit here, on a foggy beach, being held.

"How ya doing?" Jack cranes to look down at me. I sit back, shrug, and smile.

"Better." I hate to end this wonderful moment, but my logical brain is already kicking back into gear. "We should set up camp." I roll out from under Jack's arm. "Where should we put the tent, do you think?" I look up and down the beach. There's a fairly level sandbar at the river mouth, above the tide line. I point toward it. "How 'bout up there?"

Jack looks undisturbed by my sudden focus on practicalities. "Looks good to me." He holds his hand out so I can pull him up. "Just tell me what you want me to do." He picks up both our packs and walks toward the sand bar.

With Jack's help, the tent is up in less than ten minutes. The tent pegs are useless in the sand, so Jack moves four large rocks into place and ties the fly ropes to them. With the tent secured, we unroll the mattress pad and let it self-inflate inside the tent. Finally, Jack and I stand back to admire our handiwork.

"Well," I say, "That's done." The tent is a flash of color in a vista that could be a black-and-white photo. The orange dome sits atop gray sand, surrounded by stacks of silver driftwood logs, in front of a black tree line, all smudged by the dense fog. Droplets speckle our hoodies, so I put on my rain jacket and ask Jack to do the same. It'll be a chilly night if our layers get any damper. "We should make a fire. Maybe warm up some water for a bag dinner?" I scan the beach around for a sheltered spot.

"What about over there?" Jack points toward the wooden stairs. A huge fir tree is leaning over the beach and its dark boughs deflect most of the drizzle. I nod, and we wander the beach, collecting driftwood and small logs. A moment later, Jack calls out, pointing at the ground. I carry my armload of wood to him. Jack is kneeling beside a footprint in the sand. He looks up at me, eyes wide. "Is this what I think it is?"

"Black bear." I look up the beach, following the tracks. The rounded pad of the bear's footprint is rimmed with the impressions of five toes. In front of each toe print are five sand mounds where pointed claws dug in as the bear walked. The offset pattern of tracks heads north. The bear wandered to a kelp pile in the sand, where it stopped for a snack. "It was here recently," I say. "See how crisp the edges of the print are?" I search through the haze for the familiar silhouette of the bear. But I see nothing.

"What do we do?" Jack follows my gaze uncomfortably.

"Nothing." I give a small shrug. "It's nothing to worry about. It'll leave us alone. We'll hang our food and it will have no reason to bother with us."

Jack places both his hands inside the footprint, shaking his head as he imagines the bear's size. Then he wipes his sandy palms against his pants, standing.

"Let's go light that fire." I pick up another chunk of driftwood, and Jack follows me wordlessly. I can feel his worry. But there are more dangerous things to worry about here.

Large driftwood logs line the top of the beach. We clamber over them to the fire spot we picked earlier. I take out my jackknife and carve another fire-starting stick while Jack gets the dinner supplies from the tent.

I finish making a pile of cedar shavings when Jack's movements in the distance catch my eye. He walks toward me, a silver pouch of freeze-dried food in each hand. The water bottle is wedged under one arm and his gait is an uneven limp. Concern for Jack tightens my gut in a way I've never felt for any other guest. I rub my palms together and blow into my cupped hands, trying to warm them up. The scar on my right hand always throbs when chilled.

Jack looks up when he gets to the driftwood barrier. He gives me a grin that makes my lower belly tumble and my heart jumps over a beat. Oh boy.

"Beef stew? Or Pad Thai chicken?" Jack reads off the labels, as he holds up each choice and scrambles over the logs.

"I like them both." Jack settles into the sand beside me. He throws aside a few rocks and pushes sand up against the log as a backrest. When he sits down, he stretches his legs out in front of him. "How are your feet?" I ask, going back to carving bigger splinters of cedar.

"Not too bad." Jack's loosening his laces. "I mean, I feel them. But they're way better than before you taped them up."

"Tell me if they get worse." I give him a stern look from under my hood.

"Yes, ma'am." Jack gives me a grin and a small salute. "You ready for the lighter?" I build a tepee of small sticks over my fire-starting block, then add some cedar shavings. A few clicks later, we have a nice blaze. I add bigger sticks and then finally a couple of small logs until the flames lick up above our heads. Moving back, I settle beside Jack, my back against the log, knees bent. We sit in silence, watching the yellow-orange flames twist and dance among the blackening logs. The wood cracks loudly, sending sparks and embers into the air and sand. I wrap my arms around my shins and rest my chin on my knees. With the crackling heat warming my face and the fog muting our view, I could doze off right now.

"What're you thinking?" Jack asks. He cracks a twig off the branch he's fiddling with and tosses it into the fire, looking down at me gently. There are so many suitable answers, but I shyly deflect.

"I'm thinking I'm hungry."

"Let me." Jack puts his hand on my arm, pushing me back to sitting. "Just tell me how," he says. So I coach him to build a shelf of rocks for the stainless steel coffee mug. Jack fills the mug and we wait for the water to heat. After twenty minutes, it's finally warm enough. The beef stew smells ridiculously good as Jack pours the warm water into the pouch and reseals it.

While we wait impatiently for the meal to rehydrate, I carve another spoon-ish tool. The damp cold makes it difficult for me to grip the knife between my thumb and two fingers, and I pause often to warm my hands over the fire.

When Jack pours the second mug of water into the Pad Thai pouch, he declares the stew ready to eat. "Here," he says, "You go first."

"Man, that's good," I say. "'Course, I could eat cardboard and it would taste good after a six-hour hike." I hand the pouch and stick-spoon over to Jack.

"It really is pretty good." He takes a few bites and licks the spoon. I give the water bottle to Jack after taking a sip. It's funny. In a restaurant, we would never share utensils and cups. But out here, using the same spoon and bottle doesn't phase Jack. And I'm glad. He hasn't been much of an 'indoor human' at all. "What're you smiling about?" Jack asks now.

"I was just thinking that you're not as much of a city slicker as I expected," I say.

"Shut up." Jack tosses a stick at me. And as I hold up my hand to deflect the flying piece of wood, I hear a new sound floating out of the fog and my pulse quickens.

Chapter 13

"**S**hit!" I jump over the driftwood logs and sprint toward the tent. Yes! That's a boat motor. I rip open the zipper of the tent fly and dig through my pack furiously. Near the bottom, I feel the waxy cylinders of the flares. I pull one out and race down the beach, cursing myself for not being ready.

The boat motor drones, seeming to come from everywhere. As I run, I twist the short plastic cap off the end of the flare and flip it over so I can rub the ignition button against the coarse striking surface. Lighting a flare is like lighting a match, only way bigger.

I'm right down at the waterline now and on the third try, the flare finally sparks. It sputters, then roars to life like a blowtorch. A bright red flame shoots away from me and I wave it over my head in an arc. I scan the dense fog for any sign of the boat. But I see nothing. I still hear the motor, but it's getting quieter. Shit. Farther away. Double shit. I swing the flare back and forth, back and forth. A short minute later, the flare fizzles and dies out, leaving a smoking stub in my left hand. My arms drop and I scour the ocean once more. Nothing. Just the acrid sulphuric smell of burnt flare. And a terrible silence.

"Do you think they saw you?" Jack jogs up beside me. I just shake my head. The angled wake of the boat rolls toward us, forcing us to step back. That boat was so close!

"I should have been ready!" My jaw clenches at my lack of planning. "Maybe if I had the flare ready to go, they would have seen me. Shit!" I crouch to soak the flare in the icy seawater. Small sparks from the flare burned the back of my hand and peppered the sleeve of my jacket with little black scorch marks.

"Damn! Are you okay?" Jack squats beside me and examines my hand.

"It's fine," I say. "No blisters, just a little scalded."

"You need to be careful." Jack holds my fingers in his warm hands. "Flares can be dangerous." He locks eyes with me.

"Not dangerous at all." I repeat the same words I said to Jack back in the bog, talking about my sawmill accident. Jack laughs out loud, pulling me upright. We stare back up toward camp. Jack gently wraps his arms around me from behind. His belt buckle presses into the small of my back and he hugs me. My pulse fills my ears as his chin brushes my ear, his cheek warm against my temple.

"There will be another boat," he says softly. "And you'll be ready for it." I shake my head a little, caught between the soft comfort of Jack's touch and the exasperation of my failure.

⚘

We walk back to the tent and I take the second flare to the fire. I show Jack how to light it, so we're both ready to signal if there's another boat. I stoke the flames, add a few more logs, and sit down beside Jack again. We finish the rest of our dinners in heavy silence.

"At least there's no dishes with this stuff." Jack tries to lighten the mood. I don't respond. Everything feels heavy. My shoulders push down on my ribs, my ribs leave no room for my lungs, and the stew sits in a heavy clump in my gut. Would I have had the flare ready if this fluttering Jack nonsense didn't distract me? If he wasn't around, would my head have been in the game? I'm not sure. And it doesn't matter now.

"We should refill our water bottle. And hang our food. Before it gets dark," I say.

"Where do we get water?" Jack asks. "I can do that."

"From the river." I point past the tent. "But you need to walk upstream, above the high tide mark. Or it'll be brackish. Salty." Jack nods and heads off toward the river. I walk over to the tent and get the paracord, a nylon roll-top sack, and our food. I lay the gear beside the fire, first taking advantage of Jack's absence to pee. Behind a tree trunk, I pick a spot soft with pine needles and squat, keeping my feet wide. A small spider scrambles to escape the steaming stream. I forgot the toilet paper, so I use a crumpled tissue from my pocket.

Back on the beach, I toss the tissue into the fire. I stuff the freeze-dried meals, protein bars, and used foil bags into the sack. Re-rolling and sealing the top with the Velcro strip, I search for a place to hang the food.

The fresh bear tracks don't worry me. Black bears keep their distance. None of the wildlife likes people, but all of them like the smells of our food. Jack and I licked our dinner bags clean, but even a tiny amount of food residue will attract the bears, wolves, deer, and even cougars to our camp. Hanging the food, high and far away from our tent, is a nightly requirement.

The branches of the fir I'm sitting under are too close to the ground. I need at least twelve feet. Up the beach, there's a cedar tree that looks promising. I tie a piece of bark to the end of the paracord, then look around for Jack. He's been gone a while. A long while. I survey the river beyond the tent, where the path curves out of sight, but still don't see him. Something feels off, so I drop what I'm doing, add another log to the fire, and go look for him.

The fog is still shrouding the entire landscape in a murky haze. What's visible of the ocean is a mirrored sheet. From the sand bar past the tent, I'm finally able to see around the bend in the river. Well ahead, Jack's bright red rain jacket interrupts the gray monotone of the landscape. He's kneeling by the river, but not moving. I stop to watch. Jack's never motionless. His hand is poised above the river water, holding the water bottle. But he's statue-still, looking across the river. I follow his gaze but see nothing.

A tingle at the base of my skull quickens my pace. The terrain is rockier here. Tufts of river grass grow between enormous boulders. I'm close enough now to read the words on Jack's water bottle. He's still staring across the river. Again, I follow Jack's stare.

I freeze in my tracks. On our side, the shore of the river slopes gently, the water spreading into shallow eddies. But the far bank cuts into a steep earthy cliff. Directly across from Jack, hunkered below the brush, is a cougar. The river is narrow, so the cat is close. Its black-rimmed eyes are a brilliant bronze. The lapping tongue is a rough pinkish-gray and its black-tipped ears twitch as it drinks. In the thick salal, its golden coat stretches tight across the sharp angles of the cougar's haunches.

I shuffle toward Jack. It's safer to be together in the presence of these cats. The river is deep over there, so I don't think it'll come our way. At least I hope not.

I've only witnessed one other cougar. They're elusive animals, only seen when they're in trouble. Sick or injured. I keep my eyes on the big cat as I maneuver past the last boulder and step over a branch directly behind Jack. He still hasn't moved. "What should I do?" He's heard my approach.

"Stand up. Slowly," I say. "We want it to think we're big. Danger-ous." I unzip my jacket. Jack stands up, not taking his eyes off the cat. "Undo your jacket," I say. "Put your hands in your pockets and stretch your coat out like a cape. Makes us look bigger. Like this." I stretch out my jacket.

The cougar is still slurping river water, its bright eyes following us. We stand in the fog, flapping our coats wide, waiting for the cat to make the first move. It's huge. Its front paws are the size of my dad's slippers. It licks its chops, then stretches its jaws wide, revealing sharp, yellowed incisors as big as my thumbs. No way am I turning my back on it.

Suddenly, the cougar turns up the steep bank, showing off its eight-foot length. Beneath the matted gold-brown fur, the arching lines of its ribs and its chiseled hip bones are visible. The giant cat disappears into the forest without a sound.

"Not dangerous at all?" There's hope in Jack's soft voice. I shake my head without smiling.

"Actually, cougars can be dangerous," I say. "Something's wrong with it." I zip my jacket, watching Jack as he finally collects the fresh water he came for. "Did you see how skinny it is? It's starving." Jack screws the top onto the water bottle. "I've only seen two cougars in my life," I say. "This is number two. But I'm sure plenty of cougars have seen me." I glance over my shoulder as we start back toward camp. "When they're healthy, you won't see them. They might track you, but you'll never see them. When you see a cougar, it's in bad shape. Which makes it unpredictable. Don't like it." I step over a branch and shake my head again.

"They're beautiful animals, though." Jack looks off toward the forest where the cat disappeared. "Did you see her eyes?" he asks. "I felt like I could see right into her soul, the way she stared at me." Jack's voice carries quiet awe. "Still," he says, "I hope we never see her again."

Jack takes my hand and we walk back to the fire. His warm touch makes my scars tingle. I can't decide if my heart's hammering because we just stared down a cougar. Or because I'm falling for this very nice boy beside me.

Chapter 14

The fire's still burning well, appearing brighter now, as the sky darkens. Somewhere, beyond all this fog, the sun is setting. We still need to hang the food, so I lead Jack over to the cedar tree.

"This one should work." I point up at the thick silver limbs. "Can you loop the rope over that branch?" I hand Jack the bark I tied to the end of the cord. He tosses it overhand, but it boomerangs back, the cord snapping tight as the coil in his hand gets tangled. Jack carefully unwinds a bunch of line, puddling it loosely at his feet. When he tosses the bark underhand this time, the line follows in a perfect arc over the limb.

"Nice shot!" I say. "Now pull it this way… away from the tree trunk." Jack looks over at me with a furrowed brow. "Bears are excellent climbers," I say. "We need the food to hang out of reach, at least six feet from the trunk." Jack holds both ends of the paracord and flips it sideways along the limb.

"Perfect." I hand Jack the food sack. He secures it to the cord, then pulls the bag to hang below the branch. "That's good," I say. "Now we just need to tie this end down."

Jack walks over to the contorted roots of a big driftwood log. He looks over at me with raised eyebrows.

"That works," I say, and he secures the cord to the root ball.

"Done." Jack wipes his hands on his pants. He looks toward the forest. "I gotta take a leak."

"Help yourself." I wave my hand, palm up, across the whole beach like I'm introducing merchandise on a game show. "We gotta bury or sink poop. Otherwise, you're good to go anywhere." I grin in his direction. "But stay close." Concern tinges my voice as I think about the cougar. "We really should stick together, especially as it gets darker. I don't like knowing that hungry cat is out there."

"No problem," Jack says. "Rule #1: Stick together. Got it." He clambers up the short bank that separates the beach from the forest. The brush is so thick he's out of sight immediately. "No cougars here. I'm fine." His rain jacket rustles. "Still fine," Jack calls again. I know how he feels. Making a lot of noise seems like it will keep the wildlife at bay. I sing or talk out loud on my own.

Moments later, Jack hops back down onto the beach. "Let's sit by the fire for a bit," I say. "Then we should bed down before it's too dark to see." We walk the short distance back to the fire. I wish we had the headlamp with us. But I'm glad we insisted Anna keep it so she can help my dad.

"So, about that," Jack says. "Both in the same tent?"

"No choice," I say. "With this fog and drizzle, sleeping outside is not an option." If we hadn't had the disastrous boat fire, we'd each have our own tent and sleeping bag. But the fire *did* happen. And we *don't* have that gear. "It'll be fine." I settle into the sand by the fire. "It's a two-man tent. Lots of room. Plus, having both of us in there will keep it warmer." I hold my hands out over the edge of the fire, a little shiver running through me. Where does Jack want this hugging stuff to go? I'm not ready for more. Yet another part of me craves his touch. Jack sits down beside me, warming his cold red hands, too.

"I wonder what they're doing." I stare into the center of the fire, where blue flames dance around the white-hot coals on the sand. "My dad. And Anna," I say, "I wonder what they're doing right now." Jack is quiet for a moment, also staring at the fire.

"I guess they're doing about the same things we are," Jack says. I smile to myself, thinking of his embrace. But I know that's not what Jack means. "And I sure hope she's keeping the fire going over there," he says. I nod, remembering we took the only lighter.

"My dad will go crazy, just waiting." I can picture his tension. "He vibrates when he doesn't have work to do. And he's a terrible patient," I say, "but I get the feeling your mom can handle his type."

"She's definitely dealt with all kinds at her work." Jack glances over at me. The fire's golden glow reflects in his dark eyes and carves shadows on his cheekbones. Well, shit... he's... gorgeous. My heavy heart skips a beat. I stare back into the fire, letting out a long breath. "It'll be okay," Jack says. "The fog will lift. You'll flag down one of those fishing boats. By lunchtime tomorrow, we'll have your dad at a hospital. You'll see." My throat closes and warm prickles behind my eyelids surprise me. Shit. Jack's watching me in the fading light. I scoop a handful of sand, studying the iridescent grains, hoping the tears don't roll down my cheeks. Suddenly, the logs collapse into the fire, shooting an array of sparks into the fir boughs above us.

"I can't believe all the things we saw today." Jack's gaze follows the dancing light specks. "It was hard. The hike. Really hard. But so cool. The animals... the different trees... the tiny mosses. The smells. Even this weather." He looks up into the darkening sky. "I dunno. I feel it... connected to it... you know?"

"I do... I know." I don't need Jack to explain what he means by 'it'. Being surrounded by nature orders my thoughts, calms my anger.

Whenever one of us was agitated, my mum used to say 'let's go take a forest bath'. And it always helped. Still does.

"Do you believe in God, Jack?" I'm curious if his comments are rooted in religion. These first nights are often when guests share their faith. This place connects souls to the earth, prompting fascinating conversations. Humans have so many ways to trust in a higher power.

"Not really," Jack says, "We're not religious. You?"

"No. I don't know what I believe... but it's not in God... not exactly." I try to explain. "I don't buy all the rules connected with some religions." Like my ex-best friend Nora and her rigid commandments. "But I know there's something... something bigger than me... out here... I feel it too," I say. "The indigenous peoples... they believe the natural world is connected with the supernatural world... out here, I get why they think that."

"We could use a little help from nature and the spirits... kinda makes me wish I believed," Jack says. And again, I know exactly what he means. It has crossed my mind that having faith in a higher power would make understanding this world a lot simpler. But I don't have that faith.

"We could definitely use some help." I'm not sure if my words are responding to Jack or asking the universe for support. The dark is closing in. With a stick, I move what's left of the red-hot logs apart, snuffing out the fire. The last flames flicker out, leaving a glowing mass of orange coals in the sand. "Normally I'd pour seawater on these coals. But with this drizzle, it will be out in no time." I stand up, watching the glow already fading. "Ready to head to bed?"

"Sure." Jack kicks his feet out and rolls up to standing. I gaze in the ocean's direction. No spectacular sunset tonight. Just a slow dimmer switch fading from the gray day to black night. I carefully cross over the jumble of logs surrounding the fire, then wait for Jack to pick his way over them, too. We walk toward the tent in silence side by side.

We go to separate ends of the tent. On my side, I zip open the fly and shuffle into the tiny, but dry, vestibule. Crouching awkwardly, I peel off my rain jacket and lay it flat in the sand. Sitting on the jacket, I rummage through my pack, feeling for Anna's fleece pullover. I pull it on, then lift my butt inside the tent, keeping my feet outside. I ease my achy feet out of the filthy boots. They're wet and so are my wool socks, but I can't tell if from rain or sweat. Jack's wearing our only spare socks, so my feet will have a damp night.

Jack swears under his breath. "You doing okay?" I ask over my shoulder.

"I feel like a giant. It's impossible to get my wet stuff off without flicking sand onto everything. And I'm getting my dry stuff wet. Damn it!" he says. I swing my feet inside, groping until my fingers brush the smooth stuff-sack of the sleeping bag. I pull on the spring tab and give the sack a tug, spilling out the sleeping bag. It's puffy and dry, and I'm suddenly exhausted. As Jack unzips his tent door, I fold the sleeping bag open.

"Bum first," I say. "Keep those boots outside." Jack says nothing, but follows my direction. He shuffles and grunts as he wrestles out of his boots. Finally, he zips his tent door.

"Where are you?" he asks.

"Here, climb under." I lift the edge of the sleeping bag. Our hands touch, and a spark runs down my spine as I settle into the darkness.

"I'm... so... tired," he says. He's rolled to face me. His soft voice is close and the covers tighten over my shoulder.

"Good night, Jack. You did good today." I fight off a sudden urge to touch him. He's only inches away.

"G'night, Maia," he says. "Sucks to be in this mess. But I'm glad I'm in it with you." The smile in his voice sparks another warm flutter in my heart. Under the covers, Jack finds my hand and gives it a quick squeeze. I'm relieved... and a little disappointed when he stops there. The tent's rustling and Jack's hushed breathing is a steady lullaby. I hear him fall asleep, his breaths deepening and lengthening, then giving way to a slight snore.

I really like him, I let myself admit. The faint scent of campfire smoke wafts from my sleeves as I tuck my hands under my cheek. For the first night in weeks, tears don't accompany my thoughts as I fade into sleep. I really like him.

Chapter 15

A snapping racket startles me awake. I can't figure out where I am. The ground is hard and there's shiny, cool fabric under my chin. Then it all rushes back. The smoke, the fireball, the charred flesh. Hiking to the beach. Hearing a boat. Utter disappointment. And thick fog everywhere.

Jack stirs beside me and a warm flush shoots from my belly to my face. The flapping outside gets louder and the tent poles creak as they flex around us.

"What's goin' on?" Jack's words are a sleepy croak.

"The tent fly's loose," I say. "I'll go fix it."

"Lemme come help."

"You stay put," I say, "No point both of us getting wet." I fumble in the dark, finally pulling my boots, rain pants, and jacket on. It's black outside and the sharp wind drives needles of rain into me. I feel my way to Jack's side of the tent and grope for the broken rope. It's pulled off the rock tie down. After a few attempts, I'm able to wrap the rope securely around the rock, then I drag it away from the tent until the fly is taut and the flapping stops. I shuffle back to my side of the tent, careful not to trip in the darkness.

Back under the fly, I take off my gear, then crawl back into the tent and under the sleeping bag, shivering.

"Everything okay?" Jack asks.

"Everything's fine. Go back to sleep." Until today, when something needed attention in the middle of the night, my mum or dad had dealt with it. Usually, I'm the groggy voice in the dark asking if everything is okay. Funny.

I lay awake, listening to the howling gusts and the pelting raindrops. If this gale continues, the seas will build to an unmanageable swell and none of the charter guys will be out in the morning. It's almost impossible to troll in this kind of wind, and paying customers don't enjoy the rough seas.

A loud crash of a treetop snapping startles me back to the present. I'm glad we're not sleeping near the forest. Please Mama Nature, please make this wind die down before daybreak.

I slip into a restless sleep, the howling storm waking me often. Eventually, the morning light reveals the shadowy arch of the tent. On my right Jack lies on one side, tufts of his dark hair sticking up from his silhouette.

The crashing of the storm is rowdier than it was in the middle of the night.

"Shit." I groan out the word as my stomach growls.

"Is it time to get up?" Jack rolls to face me.

"No rush," I say. "But I'm hungry. Maybe I'll go get our food sack down."

"You're always hungry." Jack rolls towards me, his voice teasing. "I'll come with you. Rule #1: Stick together, remember?" He rubs his eyes. "What's going on out there?" The tent leans over in another gust.

"It's blowing hard." I sit up next to him without explaining my fears. The bad news can wait. With a sleepy smile, Jack reaches over and tucks a piece of my hair behind my ear. Color flashes on his wrist as the sleeve of his hoodie pulls up. I hold his arm between us, fingering the soft cotton threads of a friendship bracelet in shades of blue, turquoise, and brown.

"It's pretty," I say. "Where did you get that?" My empty stomach churns. If the dumb teenage traditions at his school are anything like mine, this bracelet can mean only one thing.

"Liv made it for me. She's my... she's a friend." Jack stumbles over his answer, dropping his chin to his chest. His words fall like shrapnel and I give him a cool glance before jerking out of the tent. "Maia, wait..." Jack says something else. But his words get lost in the howling wind and roaring in my head. I just need to get away from his excuses. Under the tent fly, I yank on my rain pants and boots, then snatch my jacket.

Out in the rainy wind, I flip up my hood and stuff my hands in my pockets. Low-lying clouds have replaced the thick fog from yesterday. Swirling rain buffets my cheeks and eyes. The ocean is black and churning. Along the shore, waves taller than Jack crash up the sand in a foamy white mess. I kick a cobble as I think his name again. Jack. Shit! Every time. Every time I let someone in, they disappoint me. Leave me.

Ignoring Rule #1, I stomp toward the food sack, leaning my body into the lashing rain. At the cedar tree, I untie the rope and lower the red bag from where it's spinning in the wind, then wrap the cord into a neat loop around my palm and elbow.

I return to our fire pit with our food and sit under the fir. At its base, a huge exposed root twists down into the beach. I huddle behind this root, leaning against the chunky bark, my butt in the sand. The rain drips through the tree branches, but at least I'm sheltered from the wind.

Jack's bitter letdown flashes me back to my final conversation with Nora. I had really expected her to understand, had trusted her to be on my side. But she isn't who I thought she was. Now, as I wrap my arms around the icy hollow in my gut, I can't believe I'm feeling this way again. Assholes!

I dig for a protein bar. In this weather, it's not worth building a cooking fire. As I unwrap the bar, there's movement near the tent. Jack chases after his ball cap, which tumbles hopelessly away in a powerful gust. The wind lifts the hat high, and it hits the ocean out in the surf. Jack lurches to a stop, his back to me, presumably watching the cap disappear. When he finally gives up and stomps up the shore, I wave him over. All in all, I'm madder at myself than at him. Besides, he's still a guest, so I can't exactly shut him out.

But I can't believe I didn't ask Jack about other girls in his life. I wouldn't need to ask the boys in town. Everyone knows everything about everyone. With Jack, I should have been more careful. Asked more questions. Then again, I didn't expect this to happen. My stomach somersaults and my pulse throbs in my temple as I recall how he held me. How did I actually let myself imagine having a boyfriend like Jack? All that's done now. Done.

He sits down in the sand a few feet away from me.

"That was my favorite hat," Jack says. I avoid his eyes and wordlessly pass him a protein bar as he grumbles. We chomp on our breakfast, not speaking, watching the swirling rain and the crashing ocean. I tear off another bite and chew for a long time. Jack offers me the water he brought from the tent.

"I got that hat at a hockey game... with my dad. He got Potvin stitched on the back for me." Jack finally breaks the thick silence between us. I have no idea what he's talking about, but I had noticed the sweat stains and worn brim fabric under the 'c'-shaped orca logo. That hat was the only piece of Jack's attire that wasn't pristine when he started this trip. "He's my favorite goalie." He shakes his head, kicking at the sand with his heel. "So. What's the plan, anyway?"

"We keep hiking." I pick at a hangnail. "It's the fastest way to get help."

"What? You want to keep going?" Jack asks. "Why? What for?" I finally look at him. He puckers his forehead, his eyes wide.

"I need to get help for my dad. Fast." My words are steady, calmer than I feel. "No boats are coming. Not today… not in this gale." I fold and refold the protein bar wrapper. "The fog is gone, but there won't be anyone to flag down today. It's too rough." I tuck the wrapper back into the food sack. Jack shakes his head, disbelieving.

Jack and I started on this journey to get help sooner than just waiting. Yesterday the worst-case scenario was flagging down a boat this morning. Today, the weather will prevent a rescue. So we need to walk toward help.

"I can't just sit here and wait, Jack." I narrow my eyes at him. "If we walk, we increase our chances. We might see other hikers. Someone could have a hand-held VHF. And there's a ranger's station… a yurt… two days' hike from here." My words tumble out. "This storm could hold for days. If it does, and we walk, we'll be able to call for help by Sunday. That's still two days sooner than the water taxi." I gauge Jack's reaction. He looks out over the waves and the dark gray sky, considering my logic.

"Okay, Maia," Jack says. "We'll walk… no matter what I say, you're going." He tilts his head at me with a half-smile. "I can see that. And I'm not breaking Rule #1." My eyes close for a second before I push up off the sand. I'm still mad at him. Furious with him. But I also need him to come along. For two reasons: he's still technically our guest, so I can't just leave him, and I'd rather not attempt the next section of trail on my own.

"How are your blisters doing?" I look down at Jack's feet, laced into my dad's boots.

"Fine. The moleskin was peeling off. So I added another layer. And I wrapped fresh tape around my foot before I put my boots on just now."

"Good," I say. "Let me know if they start to feel worse." I walk down the beach away from him.

"How the heck would we be kayaking in this stuff?" Jack changes the subject when he catches up to me, watching a huge wave crash up the beach.

"We wouldn't be." I glance up at him. "I don't know where this storm came from. It wasn't in the forecast. My dad wouldn't take us out here if he knew it was coming. But it happens this way sometimes." I shrug. Just another piece of bad luck.

We walk back to the tent, which is still straining against the ropes and rocks tying it down. Without taking off our rain gear, we stuff the sleeping bag into its sack and deflate the mat. Then we fight the wind to dismantle the tent, but we finally get it all stuffed into its bag.

With everything back in our packs, we adjust our straps and grimace as our loads pinch sore spots from yesterday. The next section of trail follows the beach. There's an alternate route through the forest, necessary when the tide is high. But today, I'm most concerned about keeping the shoreline in view. If there's a captain crazy enough to be out today, we'll be able to signal his boat if we stay on the shore.

We trudge along the rugged beach, waves crashing on our right, the dense tree line on our left. Even through sheets of rain, this landscape lifts me up. It's breathtaking. Wide-open, solitary, and stunning. The beach curves ahead of us, mostly sand with the odd boulder. I flip over a barnacle-covered rock, and Jack grins as the tiny crabs scramble back under the safety of the overturned rock. Carefully, I put the rock back in its indent in the sand, the crabs retreating under it again.

Jack points to our left. Perched on the stump marking the entrance to the upland trail is another raven. Its dark feathers are puffed and wet from the downpour. With a short throaty caw, it hops down onto the path, moving along it before looking back at us with shiny black eyes.

"He looks like he wants to lead the way," Jack says. But I shake my head — we need to stay on the beach.

The wet raven turns my thoughts to my mum. She loved this kind of weather. Rain walks were her favorite. Just as beautiful as a walk in the sunshine, she'd say. My mum believed there was no bad weather, just bad gear. She was so tough. And hard-working. And stubborn. I still can't understand her last choice.

We continue in silence, and I wonder how long Jack's had this girlfriend. A sudden hatred for a girl I've never even met rises through me. I imagine her to be thin and blond, with boobs that fill out more than a training bra. I glance over at Jack. He flashes me a smile that I don't return. His smile fades, but his eyes stay on mine until I turn away.

I pick up a rock and throw it hard out into the waves. The tide is rising, the rollers already reaching the logs lining the top of the beach. Jack takes in my dark expression. "What's on your mind?" he asks. I consider my options. Jack deserves the silent treatment from me, but this hike will drag on forever without conversation.

"Tell me about Liv." I surprise myself. Now, why would I say that?

"What do you wanna know?"

"How'd you meet? Does she go to your school?"

"Yeah, she was in my English class last year," Jack says. "It's a big school, so I kinda knew who she was, but never talked to her before."

"Kinda knew who she was?" I ask, "What does that mean?"

"She's on the cheer team," Jack says, "so you know, me and the guys know those girls." I roll my eyes. "What?" Jack asks.

"Nothing... it's just I imagined your Liv to be some big-boobed blonde cheerleader, and it sounds like I was right." I shake my head, smirking down at the ground.

"She's not blonde." But Jack doesn't argue with the rest of my summary.

"How did you guys get together?" I'm actually curious.

"I got partnered up with her for a project." Jack steps over a big log. "Liv decided she liked me, I guess. Next thing I knew, I was taking her to the winter dance, and she was wearing my hockey jacket."

"What is she like?" I ask, wanting him to keep talking.

"What is she like?" Jack repeats my words slowly, reflecting. "She's fun. And bossy. She and her friends decide what we do on the weekends and stuff." Jack frowns as he continues. "It's all right, I guess." I watch him with raised eyebrows. "I sound like a pushover," — Jack looks over with a sheepish grin — "when I put it like that. But it's been good."

"And you guys are still together?" I ask, "Like right now... before you left the city... you guys are together?"

"Yeah." Jack kicks at a clam shell.

I look straight ahead, the raindrops nailing my hood, and say, "There will be no more hugging. No hand-holding. None of that." I stop, turning to Jack. His expression dulls as he meets my gaze. "You're not being fair, Jack. Not to Liv. And you're not being fair to me. Okay?"

"I guess." Jack kicks another rock and watches it bounce across the sand.

"We will walk and talk and get my dad help. And I will show you all the things I would on a normal guiding trip. But that other stuff stops." My voice is stern. "Deal?"

"I'm sorry, Maia," Jack says. "I didn't mean... I mean... I don't know...". His words get lost in the wind and he stares down the beach at the crashing waves. Jack takes a deep breath and looks at me. "I've never met anyone like you. We talk... and it's easy... and you make me laugh." His soft words stumble. "I'm really sorry I didn't tell you about Liv." I nod, turning away from him, glad he's feeling sorry. But feeling sorry doesn't change what is.

Chapter 16

A bitter heaviness hunches my shoulders as I falter away from Jack. I meant what I said. I do. Imposing a normal guide and client relationship is absolutely the right thing to do. Absolutely.

Up ahead, the rollers are crashing against the steep cliff below the forest edge. Alarmed, I look behind us. Same problem. We're on a small piece of beach, but behind and ahead of us, the tide covers the base of the cliff.

"Shit." I stare ahead of us again.

"What?" Jack takes in my wide eyes.

"We need to hurry!" I grab his arm and propel him forward. "Follow me!" I brace against the wind and jog up the beach. My pack is heavy and bruises my hips with every step. The cobbly sand slows our pace. I'm cursing myself for misreading the tide and for not taking the safer overland trail up in the forest. If we aren't quick enough, we'll be trapped for hours on this little piece of beach until the tide goes out again. But it's too late now to go back, with the way to the upland trail behind us blocked by the rising ocean water.

Jack jogs alongside me. I stop where the crashing waves block our path. "See that yellow rope over there? And that orange buoy?" A hundred meters away, someone has placed a buoy to mark the trail entrance. "That's where we need to get to."

We're both breathless. Jack stares at the waves rolling right up to the black rock cliff face in front of us. He looks behind us, where the finger of beach we're on is shrinking with every minute the tide rises. I study the rhythm of the waves for a moment.

"If we run to that spot while the waves roll out," — I point to a sharp black outcrop halfway to the trail, — "we can get up on that rock... then sprint the trail between the next set of waves." I size up our chances. "With any luck, we won't get wet." I give Jack a tight smile.

"One at a time?" he asks, "Or together?"

"I'll go first." I decide sprinting to the rock on our own is best. The narrow strip of beach between the cliff and the receding water is full of boulders. Less chance for disaster if we stay out of each other's way.

⚘

I tighten the hip and shoulder straps of my pack. Then, as the next roller recedes, I run. Seawater splashes to my knees as I stomp through the ebbing wave. At school I run track and the 100-meter sprint is my best event. But this fifty meters feels infinitely longer than any race I've run. As I near the rock, a huge wave rolls from my right, the leading edge already foaming white. I take one last step, then leap up onto the rock just as the wave crashes around it. I get splashed, but otherwise, I'm safe.

I gaze back at Jack and give him a thumbs up. He watches the waves for a few more cycles, then sprints toward the rock. He's faster than I am and bounds onto the rock beside me easily. We've both made it halfway.

We catch our breath, then I nod at Jack. As the next wave recedes, I hop onto the sand and run for the trail entrance. I'm almost there when my rain pants snag on a half-buried stick. I fall. Fast and hard. There's barely time to get my hands up to protect my face. My pack knocks the wind out of me. I lie face down, stunned. Before I can react, an icy wave sweeps me to the top of the beach like a piece of driftwood.

The receding water rolls me down the beach when Jack's footsteps splash near my head. He grabs my bicep, yanking me to my feet. Yelling at me to run. So I try. With Jack dragging my soaking body, I stumble toward the trail entrance. I manage one last step near the buoy marker, then collapse on my side, breathless in the soft brown muck of the trail.

"Are you okay?" Jack drops his pack and kneels beside me. I can't catch my breath. Can't speak. "Maia, say something. Are you okay?" The concern in his voice grows, and I try to say I'm fine. But only manage a rough groan. "Here, let's take your pack off." Jack reaches across to unbuckle it and rolls the pack into the dirt. "Can I sit you up?" Jack asks. His voice echoes from far away. I nod inside my hood. Jack grips my upper arm to pull me upright, my legs straight out in front of me. "Damn." Jack breathes out a low whistle. "Your hands, you're bleeding," he says. I turn my hands, palm up, watching the raindrops splash into the bright red streaks of blood, then drip into the muck.

There's still a weight on my chest. I force a slow exhale, then attempt an inhale. Finally, a bit of damp briny air is coaxed into my lungs, near my racing heart. Jack's worry is written all over his face. I nod, signaling I'm good, but still can't find my voice. Then I inhale again.

As my breath returns, I also notice the sharp stinging of my hands. And the wet cold of my back and chest. I examine my hands first. On my left, the meaty part of the palm has a deep, jagged tear. The flap of loose skin is filled with black grains of sand. I wince as I try to clean it out. The knuckles on my right hand are also scraped raw. I must have made a fist when I went down.

Jack kneels at my side with the first aid kit. He tears open a sterile wipe and holds out his hand, silently asking to help. I hesitate, then place my right hand in his palm. Jack wipes the blood and grime from my knuckles and gnarled scar. I watch, wincing and flinching. Jack keeps a firm grip, then dabs antiseptic cream on the scrapes. After he wraps bandages around each finger and across my stumps, he holds my hand between his, offering a light squeeze. He wants acknowledgment, but I refuse to look up.

Wordlessly moving to my other side, Jack whistles again at the gouge in my palm. "Damn, Maia," he says. "This is an ugly one." He tries to flick the sand out of the wound with a fresh wipe, and I gasp at the stabbing pain. Jack finally shakes his head. "I think we should flush it with water first." I sit obediently as Jack washes the sand out of my palm with water from the coffee mug.

Getting the bandages to stick over the larger wound is tough. Everything is wet, the rain still swirling around us. Jack places the bandages over the hole in my palm, then wraps first aid tape right around my hand.

"Thanks." I pull my hand away as a violent shiver runs through me.

"You're freezing," Jack says, watching me shudder.

"My legs are dry." Which is surprisingly true. "But my top is soaked." Jack finds two of Anna's tops in my bag. My palms ache and I let him help me out of my rain jacket. He pulls my hoodie over my head, as if I were a little kid. I shiver again, sitting there in my sports bra until Jack tucks me into a dry base layer and fleece without comment.

CHAPTER 17

Jack pulls me up and steps back as I tuck my dry shirt into my rain pants. I move slowly, careful not to wreck the bandaging Jack just finished. Then I try to zip my jacket, fumbling with my numb, bandaged fingers. Jack moves in to help, but I wave him off. He shrugs, shakes his head, and walks away. I zip up to my chin and secure my hood, then stuff my hands into the fuzz-lined pockets of my jacket. Luckily, the pockets were zipped shut before I went for my accidental swim.

On a rock outcrop beyond our gear, Jack is studying the crumpled map. I walk over to him, watching the waves crash against the cliff face.

"I'm sorry Jack." The beach we just ran across is now covered in a foot of water, the sand shifting with every wave. "That was really stupid. I should have taken you on the overland route," I say. "I was so worried about staying on the beach. So we could see boats. But that wasn't the right choice. It wasn't safe."

Jack thrusts the map between us. "Show me." I trace our route with my thumbnail, beginning at the yellow star at the trailhead, then along the trail to our current location. "And where are we going?" I move along the trail to a symbol of a cabin. "Not too far now." He's right. We're over halfway there. "And what's this?" Jack points to an unlabeled red dot between our location and the ranger's yurt.

"It's our supply cache." I peer down at the map, recalling my dad's reference to it. It's there if you need it, he'd said. He must have suspected this storm would hit, must have guessed signaling from the first beach wouldn't work. The plan he and I discussed didn't involve us coming this far along the trail. I shake off the quiver that runs through me when I think about how we got into this mess.

Jack just nods, then turns toward the yellow rope at the next climb, folding the map closed.

"I'm going to go up first. With your pack," — he holds up his palm, silencing my protest — "No arguments, Maia. You're hurt and cold. And holding onto that rope is going to be hard enough." He glances toward my right hand, tucked in my pocket. "I'll go up, drop your pack, then come for my pack. Okay?"

"Okay," I say softly, staring at the ground. It's a good plan. The right plan. I hate needing help. But I know Jack's correct. And I'm glad he's not questioning my ability to make the climb — he just acknowledges it will be hard. In my pocket, I wiggle my fingers, and flashes of hot pain pierce up my arms.

Jack shoves the map inside his jacket and throws my pack on. He smiles before he grabs the rope and starts a careful climb. This cliff is not as high as the ones from yesterday. Jack disappears over the top edge for a moment where he drops the gear, then he descends. He rappels with ease, leaning back and holding the rope the way I showed him, then hops down beside me.

"Nice," I say. "You've gotten better at that without any actual practice."

"Your turn." Jack grins at my compliment. "Watch that middle section. You'll need lots of grip strength there. Maybe you can wrap the rope around your arm? Or behind your back?"

"I'll see." I pull my hands from my pocket and take the rope. Stabbing pain drills into my palm.

"Go slow. Be sure of each step," Jack says. I almost smile. Who's supposed to be the expert here? Jack is quickly becoming an outdoor human, I think, while grimacing at more wrenching pain.

"I will," I say. Near the bottom, I slip and have to grip the rope hard. Sweat beads on my forehead and my breaths are raspy. I just need to get to the top of this cliff. Nothing more. Just the top of this cliff. And I finally do. Cresting the bank, I sink onto a rotting, moss-covered log, exhausted. I rest my elbows on my knees, palms up, willing the throbbing to stop. Deep breath in, deep breath out. Steady heart.

A few minutes later, Jack's red, smiling face tops the bank. He clambers onto flat ground, drops his pack, and sits beside me on the log. His breathing returns to normal quickly, showing off his fitness level.

"You want to share the last protein bar?" he asks. "And have some water?" I nod and he digs out the supplies. "Blueberry Boomdizzle." Jack reads off the bar packaging. "Kind of sounds like our day so far." He tears the bar in half and hands me a piece.

"Is that what we're calling my fall?" I ask. "A boomdizzle?" Jack shrugs at me, grinning as he takes a big bite of his bar. Man... that smile. Things would be so much simpler if that smile didn't heat my insides. We sit shoulder to shoulder as we eat, sharing sips from the water bottle. "Thanks, Jack." I hold his dark gaze as we finish. "Thanks for all of it."

Jack shifts on the log so his shoulder bumps against mine playfully. I'm not changing my position on the whole Liv situation. But I *am* very glad Jack is here with me.

We're walking again, the trail now weaves through forest, along the cliff edge, overlooking the beach below. I'm still rattled by the danger I put Jack and me in this morning. It will not impress my dad when he hears about it. He has always let me do things many people consider dangerous. I think it comes from growing up on a farm, where his experience showed him the best way to stay safe is to *pay attention*. To have your head in the game, as my mum had been fond of saying. But this morning, I didn't have my head in the game. I let the need to get help for my dad outweigh our safety. Thankfully, nothing worse happened. I put Jack at risk by tripping. I tripped because we needed to rush. We needed to rush because I took the wrong trail. And I took the wrong trail because I felt pressured to stay where we could signal passing boats. No excuses. But that's what happened. I caused it.

A grunt from behind me makes me turn.

"You okay?" I raise my eyebrows at Jack. Every muscle in his body will be achy today. He hasn't complained, but it's normal for even the fittest guests to lose their enthusiasm on their second day of hiking.

"Totally okay." Jack gives a little hop to reposition his pack, unable to hide a wince. "Lead the way." If he's going to put on a brave ego face, I will not push for the truth about his pain.

And so I keep walking, distracted by a gut feeling I'm still making the wrong choices. This poor decision was because I'm afraid for my dad. Anna rattled me yesterday by insisting any delay could risk my dad's fingers. And hands. My stomach churns at the thought of him being permanently maimed. Or worse.

My brain flashes back to the last time I made a series of bad choices. It had been a cool, crisp fall day out in our rear acreage. We had a dimensional sawmill set up there. The kind where you position a log and then the mill runs the length of it to cut lumber. Two giant circular blades, each with thirty-two teeth, which I sharpened with a special file every morning. My dad had sold the log on the mill to a neighbor down the street, who was building himself a woodshed. The order was mostly smaller strapping and siding, but bigger pieces for the roof rafters, posts, and beams were on the cut list, too. I got paid by the board foot, so the beams were much more lucrative per cut than the crummy little strapping boards.

The air was chilly that morning, with frost sparkling on the ground and plumes of my breath hanging in the sunlight. The sharp, woodsy scent of the red cedar log I had milled the day before hung in the air. I left the house to end a conversation with mum. I just couldn't agree with her. She was wrong. And she was fading away: eyes sunken, ribs showing, her walk a shuffle. I couldn't bear to fight with this shadow of her. So I left to soothe myself with hard physical work.

The start-up process for the mill was routine, and I had done it without thinking. The big fir log was already leveled and set. My dad and I did that the previous evening. The end of the log facing me was almost four feet in diameter. Old-growth, harvested to make room for our house, with over two hundred tree rings witnessing its seasons. A light-colored ring of new wood grew each spring and a darker ring of slower growth formed each summer. I was noting a season about a hundred years ago when the fir endured a forest fire, marked by a slim, charcoal tree ring. Farther out, three wide tree rings mark good growing seasons, probably a time when the stand around this giant had been logged, letting it flourish.

I had fingered the tree rings, imagining what this land must have looked like when this fir had been a sapling centuries ago. Back to my task, I visualized how the stacks of rectangles would fit inside the circle of the tree trunk. These rectangles would become the cut pieces of lumber, and I set up the saw blades to make the first cut. With a clunk and a loud whine, the saw made its way across the immense tree, cutting a flat surface just under the bark. When the saw got to the end of the log, I stopped it while I dragged the heavy piece of outer wood to the scrap pile.

As the saw returned on the track, my dad had rounded the corner by our storage shed. With one glance, I knew he wanted to talk. Knew what he was going to say. And I wasn't ready to hear it. I turned my back on him, rotated the cranks to position the two blades for the next cut, and engaged the saw again. I felt my dad watching me as the sawdust spit out along the cut. After the blades finally returned, he stood beside me, signaling for me to remove my ear muffs. When I shook my head in defiance, a flurry of emotions chased across his face. The raw agony in his puffed eyes made me look away. The rage in his tight jawline frightened me. How were the two of us ever going to make it alone?

Frustrated by my rebellion, my dad had grabbed my upper arm to spin me around, pulling the earmuffs off my head with the other hand. "She's picked her day, Maia," he said hoarsely. "Go see her. She's asking for you." I looked into his red-rimmed gray-blue eyes, unable to accept mum was ready to end her... to leave us. "Go. Now." He shoved me toward the house.

"I won't!" I stormed past him to get back to work. He grabbed for me again. I jerked away in a rage. And then... then I was falling. Falling fast toward the giant, glinting blades. I protected my face with my right hand. That's how it happened.

It had been so swift. A hard pull and the snapping of bones as the blades caught my last two fingers and yanked them free. The thud of my body hitting the sawdust-covered earth under the sawmill. The shout from my dad, pulling off his mack jacket, wrapping my hand. I watched it all in slow motion through an underwater kaleidoscope.

The pain hadn't come until we were in the truck halfway to town. My dad plopped my fingers in an old Mason jar he took from the shed. He hauled me to my feet and braced my tottering trip to the truck, his eyes saucers of disbelief in an ashen face.

I had never seen him drive so fast, blow so many stop signs, the Mason jar wedged between his thighs on the driver's seat. I remember how he hollered for Cindy, the intake nurse, as the truck door slammed in front of emergency. Then dad's musky scent as he carried me inside and laid me gently on a gurney.

Much later I woke up, cool white sheets covering me. Mum sat propped in a chair beside the bed with pillows around her, eyes closed. Dad stood behind her, his back to me, glaring out the hospital window at the ravens drifting in the wind over an unfamiliar town down-island.

A loud creak from above us now jerks my focus to the trail. I stare up at the tree canopy, where dark green boughs are jostling in the gusts. I stop, realizing how fast I've been moving, and wait for Jack to catch up. Anything to distract my mind from another replay of The Worst Day.

I've never spoken to anyone about the labels I've given the events of the past thirteen months. But in my mind, I capitalize the words. Proper nouns, as Mr. Lanahan, my English teacher, would say. First came The Diagnosis. A sunny day in early May when the word "cancer" had entered our family's daily vocabulary. And last summer, throughout The Summer of Hell, we watched powerlessly as my mum fought, weakened, rallied, and then faded again. The Worst Day actually happened over two days. It started the afternoon I fell into the sawmill and ended the next morning, while I lay propped in a hospital bed, with my mum sharing the details of how she would end her life. The day I'll forever call The Last Day.

Chapter 18

"You okay?" I ask Jack as he approaches. He smiles, then he shakes his upper body. Raindrops fly off him in all directions, like a dog shaking after a swim. Despite my heavy mood, I crack a thin smile at his goofy grin.

"This rain could stop any time!" He looks skyward. "Does it always fall so thick here?"

"Not always. But a lot."

"And this wind," Jack says, "it's totally wild." Another gust hits the treetops and the giant timbers creak in protest. Drips fall in loud splats against our rain gear and the salal leaves around us. "Where do the animals go in this weather?" Jack asks. We continue walking, sidestepping the deepest mud holes.

"I'm not sure," I say. "I think most of them just hunker down and nap. They're used to this." I balance on a large root to cross another mud pit. We round a corner, where the remains of an old cabin are evident. The crumpled walls are now a square, moss-covered hump in the small clearing. Along one wall, the rusty remnants of a stove and stovepipe lay on their side.

"Cool," Jack says, "But what a lonely place to build a cabin."

"It is." I point ahead of us at the wider and flatter trail. "Here, the new trail meets the old settler's road. This cabin would have been on the main road a hundred years ago," I say, "and before that, the indigenous people were out here too. See that?" I point to a tall cedar tree with a long scar running up its side. We place our hands on the bark-free scar, feeling the smooth inner wood where, hundreds of years ago, the bark was removed. The patch is wide at the base, running up the tree, where it tapers to a point fifteen feet from the ground. "It's a culturally modified tree. Well... that's what we call it now. The indigenous people cut through the bark at the bottom... here." I crouch and finger the scar base. "Then pulled off the soft inner bark to make clothing and blankets, baskets and ropes. It didn't hurt the tree... the tree just kept growing. You can see how the new bark is curling to grow around the scar." I cup the curve of the scar lobe in my palm.

"Neat," Jack says. "It's so hard to imagine living out here... just off the land... they had to be tough. And smart."

We continue, now walking on the long-abandoned settler's road. Ferns, alders, and salmonberry bushes grow tangled across the width of the flat path, our trail punching through the middle. With the big trees set back on both sides, more light gets to the road. And today, so does the rain. But the trekking is easier, without mud holes and roots to trip on.

"Do you like living up here?" Jack asks.

"I guess." After some consideration, I answer. "I mean, I have no idea what it's like to grow up anywhere else." Jack's life in the city must be so different from my life in town. "There's not a lot of privacy. Like there's no way I wouldn't know someone my own age. And when things happen, everyone knows your business." There were endless sidelong glances and silenced conversations when I returned to school after The Worst Day.

"It must be kind of nice," Jack says. "Knowing everyone, I mean." He kicks a mossy branch as he walks. "I don't know anyone in our new neighborhood." I think about this and can't imagine not knowing who my neighbors are or how long they've lived here. And what they do for a living.

"There is some good in it." During our hardest days, so many in town showed us kindness and concern. Not in sympathy cards or flower bouquets. Kindness was waking up to a shoveled driveway, finding a load of chopped firewood stacked in the woodshed, and coming home to a pile of teen magazines left on the front step. There were, of course, the obligatory hot meals. Meals that sustained my dad and me those first few weeks. We have no family in this country, but after The Last Day, there were plenty of people who cared enough to feed us.

"People look out for each other," I say, "even if they don't know you super well." I reflect on the reasons. "Around here, no one's a total stranger." Jack nods as he walks beside me, holding out his palm for a minute, watching the raindrops dance on it.

"Yeah," Jack says. "My dad wouldn't get away with fooling around on my mum in a place like this." He sighs, then asks, "What would you do, Maia?"

"About what?"

"About telling my mum what my dad's doing with that pencil skirt woman." Jack pounds the ground with his walking stick as we trudge along the old settler's trail. "I can't keep a secret from my mum." Jack's nostrils flare and his knuckles whiten as he grips his stick. "But I also shouldn't have to be the one to tell her."

"It's not fair." My voice is soft. "This shouldn't be *your* problem at all. But it is. So... what would I do?" I consider the facts for a long while, rubbing my sore neck. Our conversation distracts us from how our bodies ache. "I would tell your dad you saw him. And that he has to tell your mum." I shake my head a little, thinking of Anna's kind eyes.

"Erg!" Jack's response is a throaty grunt. "It's going to kill her." He glances over at me, realizing his poor choice of words. "I mean... it's going to hurt her so much... sorry, Maia. I shouldn't have said it like that," Jack says.

"It's fine." I wave a hand at him.

"Still, I'm sorry," Jack repeats. He really is a nice guy. Shit. "What was she like, your mum?" he asks. The trail makes a sharp right off the old settler's road now, and back onto a narrower footpath downhill.

"She was adventurous, loved being outside. Hiking, skiing. Loved doing these trips," I say. "And she evened us out. My dad and I understand each other well. I talk to him about most things. And I can tell what he's thinking. But we also fight. A lot. We're both stubborn. So my mum balanced out our family." I suddenly realize this is true. "I wouldn't have to fight to go away to school next year if my mum was still here. She would have straightened my dad out," I say. "She was also a great cook. She had a huge garden and made the best meals... at home... and out here." I smile across at Jack.

"You must miss her."

"Yeah." Yet despite my upbeat description, I feel a flash of anger cross my face, my jaw clenching.

"Are you mad at her?" Jack asks, his brow scrunched.

"Furious!" I stomp along the trail a few steps. Then I stop and whirl to face Jack. He's puzzled, and I need him to understand. Need him to see. I rub the bandaged stump of my injured hand, deciding to share. "Let me tell you about The Worst Day."

And so I tell Jack how beautiful it was when The Worst Day started, sunny and frosty. That I went outside to avoid my mum. I tell him about how I checked out the old log and its tree rings before I worked the sawmill. How my dad came outside, that we fought. And then I tell Jack everything I remember about falling. The blades, the Mason jar, the truck ride. And how I woke up under those white sheets, with mum and dad beside me in the big hospital down-island.

Chapter 19

"Jesus, Maia. That's horrible." Jack's voice falters from behind me as I finish. Our pace is faster here, the trail heading toward the beach again, fishy seaweed in the air. The rain still beats down in gusty sheets, filling the forest with rushes of drumming.

"What in the world were you guys fighting about?" Jack asks. He stayed silent throughout my story. I maneuver over a rivulet carving a trench across the muddy trail, walking a while before answering.

"It was about my mum choosing her day to die." I glance back at Jack. He tilts his head, frowning. "She just stopped fighting, picked a date, and then she was gone." My voice cracks. "And somehow, I was supposed to be okay with that!" I hack at the brush with my walking stick and shout up into the swirling deluge. "How the hell am I supposed to be okay with that!?" I'm yelling now. Warm tears mix with raindrops on my cold cheeks. Still facing away from Jack, I stop as my vision blurs into a murky concoction of browns and greens.

Jack comes up beside me. He says nothing; doesn't touch me. But his calm presence is welcome, soothing. We stand unmoving as the steady rain pelts down on our gear. Finally, with a muffled sniff, I get my breathing level and blink until the trees come into focus again.

"So yeah," I say hoarsely. "I'm pretty pissed at her. Still." Jack nods, his eyes soft. He's quiet for a long while, then swallows hard.

"I'd like to hear about it." His expression is full of questions. But I'm suddenly exhausted.

"Let's go down to the beach and have a drink." I motion in the ocean's direction. Jack takes the lead, and I follow his careful progress. The trail steepens from a slippery slope to a section of steps carved into the roots and rock. Soon we get to the vertical cliff face separating forest from beach, where a ladder has been built to suit the spot. Slimy two-by-four rungs are nailed to timber rails extending above the top of the cliff.

Jack assesses the ladder, looking past the drooping ferns, down to the cobbly beach below. "Not dangerous at all." He looks up at me with his lopsided grin, trying to cheer me up. I feel the corners of my eyes crinkle. How does he do it, I wonder? This boy can make me smile through tears. It's nice. Very nice. Damn that city girlfriend of his, anyway.

"Do you want me to take your pack?" Jack glances at my bandaged hands.

"I'm fine," I say. "You go ahead."

Jack carefully steps onto the ladder, gripping the stringers and bouncing it a little, but the ladder hardly moves. When Jack hops onto the beach, I grip the rails tightly to get onto the rungs, grimacing at the stabbing in my palm.

Age and mildew blacken the rungs. Soft green moss and white lichen grow on the rails where hikers' climbing feet and hands don't rub it off. Ferns overhang the cliff face, their shiny foliage dancing in the wind. As I near the bottom, a dark green spongy moss covers the rock beyond the ladder, rainwater soaking everything.

I hop off the last rung and my feet crunch into the sand, tinged a deep purple with broken mussel shells. Jack is peering across the short cobblestone beach that shapes a small bay. It's rougher than the last beach. Across the way, there's a campsite, marked by another faded buoy and a sign.

Jack pulls the water bottle from his pack, offering me some. I take a long swallow before lowering it from my lips. Without warning, the water bottle falls onto the cobbles with a metallic clunk, slipping from my bandaged grip. I watch in horror as the rest of our drinking water disappears into the sand.

"Shit!"

"It's okay." Jack jumps to grab the bottle and looks up as he screws the lid back on.

"It's not okay!" I'm frustrated at my clumsiness. "That's all of our water. Shit." I shake my head, my throat closing up again.

"Seriously?" Jack's reply is calm, as he shoots me a concerned glance from under raised eyebrows. "Look around. We're not gonna dehydrate." And he's right, of course. I'm overreacting. Water is coming at us from all directions. I grunt an unintelligible response and step over a log.

We traverse the beach carefully, leaning on our walking sticks. The barnacle-covered round rocks are perfect ankle crunchers. Rollers crash on our right, pounding the shore with a force we can feel in our feet. The wind has been blowing a gale for hours, building the swell to over ten feet.

"Boogie boarding those things would be fun," Jack says, "Except for the chompy landing in the rocks."

"Not dangerous at all," I say. Jack grins, accepting my unspoken apology for flipping out earlier.

There are two tent pads near the edge of the forest. But there's no hint of other hikers as we pass the park sign, empty food locker, and outhouse.

Here the trail cuts inland, following the bank of a much bigger river boiling on our right. Between the trail and the river mouth lies a swampy grassland. Usually, it's a beautiful spot for a break when we're kayaking. The last time I was here, the river was mirror-flat, with steam hovering over the water. Today, the swollen river is murky with a two-foot chop. A curtain of rain dances by in a gust, the blast stinging my eyes. Squinting, I lean hard into the wind to keep my balance.

A steep climb puts us back in the relative shelter of the forest, to a spot where the river mouth narrows to a passable width.

"Holy crap!" Jack's tone fills with the excitement of a toddler at an amusement park. "Do we get to ride that?" He points and stares up at a small manual cable car, docked against the steel support platform, two stories above our heads.

Chapter 20

The cable car itself is a small aluminum box, two feet by four feet, made of square metal tubing. There's a seat at either end, each big enough for one person. The side rails are low — waist height when you're sitting. With two people in the car, your gear crams between your feet on the floor made of the same metal grating as the platform. A vertical ladder welded to the platform leads up to a metal grate landing surrounded by a sparse guardrail. Beside the ladder, the structure is anchored into the ground behind us with massive cables.

A thick cable runs across the river, connected to another tall steel platform on the far bank. The whole cable car is suspended from two sheaves. Hanging below the cable is a blue nylon rope, one end tied to the front of the passenger box. It spans the river, wraps around pulleys on both banks, and ties to the back of the box. A miniature, hand-powered gondola.

"Are we riding this?" Jack has already scaled the ladder to the steel platform, his gaze following the thick cable to the far bank. I nod silently, still agitated about losing our drinking water. There's a freshwater source farther up this river once we cross. But it'll likely be undrinkable because of the volume of silty rain run-off. We'll collect rainwater if we need to. But I'm pissed I made another error.

I had chosen not to tell Jack about the cable car. This contraption is hard to describe and our guests enjoy the surprise of finding a bit of human engineering out here in the wilderness.

"I get it," Jack calls down to me as he examines the pulley system. "You ride it down, then pull yourself across with the rope. Cool!" His child-like enthusiasm is scattering the cloud hanging over me.

"It is pretty cool," I say. "Hold on to the cage, so it doesn't roll away on you. And put your pack in it. Then I'll come up. There's not a lot of room up there."

Once Jack has his pack in the cage, I start the climb. My face crests the platform where Jack is rummaging for something in his bag. Grabbing the guardrail over my head, I clamber awkwardly off the ladder and onto the platform. When I turn to drop my pack, my jacket snags on a sharp edge, throwing me off balance. I grab the guardrail to steady myself, but my sore, bandaged hands won't do the job. Suddenly I'm falling. Jack still has his back to me, leaning way over the cable car, his knees on its side rail. He gets no warning of my tumble. I hit hard, my forehead bouncing off a metal cross brace with a hollow thud as the full weight of my body lands on Jack's back and hips. Twinkles of bright light overlay the circling treetops as I scramble to get off him. I groan, touching the goose egg already forming near my temple. Through my daze, I barely register Jack's alarmed shout.

I stare in horror as the cable car slides away from the platform, with Jack hanging off the side of the mini gondola. The momentum from my fall has rolled the car along the cable. In seconds, he's over the edge of the river, legs flailing below the passenger box. Hanging by his armpits, Jack is floundering to wrap his arms through the tubing of the side rail.

"Maia!" Jack yells, then lets out a prolonged, "Oooohhhh shiiiiiit!" The cable car picks up speed as it drops along the wire rope over the murky river. Then the car slows and finally stops, as it runs out of momentum on the uphill half of the cable.

Jack's body twists under the passenger box, which sways dangerously. "Maia!" Jack's shout is strained.

"Hang on, Jack!" I yell back. "Hang on, I got you!" I crawl to the edge of the platform. My vision blurs in a wave of wooziness. Jack and the cable car swirl as my knees suddenly buckle. I grip the rail, clamp my eyes shut, and give my head a shake. Jack shouts, and I squint in his direction. Blood rushes in my ears and Jack still looks blurry, but at least he's not spinning.

I reach for the blue rope, pulling the cable car and Jack back toward me. Pain flashes through my palms as I tug hard. "Hold on! Almost here!" My biceps and shoulders burn from the panicked effort and I hardly notice my bandages rip off.

"I'm slipping." Jack's voice is shrill. He grunts, trying to get a better grasp on the bars. The cable car bounces and his legs thrash in mid-air as he struggles to hold on. Something falls from his pocket, floating like a leaf for a moment in the wind. As it drops into the rushing river, I recognize the folded shape of our map. The boiling current rips it out of sight almost instantly.

Shit! Jack can't fall in. He'll drift into the pounding ocean in a heartbeat down that river. The cable car inches closer. But so much slower than the ride down. Hand over hand, I haul on the rope, dragging Jack bit by bit to the edge of the river.

"Almost here, Jack. Hang on!" His boots kick at the bush tops as he reaches the bank. He's no longer over the rushing water, but the forest floor is savage. Blow-downs with pointed broken branches crisscross the ground twenty feet below him. "Just a few more seconds." Jack lurches lower, losing his grip. "Hold on!" Please don't fall, I think, hoping he's unaware of the spears of sharp debris under him.

Jack's only reply is a strained groan. He's holding on with all he has. Finally, the cable car is close enough for me to grab the aluminum cage. I pull it close, but Jack's body hanging off the side prevents the cable car from parking like it's supposed to.

By wrapping the blue rope around one arm, I secure the car. Laying down on the platform, I reach out under the bottom guardrail for Jack with my other arm. "I think I can grab your belt." I strain to hold the rope and clutch Jack's waistband. "Pull up!" I focus everything on lugging Jack to safety. I'm being ripped in half, the wrapped rope cutting into one arm and most of Jack's weight hanging from my weak, injured fist. Jack climbs, inching toward the cable car's side rail. Finally, he flops into the cage, flushed and breathless.

I let go of his belt and roll over on my back, panting, the rope still binding my arm. Tears well up behind my eyelids, my thoughts jumbled. I try to block out the wide-eyed terror on Jack's face. I caused that. My shoulders shake and silent tears spill down my temples. A wave of searing anger boils from my belly. I caused that! The treetops dance and jerk in the wind above me. Raindrops fall in streaks, and I squint as the pinpricks hit my face.

Jack groans from the cable car, and I feel a tug on the rope as he sits up. I sense him looking over at me, but I don't move. Don't speak. I caused that. Clamping my eyes shut again, I turn away.

"Maia," Jack says softly, "Are you okay?" The rope jerks at my arm again. Jack's boots clang onto the metal grating of the platform beside my head. There's a clunk as he pulls the cable car to its parking spot. Kneeling, Jack wordlessly unwraps the rope from my arm. He sits down against the far guardrail beside my outstretched legs. Jack's quiet for a long moment before he murmurs, "That was... not dangerous at all."

But this time, our shared joke doesn't make me feel better. Not even a bit.

Chapter 21

Gusts rush through the trees, the rain still hitting my face as I lie on my back. After a while, I prop myself up and peer across the platform at Jack.

"Jesus!" He crouches in front of me. "Your forehead." He reaches toward my face with concern. I jerk away, gingerly feeling the lump with a fingertip. Blood has crusted over the golf-ball-sized bump above my left eyebrow.

"I'm fine." But I wince as I wrinkle my brow. Jack's lips press together and he crosses his arms.

"Are you dizzy at all?" he asks. "How's your vision? Seeing spots or stars? Blurry?" Shit, I think groggily. Is this guy a mind reader?

"It's better now." I don't admit the world is still swirling around me. "Are you okay?" I don't meet his eyes. "You're the one that almost died."

"I'm fine." Jack holds his palm to his upper chest. "Yep, my heart has settled down. And the other bruises will heal — no worse than taking five hundred pucks in a practice." He pats down the rest of himself. I consider him curiously.

"You should be pissed," I say. "Seriously! I don't get you." I give a slight head shake and feel my eyebrows squish together. His upbeat attitude is infuriating.

"Look at your hands," Jack says. "You didn't do it on purpose. Mistakes happen. You move on." He reaches into the cable car for his pack. "Like my goalie coach says — shake it off and refocus. You can't change the past, Maia." I study him, still perplexed. He holds up the zipper bag of bandages and motions me over. "Now, let me fix your hands again," Jack says. So he's noticed my bleeding hands. Fine, I think. Fine! It's pointless to resist this whirlwind of positive energy. Jesus.

When my hands are bandaged, I say, "We need to get going." My gut clenches. Every minute we waste here is a minute longer my dad waits in pain. I haul myself up, but sway dangerously, losing my balance.

"Whoa, there." Jack jumps over to grab my arm. I steady myself against the guardrail, brushing off his support. Shit. "Just let me help you get in," he says. "We don't need another adventure."

Jack settles me onto the front bench, then climbs in opposite me. "Ready?" He grins and pushes us off. The car rolls down the cable for just a few quick seconds before it stops over the center of the river. We can see down to the river mouth from here. The ocean waves are still huge, breaking thunderously into white foam on the beach. After taking in the view, Jack pulls us along the rope to the other side. He insists on doing this part, and I let him. My hands and arms are throbbing.

This ride should have been a fun break from our exhausting hike. Instead, the passage over the murky water is solemn. My clumsiness has taken another piece of joy from Jack's day.

Jack maneuvers us up against the platform on the opposite bank and climbs out. He holds out a hand to steady me. I accept his help with a glower, trying to hide my dizziness. "I won't risk you falling from up here. You're probably a little concussed," Jack says, taking in my look. "I'll leave you alone once we're back down on solid ground, promise." Without a word, I step onto the platform and let him help me climb down the ladder. I'm relieved when I'm on the spongy forest floor.

Jack makes two trips to carry both sets of gear down from the platform. We both wince as we hoist our packs, wrestling straps over tender body parts. Something makes me take a slow look over my shoulder at the forest surrounding the platform tower. Giving my foggy head a shake, I stomp up the trail after Jack. But I still have that tingly feeling of someone... or something... watching us.

Chapter 22

"We should refill the water." I jog to catch up. We're following the trail downstream, the river now on our right. I fall into stride behind Jack. His closeness shakes the creepy, tingly feeling. "There's a spot... up ahead... maybe ten minutes away." He nods and we walk in silence for a while, Jack leading. The trail moves away from the river and deeper into the forest. It's muddy, but better than the previous stretch. Sword ferns droop onto the path, twisting in the wind gusts that reach us even in the dense forest's shelter. And the rain. The rain never stops. The patter of drops on my hood and the splatter of drips from the boughs above are a steady soundtrack.

As we round a bend in the path, Jack stops suddenly. Near the trail's edge is the ragged blue-black body of a feathered Stellar's jay. The bird is lying still with its back toward us, a twisted inky claw curled underneath it. We move closer, staying on the far side of the path.

Its head is turned, just one eye facing us. When we approach, it flinches, startled, but can't seem to move much more. Its shiny black eye widens for a moment, then returns to an exhausted half-squint. There are bald patches in its charcoal crest. The usually beautiful, aligned blue feathers of its tail are sticking out haphazardly, wet and battered.

"What do we do?" Jack whispers. He crouches close to the teeny thing, his eyebrows pulling down in concentration. I look away from the bird's dark eye, knowing the light will soon fade from it.

"Nothing," I say. "There's nothing we can do." I falter away, sudden memories of my mum's last day crushing me. The tiny smile on her cracked lips. The paper-thin crinkled skin of her cheekbones. Her withered hand giving mine a faint squeeze. The loving glow in her blue eyes dimming to a blank stare.

I stumble, then lean against a big hemlock. I double over, arms wrapping around my gut, blood pounding in my ears, rocking up and down. Deep breath in, deep breath out, I chant silently.

Soon the tightness in my chest subsides, and the tingling in my arms fades. I pull myself upright. Jack is standing in the path, his puzzled gaze moving from the dying bird to me, and back to the Stellar's jay. He walks toward me, his eyes flickering with slow understanding.

"Tell me about it," Jack says. "Let's walk" — he lays a gentle hand on my shoulder, pushing me into motion — "and you tell me about it. If you want."

I've only told one person about The Last Day. Parts of it, at least. That conversation ended with Nora accusing us of murder. I miss her friendship fiercely and if I could take back that talk, I would. But as we plod along this trail, cold and wet, the story of The Last Day tumbles out. I can trust Jack with it.

Chapter 23

"She picked November 11th as the day she would die." I follow Jack along the trail. "Remembrance Day. The date... it wasn't really on purpose, I don't think. She waited for what she called her ten-day 'period of reflection'." I pause as we clamber over a blow-down. The red poppies we all wear those early weeks in November, to honor Canadian war veterans, will now forever remind me of The Last Day. "That day I woke up in the hospital... after my sawmill accident... that was the day after Halloween." I pause again, replaying those initial moments of consciousness tucked under crisp white sheets.

My parents hadn't noticed I was awake. Mum was so gaunt, fragile, and pale. Even as she dozed in that hospital chair, soft pillows propping her up, pain tensed her face. And my dad's profile, as he watched the ravens outside, held an electric jumble of rage and sadness, the energy visible on him. At least to me.

"She told me the cancer had spread to her bones," I say to Jack, "In the hospital... where I couldn't run away from her and her news. That's when she told me. About the bone cancer... and her decision. She was so sure she was doing the right thing." I shake my head.

"Was she in pain?" Jack's words are slow and soft as he glances back at me.

"Some." I shrug. "The last days got worse. She couldn't walk any-more. Couldn't eat. Had to wear a diaper. It was awful." A shudder runs through me. It's another memory I wish I could burn from my brain, like a photo in a fireplace. "By then, she spent day and night in a rented hospital bed. My dad set it up in the living room. In front of the bay window... like she wanted. So she could watch the trees and the birds and the ocean in between her naps." It had been the longest, shortest time. Her minutes of scorching pain seemed to last for hours. But now, those last ten days are barely a heartbeat.

"On the day..." My voice breaks and I start again. "On the day... my dad went to her just after lunch. It was blustery, like this. Chunky rain pelting at the bay window." That pattering sound puts shivers up my spine whenever I hear it now. "He talked to my mum... one last time, alone. To make sure she hadn't changed her mind, I guess. And she hadn't... she was ready to go." My eyes sting. "But she was the only one ready. I wasn't ready." I choke out these words, tears blurring my vision. "Dad sure as shit wasn't ready!"

I pull out the sleeve of my hoodie to wipe my eyes, snuffling. Jack stops too. At his sides, his fists clench and unclench. When I can see again, I shuffle on, Jack following a couple of paces behind me. The trail continues to climb and we must be close to that freshwater site.

"Dad finally called me in," I say, "and we sat on either side of her... and just held her hands. She said nothing. Not then. We were all talked out, I guess. We'd been talking for days. She just gave each of us a little smile, squeezed my hand... and then her eyes just kinda blanked." I look up at Jack. "That's how she died."

I don't tell Jack the rest. The hushed conversations mum and dad had with Maggie, mum's nurse, leading up to The Last Day. Mag-gie's quiet compassion around mum's decision got us through. She had shared how things would go. What it would look like... how I might react. Maggie made The Last Day bearable. I don't blame her for mum's decision. Mum would've ended her life, with or without Maggie's help. I'm pretty sure Maggie showed Dad how to turn up the IV doses, but we've never discussed it. In any case, Maggie has entrusted us with something that could end her career. I know this. Yet I stupidly shared details with Nora. Look how that ended — I'll never tell anyone else the whole story.

Then, while we had waited for the crematorium, my dad sat with my mum for hours. I checked on him often, peeking through the stair risers into the living room. Sometimes he sat motionless. Other times he held her hand in both of his, silent tears streaking his face. Once, he was whispering urgently in her ear, his forehead resting against her temple.

When they finally showed up to take her away, he had his eyes closed, his cheek on her chest. One hand enveloped hers, and his other cupped the back of her head. I couldn't watch when the workers went to him. To ask him to move. I... couldn't. My throat feels thick, and I shake myself back to the present.

Now, on our right, is a stream. "That's the path. To the water," I say. Just a few steps below us, the water burbles. As I feared, it's pretty silty. "Maybe not." I look down into the brown murky water and shake my head, blinking. We need water. But this won't work.

"Let's just keep an eye out. We'll get rainwater somewhere," Jack says. "It's not like this is our only option." He's right, of course. But I really don't like when my plans don't pan out.

Jack tucks the water bottle into his pack, and we continue through the soggy forest in companionable silence. The terrain continues to climb and our breathing is heavy. Jack's footsteps behind me stop, so I look back at him. His expression is unreadable.

"Maybe choosing her day was a favor to you guys." Jack speaks softly after a long silence.

"Why would you say that?" A wave of fury rises in me. Sharing my story had loosened the heavy knot inside me. Just a little. But Jack's words bind me right up again. He shrugs.

"She was in pain... she was going to die... soon, anyway. And she saved herself from some pretty undignified help. Plus, she got to die at home, with her favorite people," Jack says. "I think she was smart... brave... to take the choice."

I turn on my heel, heat flushing through my body. I lurch away, needing distance between me and Jack's ludicrous opinions. A long while later, where the trail peaks, my breath comes in quick gasps. I finally stop, leaning against a tree and running my icy fingers gingerly over my aching goose egg.

This spot can be stunning, overlooking the forest, ocean, and mainland mountains. Today, the heavy rain and clouds limit visibility. The angry coast below me dominates the view, the rollers already an enormous size. Probably fifteen feet. In front of me, sheets of rain get shaped by the wind gusts, the raindrops swarming like a flock of birds.

When Jack finally rounds the bend and joins me at the overlook, my breath has recovered. He says nothing, just takes in the view, standing well away from me. As Jack catches his breath, I consider his earlier words, realizing he can't possibly know what it was like. No one who wasn't there ever can. The numb loneliness surges into a solid ache as I stare into the rain.

Chapter 24

My stomach growls as my heart thaws a little. It's not fair to be angry with Jack. But I'm mad, anyway. He's quiet, fidgeting from side to side, picking at his cuticles. Finally, he looks up and I raise my eyebrows. What's on your mind, Jack?

"Should we… maybe… the supply cache? Should we go there now? It's the next left, isn't it?" Jack rubs his eyebrow. I turn back to the pounding ocean below us, feeling a shift. This is Jack's first suggestion. Is he losing trust in me? Understandable after endangering him twice in a single morning. I let out a deep breath, shrug my shoulders, and start walking without responding. Jack follows, his footsteps plodding and rain gear rustling along behind me.

I'm not sure what to do. My stomach growls again, unsatisfied by the one-and-a-half protein bars I've eaten today. The supply cache will have food. But going there will take time. Time my dad might not have. On the other hand, if anything else goes wrong, we will need food. Going to the supply cache now will take less time than backtracking.

Past a rotting stump, the trail descends toward a steep embankment. Mini waterfalls run down the middle of the path, over the tree roots and boulders. Avoiding the soft mud forming everywhere, I continue carefully until we reach a small clearing. Two wooden tent pads perch above the soaked ground. Picturesque camping spots under the massive old growth. To our right, the trail continues to a timber and packed-earth staircase, twisting down to the beach.

Jack stops beside me, turning to look in every direction of the clearing. "Where's the trail to the cache?" he asks. The only obvious trail is the one leading to the beach. I dump my pack off my back onto the nearest tent pad. I sit, leaning my elbows on my knees, head in my hands. My palms are cool on my temples, where blood pounds rhythmically over the goose egg. Raindrops pelt my pants and roll off in tiny rivers, plopping into the murky water of my boot print. My chin hits my chest and my shoulders hunch. What should we do?

Jack hesitates, then dumps his pack beside me. My hood blocks all but his mud-covered boots from my view. The boots take a step back, then stop, toes pointing toward me. He's watching me. But I'm still not ready to meet his questions.

So many thoughts swirl through my throbbing brain. I want to run away. Away from Jack and his opinions and the skepticism he must feel right now. But I can't. My dad needs me to shake it off. To get my head in the game. My eyes close. I don't know what to do.

"Hey," Jack says now. "Maia? Look. I'm sorry. I'm sorry I said that about your mum. I... I didn't mean anything by it. I know... I can't know what you and your dad went through. Or your mum. Maia?" Jack says my name gently, a caress, and my chest releases a little. Without thinking, my eyes open and I look up at him. "Let's go to the supply cache. It didn't look far on the map. We need the food and first aid supplies. Who knows what other..." Jack hesitates, smirking. "What other... obstacles nature will throw at us between here and the ranger's station?" His eyes twinkle with mischief. I shake my head. This guy's positive attitude is unbelievable. And exactly what I need.

"Fine," I say. "Fine. Let's go to the cache. It's a good idea, Jack." It would be silly to pass up an opportunity to restock our food supply. Jack swallows and gives me a grateful smile. I realize I haven't said a word since my outburst, long before the overlook. Well, you're still wrong Jack. But I can't stay silent forever.

I stand up, then sit right back down as a wave of light-headedness washes over me, crushing my eyelids closed. Jack's beside me in an instant.

"Are you okay? Maia?" He leans in, reaching his hand toward me. Then grows still before touching me. I open my eyes. The world has stopped swirling. I nod and stand up again. Slowly.

"The path starts between the tent pads." I step away without answering Jack. It won't help for him to know how much my head pounds and my stomach churns. "We can leave our packs here. It won't take long to get back — it's only a couple hundred meters up the hill." Jack frowns, looking at our gear, then turns to follow me.

The path to the supply cache is unmarked on purpose. Technically, no one is allowed to leave anything in provincial parks. But my dad is not a rule follower. Leaving an emergency stash along the trail makes sense for the safety of our guests. And if the authorities don't know, it can't bother them.

I grin to myself, recalling a story my mum liked to tell about building our house. When they were halfway through pouring the strip footings, the district inspector had shown up, asking my dad for his building permit. My dad had shrugged, still shoveling sand and cement into the concrete mixer. "Don't got one yet, Paul. Will ya fill it out and bring it to me?"

The crazy part is, that's exactly what Paul did. He knew my dad wouldn't stop work to complete the required applications, even if he issued a 'Stop Work' order. So, after Paul made sure our building plans met all the setback and floor space ratio rules, Paul did the paperwork for dad. I'm still not sure why. Small town advantage? Or the hassle of issuing and rescinding an order? Or the respect my dad had gained with Paul for backing him up at town meetings? Probably a little of everything.

I push aside some long branches now and hold them until Jack catches up so they don't snap back and whack him. This path isn't really a path at all. The ground is unmarred by human footprints and the branches cut last summer have filled in with fresh growth. I've only been to the cache once, years ago, when I helped my dad lug in the container. And at that time, I wasn't leading the way. Nothing looks familiar.

A cedar tree, growing a huge burl, towers over us. My stomach flutters — I don't remember this tree. And I *would* remember this tree. I pause a moment, then walk past the cedar on the right. A few steps farther and the ground falls away, downhill. This is definitely not right. I freeze, a cold sweat forming between my tightening shoulders.

"What?" Jack stops behind me.

"This isn't right," I say. "The cache is up-slope from the tent landing. Not down. We're not on the right trail." Jack's eyebrows raise and his eyes widen a little.

"I wouldn't exactly call this a trail," he says. "I don't know how you decided where to go."

We backtrack to the cedar burl, and I look around. The salal and salmonberry bushes rise in walls of green all around us. My breath quickens as spots cloud my vision. I don't know where to go. My fingers tingle. We're lost.

Are my emotions obvious to Jack? He's staring down at my clenched fists with furrowed brows. No use pretending, I decide. "I don't know where we are," I say. "I'm not even sure which way we came from." My words rush out.

"We came from over there." Jack's voice is low and sure. "Come on." I follow Jack as he backtracks our route. He pauses occasionally, examining the ground and fingering the brush. About fifty meters back, he stops, pointing to a break in the bushes on our right. "Do you think that's the way?" While I had my mind on other things, Jack had clearly been paying attention to our route on the way in. I recognize the moss-covered blowdown with a three-foot wide chain saw notch carved into it. On our first trip, my dad had taken a few minutes to do that. It had been easier to cut a path through the log than haul the big metal toolbox over it.

"That's the way. We're almost there." There's relief in my voice, and Jack pushes through the brush as soon as I answer. I follow behind his confident stride, wet leaves slapping my cheeks. As he leads, Jack brushes away the delicate spider webs without flinching and points out a mottled banana slug for me to avoid. I lift an eyebrow at how far he's come.

Two minutes later, we're looking up at a huge moss-covered boulder. This part I remember. I circle to the left, eyes on the base of the rock. "There!" An unnaturally square drag mark scars the forest floor. The rain hasn't removed the evidence of my dad's trip last week. I crouch, reaching into the foliage to grab the handle of the cache. Jack's immediately beside me, grunting as we lug the big steel box out from under the salal.

Jack untwists the tie-wire securing the sliding latch. Since no one else knows about this stash, there's no need for a padlock. And the tie-wire keeps the animals out, in case the scent of our food tempts them. Jack slides the latch and lifts the rusty hinged lid.

Our shoulders bump together as we both peer inside. I let out a shaky laugh and feel a slow smile spread across my cold cheeks. Jack lets out a long breath, eyes locked on the stacks of supplies. His reaction confirms he also considered other outcomes. Like not finding the cache, or finding the contents wet or rotten or gone.

I hold the lid at an angle for Jack, keeping the rain out. My stomach grumbles and my mouth waters as he pulls out a bag of protein bars. Jack rips two open, handing me one as he inhales his in two large bites. I suppress a moan as the salty chocolate melts on my tongue. Hunger makes everything taste so, so good.

Jack shifts another bag of protein bars out of the way before handing me a bag of freeze-dried food pouches. Then he ducks back under the lid. This time he hands me a zipper bag of first aid supplies. Then a smaller baggy of water-purifying tablets. A couple of space blankets. A shrink-wrapped roll of moleskin. My spirit lifts with every item I toss onto our growing pile. We can do this. We can get to the ranger station and get help for my dad. Maybe even today.

I shift the weight of the lid to my other arm just as Jack freezes. When he slowly retreats, Jack sits back on his haunches and looks up at me, frowning.

"What?" Has he found a dead mouse or something? I lean under the lid, letting my eyes adjust to the shadows. Then I see it too. In the bottom right corner is a sealed zipper bag. Inside the bag is a rectangular box, wrapped in brown kraft paper. Tied to the top with white butcher twine are three dried cornflowers. And under the flower stems, my name is written right on the kraft paper, in thick black marker.

My back stiffens and a flush of adrenaline tingles through my belly. What? How? How could my mum's handwriting be on this neatly packaged box? She's been dead for seven months. My fingers shake as I gently pull the parcel out. I step back and stare down at the familiar wrapping resting on my open palms, rain bouncing off the plastic of the zipper bag.

My mum had never bought wrapping paper. Other families have rolls for every occasion — bright primary birthday paper and holly-covered Christmas paper and wedding paper with silvery bells. But my mum had kept a single roll of thick brown kraft paper. She'd tie each neatly wrapped present with white butcher twine and top it off with natural decoration. A dahlia from her garden or a sprig of huckleberries from our backyard forest. Her presents were distinct and beautiful.

I wouldn't have needed to see my mum's writing to know she wrapped this parcel. The paper and twine are enough. The dried dark blue flowers, tied neatly on top, are ones I picked and hung to dry under her watchful eye last summer. Back then, she could still sit up in a lawn chair, bossing me about. A sudden vision of her fills my heart. She's turning her face to the sun, smiling, eyes closed. A blue batik scarf wraps around her head as she inhales the soft fragrance of the chocolate cosmos I've lain in her lap. A good memory. That's been buried under so many worse memories.

"Is it... who is it from?" Jack breaks the silence. I hug the package to my chest, nodding. I know he knows it's from my mum. "Well? Are you going to open it?"

The idea makes me shudder. I chew my bottom lip as my heart pounds against the precious parcel. What could it be? A letter? A gift? I'm super curious. And terrified. Whatever it is, I'm suddenly certain I don't want Jack watching me figure it out.

"Nope," I say, "It can wait." I place the parcel on our pile of supplies and say, "Let's get the cache secured and stashed. We've used up way too much time already." And it's true, I realize, the familiar knot growing in my stomach. My dad needs us to move.

Once we've dragged the cache back under the bushes, Jack spreads one of the space blankets across the mossy forest floor. He hands me the parcel from my mum before stacking the other supplies into the center of the blanket. Jack then gathers the four corners of the thin silver foil in a crinkly burst, slings the whole thing over his shoulder, and strides toward the invisible trail we arrived on.

With a last glance at the cache, I wipe the rain off my mum's parcel and tuck it under my jacket, wondering again how it got here. And when? And why?

Chapter 25

Jack leads the way back to the tent pads without hesitation. He dumps the crinkly sack of supplies next to our packs and spreads the space blanket open. Raindrops tinkle on the silver sheet as we divide our haul between us. Once I've arranged the heavier food in my pack, I place my mum's parcel on top, still in its plastic zipper bag.

We roll the now familiar weight of our packs onto our tired shoulders and begin another descent, soon coming to the longest staircase on this trail. There are over 250 steps. I've counted.

"I'm sure glad someone built these." Jack breaks the silence and assesses the steep bank. We climb down, watching our footing. There are no handrails. Each step is built of thick timbers, slippery with a dark green slime. Each tread is dug into the slope and backfilled with dirt. Ferns and moss grow everywhere, especially this early in the season when few boots have scuffed the vegetation.

Halfway down, the steps curve along the overhung black rock cliff. Rainwater is pouring down the face, creating crevices of waterfalls.

"Can we fill up the bottle here?" Jack asks. I look up at the rock wall. It's impossible to tell what the water flows over before it gets down here, so I cup my palms into a crack. The water is crystal clear, without sediment or floaters.

I nod over at Jack, but he's already filled the bottle. He takes a huge drink, then passes it to me, smiling.

"Here," he says, "you must be thirsty too." I take a few big swallows of the ice-cold water. Perfection. Jack refills the bottle, then tightens the cap before tucking the whole thing back in his pack.

A gust of wind reaches us, catching my hood and whipping the ends of my blond hair up into my eyes. I tuck the strands behind my ears and turn toward the ocean. The rushing of the surf below joins the ebb and flow of the storm. The wind carries the distinct scent of seaweed and bird poop. I take a deep breath. Ocean air always calms me. Another breath. Yep. Soothing.

"Let's see if we can find a sheltered spot down there," I say. "We can warm up some lunch before we move on."

We finish the climb to the beach, as I ponder my decision to make a fire. It'll take extra time. However, we can both use a break. Restocking at the cache diminished the anxiety about our food supply. But getting us lost and then finding the parcel from my mum has rattled me. I'm not thinking straight. And though I can't tell how Jack's feeling, his smile tells me a hot meal won't make things worse.

This shoreline is rocky, with only small patches of sand. The crashing surf forces us along the top of the beach. Not far away, there's a massive tree stump lying on its side. The underside of its root ball makes a vertical shelter in a position that blocks most of the gale.

We drop our packs in the strip of sand by the stump and begin the fire-starting routine. The wind blows out our tiny flame a few times, but soon we have a nice blaze going. We prop a mug of water against the stones, warming our hands as we wait. The fire's heat scatters in this wind, and I wish for the tarp we left with Anna and dad.

Dad. I wonder how he's doing. It's been about twenty-four hours since the accident. I shudder involuntarily, the charred scent of his wounds filling my nostrils. By now, the pain will make him irritable and restless. I hope Anna can handle him. Remembering how painful the recovery of my hand was, I shudder again. No matter what happens, my dad has a tough road ahead of him.

I turn back to the fire as my thoughts consider the other... the scenario where there's no recovery for my dad. A hard lump fills my stomach and I gulp down a breath to stop a sob. In front of me, the fire blurs and swirls as I force my attention back to the parcel. Did my dad put it there? Does he know what's in it? Did he mean for me to find it? Or was it all my mum? Pondering these questions suppresses my urge to flee. For now.

When the water in Anna's mug is warm, Jack pours it into a pack of Pad Thai chicken, reseals the bag, and gives it a shake. Then he props it up near the fire to keep it warm while it rehydrates. Jack's being super helpful. I think it's a silent acknowledgment that his earlier words hurt me. And I appreciate his attempt to show me he's sorry. Or maybe he's taking over because I've messed up so many things. I sit back, watching him fix us lunch, thinking about our situation.

The northwester hasn't let up since last night. The storms up here can blow for days, so the hope of signaling a boat today is fading. Which means we need to get to a radio. In relative terms, the ranger station isn't far from this spot. With any luck, a ranger will be there. They use the yurt as a base camp for trail maintenance this time of year. I know some kids from school who worked out here last summer. It's the prime season for repairs, with hardly any hikers and decent weather. Well, it's statistically *supposed* to be decent weather, I think, shaking my head. Regardless, they wouldn't leave a ranger out here without a VHF radio.

"What're you thinking about?" Jack notices my frown.

"All of it." I sigh. "My dad. Anna. I'm worried. He must be in so much pain by now," I say. "They'll expect we flagged down a boat last night. When help didn't come today, they'll both be worried about us. I just wish we could let them know we're okay." I look back into the fire. "And this stupid storm!" I shake my fist up at the swirling rain. "No boat will be out in this. Even once the wind dies down... which could be in a day or two... the rollers will be huge for hours." I shake my head in glum frustration.

"So, how far is that ranger station?" Jack asks. We haven't talked about the plan. So far, he has trusted my directions, and I'm careful not to worry him.

"Maybe two hours," I say lightly, not sharing another fear I have. It's likely the rangers have moved to their main cabin, a day up the trail, to wait out this crazy storm.

"So we'll get there this afternoon," Jack says. "We'll call for help. And with any luck, the Coast Guard will go get our parents tonight before dark." He bites his lower lip. "I'm worried about them, too. But they're tough. And they'll put the pieces together. They're parents... they're going to worry no matter what. But I don't think they're panicking right now." Jack finishes with a wan smile, pouring warm water into a bag of beef stew. "Here." He hands the re-hydrated chicken over to me. "Eat something. You'll feel better." The fragrant spice and Jack's words lift my spirits ever so slightly.

Chapter 26

We huddle behind the tree root, sitting shoulder to shoulder in the sand, our legs stretched out toward the fire. Tucked out of the wind, we watch the surf crash up the beach as we savor our lunch. My hands and head still hurt, but so do my legs, feet, and shoulders. The packs are a constant burden and it feels heavenly to be free of their weight as we eat.

Jack points to our right, up into the tree line. I follow his gaze where a bald eagle perches on a branch, glaring out over the ocean. The regal bird swivels its head back and forth. Then it lifts off and circles the water beyond the breaking surf. Suddenly, it dives, then its wings go wide as its clawed feet reach down toward the surface. The eagle disappears from our view behind a wave for a moment, and when it reappears, a huge salmon is writhing in its talons.

"Holy!" Jack looks over at me, shaking his head in disbelief. "How do they do that? How did he know there was a fish there, from way up in that tree?" I grin over at him.

"Pretty amazing, right?" I've often seen eagles hunt, but it's still magnificent every time. "And I believe the answer to your question is 'eagle eyes'."

Jack frowns for a moment, peering into his bag of stew, then laughs.

"That's where we got that saying, huh? Eagle eyes. Never put that together." Jack is still smiling as he rips open his foil bag. We both lick every scrap of food off the inside, then stuff the garbage into the food sack. As we watch, the eagle lands at the far end of the beach, the flopping salmon clamped securely in one claw. It wrenches into the fish with its hooked golden beak. Between each nibble, it glowers at the gathering seagulls with cold yellow eyes. We watch the scene mesmerized, savoring the heat of the fire and the warmth in our bellies.

"I should refill the water," Jack says eventually, standing up. "Want another drink before I go up there?" I take a gulp, then hand the bottle to Jack, wiping my mouth. He backtracks, disappearing up the stairs into the dense brush. I'm glad we stopped to take this break. I feel Jack's renewed energy feeding my own. It was the right call.

I pull out the toilet paper from my pack and stuff the roll into my pocket. May as well get my business done while Jack isn't here. I walk along the beach away from the eagles, past the base of the staircase, and around a jagged rock outcrop. Even if Jack comes back before I'm finished, I'll be out of sight. There's a perfectly sized driftwood log near the forest's edge. I unzip all my bottom layers, pulling them down to my knees. Then I perch the backs of my thighs on the cold, but smooth wet log. Nature's outhouse. I grin, my butt getting an icy draft in the swirling wind.

I pull the toilet paper from my pocket and wrap some around my palm. A couple of seagulls dive at each other, getting tossed about by a gust. The rain is still pounding and a loud rush of drops falls from the salal bushes behind me. And then, without warning, a massive bulk hits me between the shoulders. A deep, guttural snarl freezes my core as I'm thrown forward onto the rocks.

Chapter 27

I crash to the ground, my outstretched arms shielding my face from the rocks, the toilet paper flinging across the beach. A dull pressure squeezes the base of my neck as the snarling continues behind my head. Panic surges through me. I'm getting dragged. Toward the brush. Twisting my body, I flail wildly, trying to get away. I scream and yell and snarl like a beast. Frantic to stay out on the beach, in the open, I grab at the ground. My left fist closes around a rock as I'm rolled over onto my back.

The gaping chops of the cougar hang over me. It spreads its jaw wide, showing four massive fangs. It pulls its tongue back, sides curling up. A horrible hiss comes from deep in its throat. The warmth of its rancid breath brushes my face. Without thinking, I aim the rock in my fist at its head. It hits with a hollow impact, above the cougar's right eye. It jumps back in surprise. But just as quickly, it pounces on top of me again.

Its front paws dig into my chest, pushing the wind out of me. Hissing, then growling even louder, its head lowers to mine. Fierce amber eyes narrow into black slits. Its snarl wrinkles the dark brown fur of the cat's nose. Its ears twitch forward as it lunges toward my face. Again, I hit it from the left with the rock, releasing another savage scream. I grope in a frenzy with my injured hand for my next weapon. But I'm unable to grip anything.

I try to sit up. I need to sit up. Stand up. Cougars attack children and pets because they're small. I need this cat to know I'm not easy prey. I try to squirm out from under it. Rocks and barnacles scrape the skin of my bare backside. But the paws on my rib cage make escape impossible. I thrash beneath the huge cat as I wind up to hit it again with the rock, screaming. I miss it as it backs up a little, its softball-sized paws still firmly planted on my chest.

Behind the cougar, a flash of red races along the beach, around the rock outcrop. It's Jack, sprinting. Without slowing, he stoops, grabbing a thick piece of driftwood. As he gets closer, he moves the stick over one shoulder, winding up like he's holding a baseball bat. Just as Jack swings at the cat's head, the cougar jumps out of the way. Jack misses his mark, the wild swing of the driftwood pulling him off balance. He falls onto the rocks with a thump to my right. Jack's movements scare the cougar off of my chest and I scramble backward, desperately folding my legs underneath me.

The cougar lunges again, this time at Jack. It grabs his shin in its jaws and clamps down hard. I hear Jack moan as I yank up my pants, letting out another wild, savage screech. I stumble at the cat, a bigger rock in both hands now. Raising it over my head, I arch my back as if swinging an ax. Then I aim the heavy rock down toward the spine of the cat with all the force I can muster.

The cougar doesn't see my blow coming. It's focused on Jack, rolling its head left and right, ripping at Jack's leg. The rock hits its back with a satisfying thud. The cat whimpers, whirling my way, releasing Jack. Its jaws spread wide as the cougar pounces in my direction, hissing loudly. I bare my teeth, raise my arms, and charge, yelling like a crazy woman. The cat snarls and takes a step, but my blow has subdued it. I lunge again, screaming. Just as the cougar moves a step away, it turns back, tensing like it's ready to pounce.

"Get lost! Get outta here! Gaaaaahhh!" Lunging and thrusting my hands at it, I stoop briefly to pick up another rock. I throw it at the growling cat, still screaming. Finally, the cougar retreats. I follow it, finding the big stick Jack dropped, and swinging it wildly. Finally, the big cat gives me one last glimpse with its fierce amber eyes. Then it turns and disappears into the brush with a graceful pounce.

I back up toward Jack, white knuckles gripping the driftwood stick held high above my head. I glance behind me so I don't trip, my legs shaky, pants slipping down again. When there's a crack in the woods, I flinch and whirl back, expecting the cougar to jump out at us again. But there's nothing there. A few moments later, I'm kneeling at Jack's side, facing up the beach so I can watch the spot where the cat disappeared into the brush.

Jack is lying flat, his forearm over his eyes, his face clenched in pain. The cougar's big teeth have ripped his rain pants open, revealing nasty puncture wounds in his calf. "Shit!" I say under my breath, looking for some way to wrap his leg. But our gear is around the corner, past the bottom of the stairs.

"Bad?" Jack takes a sharp inhale, his jaw clenched. He's breathing too fast and his face is a greenish shade of gray. Shit, I think. What do I do? I need to do something! I fold his torn rain pants open to get a better look, trying to keep my face expressionless. There are four puncture wounds, two on each side of his shin. There's blood, but not as much as you'd think. The wounds are oval, about a centimeter wide, and three centimeters long. The cat's sharp fangs didn't just punch through Jack's skin, the teeth also ripped the flesh down to his shin bone as the cougar twisted its head back and forth.

"You're not bleeding much." No point in sharing the whole truth. I pull my arms into the body of my jacket and shirts, then remove my purple wool base layer in a few quick movements. "Let me wrap your leg with this." My words are gentle. "Then I'll go get our gear."

"No way!" Jack stares up at me from the ground, wide-eyed, gripping my arm tightly. "Together. We stay together now!" He closes his eyes, a pained grimace crossing his features, his fingers digging into my forearm.

I extract myself from his grip and pull up the leg of his pants. Folding the thin purple shirt into a rough rectangle, I lay the center over the puncture wounds. Then I wrap it around twice and tie the two sleeves together over his shin as tight as I dare.

Jack suddenly cranes his neck toward me. "Are *you* okay?" he asks.

"I think so." Focused on Jack's injury, I haven't thought about checking what the cougar did to me. I take stock of my body now. There's a sharp pinch on my left shoulder as I shrug. And my hips sting, where the barnacles scraped my bare skin. I reach inside my hood, my stiff fingers running over my tense neck muscles. When I pull my hand out, it's streaked red.

"Turn around." Jack struggles to sit up when he sees the blood. I crouch next to him. "There are a couple holes in your jacket," he says. I lower my hood and move closer so he can see. "Oh, geez." He gives a low whistle. "You got some nice tooth holes. Does it hurt?"

"Honestly, not as much as other parts of me." I glance back at him. Jack is still peering at my injury, our heads just inches apart. Now that the adrenalin from the attack is wearing off, I shiver. Jack's gaze meets mine. My pounding heart quivers as our eyes lock. The skin on my shoulder still sparkles from the touch of his fingertips.

"Jesus, Maia." Jack wraps his arms around me and pulls me into his chest. "I'm so glad you're okay," he whispers into my tangled hair. Then, lifting my chin, his cold lips meet mine.

My first kiss is slow and gentle and puts glinting butterfly wings in my belly. When Jack pulls back, his dark eyes look at me for a long moment. I don't know how to respond, just close my eyes with a deep, shaky breath. He nestles my head onto his chest. And for the second time in as many days, I let myself melt into Jack and cry.

Chapter 28

We sit bundled together until a relentless gust blows hard bits of seaweed into our faces. I pull away first. Jack is even paler than before and his eyelids droop. Shit.

"Let's get you back to our gear," I say, with a lightness I don't feel. Jack struggles to stand up on the rough beach. With my help, he gets upright. But when he tries to bear weight on his injured leg, it's bad. His knee buckles, and his jaw clenches as he collapses against me.

"I don't think... I don't think I can walk." Pain and fear slurs Jack's speech.

"One step at a time," I say. "Just use me as a crutch. We'll get you there." And we do. It seems to take forever. Although every step is a careful effort, we're soon back near the stairs.

"Dropped it." At the stairs, Jack points down at our water bottle, abandoned in the sand. "Screaming. Heard screaming." His words heave out in gasps. I pick up the water and offer him a drink, which he takes. Then, with a breathless struggle, we get Jack back to our gear. I add logs to the coals and the fire blazes as Jack sinks onto the beach beside it, winded. He flops against a log, his blanched chin dropping to his chest.

"Stay close to the fire. Stay warm." I sit down beside him. What do we do next? I know from annual first aid classes that there's a 'golden hour'. It's the reason we rush badly injured people to proper care — they have the best results when they get help in under an hour. Well, that frigging rule is getting broken. I visualize the page in the workbook where we learned how to treat shock. I need to keep Jack warm. Give him fluids. Elevate his legs above his heart. I don't remember the rest. Shit.

Why did I let him go on his own? Why did *I* decide to go on *my* own? We made all this effort to get within two hours of help, and now one huge mistake means we can't get anywhere. I shake my head, looking into the blazing fire, frightened for my dad and Jack. As I study the flames, a movement makes me turn. Beside me, Jack has slumped over, his upper body fallen away from me, into the sand.

"Jack!" I crouch over him, shaking him roughly. When he doesn't respond, I put my cheek near his mouth, hearing short, ragged breaths. I place my fingers across his wrist and his pulse is strong, so I pinch his thumb. Hard. But Jack doesn't react to the pain. Damn it. He needs shelter. Now. My heart sinks farther — we're definitely not moving on today. I roll Jack's floppy body onto his side, just in case he throws up. The recovery position, I remember from the classes, and push sand against his torso until he's stable.

The wind is still gusting terribly, and under any other circumstance, I wouldn't set up a tent here in the open. The purpose-built wooden pads at the top of the stairs would be the sensible location. But until Jack can move on his own, I don't have that choice — this is where we're stuck.

Crouching by Jack again, I shake him again and call his name, but he still doesn't respond. Other than my mum, I've never been around an unconscious person. The unmoving slackness of Jack's face makes my mouth go dry and my heart race. Focus. I need to focus. If I jam the tent up against the shelter of the upturned root ball, it might stay put. With a flat piece of wood, I smooth the sand, then unroll the tent. Before I insert the tent poles, I lift four large rocks inside the corners to keep it from blowing away in the gale.

It's easier to get Jack inside before I secure the tent fly, so I lug him the few feet, taking what's left of my energy. He's heavy. So very heavy. When I get his upper body under cover, I wrestle him out of his wet jacket. After another scuffle, I finally pull his legs inside the tent, too. The tops of his socks seem dry, so I leave his rain pants and boots on. If his leg swells overnight, we might never get this stuff back on him.

Outside in the wet wind, I anchor the tent fly by wrapping the ropes around a rock at each corner. Next, I pull out the water, food sack, and first aid kit before stacking our packs under the vestibule. Then I climb inside the tent, where I unwrap Jack's leg. To disinfect these deep puncture wounds properly, I should have peroxide or alcohol, but the first aid kit only contains prepackaged wipes. So I do the best I can. Jack moans when I apply the antiseptic cream, but doesn't wake up. I keep talking to him softly as I layer gauze over the wounds, then wrap his entire leg again with the clean side of the purple wool shirt. Before leaving Jack in the tent, I lay the sleeping bag over him, tucking it around him gently. His breathing is fast. Too fast. And shallow. I brush his bangs back from his cold, clammy forehead. Damn it. Just like they talked about in those first aid classes. "Please be okay, Jack," I whisper, "I need you... I need you to be okay." I lean over and kiss his dank cheek, a tight pain in my chest.

Chapter 29

Outside, I transfer the supplies from the cache into the food sack, then hang the bag far from our camp. As I shuffle slowly back to the fire, a couple of seagulls coast on the wind gusts high above me. Beyond the beach, the gale blows the tops right off the waves, blending seawater with rain in a misty opaque layer above the ocean. The rollers crash in rushing thunderclaps. Everything is shades of black and gray, with no color in sight. No wildlife, no boats. Just a pissed-off piece of nature. I feel tiny and utterly alone.

When I settle by the fire, a churning looseness fills my lower gut as I replay the mistakes of the past two days. I pull my knees to my chest and wrap my arms around them. My chin drops onto my wet rain pants and I stare glassy-eyed at the fire. Yet another delay to the rescue. My stomach knots further as I think of my dad. He needs a hospital. Needs to be pumped full of antibiotics so infection doesn't kill him. Maybe I've taken too long. Maybe it's already killed him. My heart skips a beat and my thoughts turn to Anna. She's out there, doing her best to keep him alive and depending on me to find help. I feel a sudden kinship with Anna, who, miles away, must be restless and afraid too.

I roll to my feet, then pull back the tent flap to check on Jack. No change. Cold, clammy, and breathing too fast, but at least he's breathing. Under the sleeping bag, his chest is warm, but his fingers and forearms are ice cold. Shit.

Back outside, I use a stick to drag two fire ring rocks away from the blaze. They're too hot to touch, but once they cool I'll carry them into the tent to keep Jack warm. I wonder if Anna's been able to keep my dad from becoming hypothermic.

If my dad's still alive, he'll be wondering what happened to us. Why help hasn't arrived yet? When... if... he hears what I've put Jack through, he'll be so disappointed. And mad. Seriously! Hanging a client off the cable car and pushing him out over the river? Going off to take a dump, causing our client to be mauled by a cougar? I'll never guide again. Who would trust me? And they'd be right. Every decision has been stupid. Stupid. Stupid!

A sharp crack from the forest above me interrupts my thoughts. A huge bough falls from a Sitka spruce, then hangs up in the adjacent tree branches for a moment before crashing to the ground. Even the trees are breaking under this gale's endless pummeling.

The warming rocks I pulled from the fire ring are now a manageable temperature, so I drag them into the tent, carefully laying one on each side of Jack. After I place his hands against the rocks, I tuck him under the sleeping bag again. My throat tightens at the sight of his damp gray face, dark circles under his closed eyes. In a choked whisper, I tell Jack how sorry I am, but he still doesn't budge.

Back at the fire, I add more driftwood, then move some cold rocks into the gaps to complete the fire ring. If we're out here all night, the fire needs to burn strong. It'll help keep that cougar away, and it'll keep Jack warm if I rotate these heated rocks inside.

Maybe I should just go get help. Right now. The ranger's yurt is only a couple of hours away. Less if I don't take a pack and move fast on the easier trail sections. I could get there this afternoon, radio help, and be back by nightfall. It should work. It could work. *If* the ranger is there with his radio. *If* I don't have any other problems on the trail. *If* the cougar stays away. If, if, if!

So far, we've had to work together many times. Jack snagged under a branch on the first rope climb. Jack stuck in that giant mud hole. Jack dragging me out of danger in the tidal zone. Jack bandaging my hands. The cable car calamity. The cougar attack.

Leaving without Jack is a bad plan. Fine. But sitting here, just waiting, is a useless torture. Then I put myself in Jack's place. How would I feel if I woke up alone? In a cold tent in the dark, with no fire outside, unable to walk, a deranged cougar stalking the beach? Um, no! I will not do *that* to Jack. If anything else happens to him... no... not taking that chance. Maybe... maybe if he was conscious. If we decided together. But I'm not leaving my passed-out friend on this beach, as nylon-wrapped cougar bait. Cross that idea off the list!

So what's the next best choice? If... when... Jack wakes up, can I help him walk to the ranger's yurt with me? It was a struggle just to get back here. A deep sob catches in my throat and I shake my head. This is hopeless! There's nothing I can do. I can't go get help alone. I can't go get help with Jack. And help can't come to us because of this stupid weather!

I close my eyes and let myself cry. Deep, soul-wrenching sobs flood out into the howling wind. My body trembles and I don't care how loud I am. Anguish pours out of me like the day I got home from the hospital. That night, I went down to the beach alone, trying to understand my mum's decision. Trying to be okay with her choice. Trying to be the daughter she needed in her last days.

But I found no understanding. Only grief, which tumbled into the night in roaring screams, stunning me. Brutal, untamed moans intertwined with gasping groans. I'd never heard anything like it. The physical pain of having two fingers ripped off my hand didn't compare to the agony of my mum choosing to go.

And then came the anger. So much fury. We hid our rage from her, my dad and me, fairly well in those last days. But boy, did we fight when we were away from her! Still do. Our interactions have basically been silence, grunts, and explosive battles since last fall. About stupid things, too. Dirty dishes, overdue milk, piles of laundry. Neither of us has ever mentioned mum. Not once. Not until yesterday in dad's tent, where we said our goodbyes. He had finally talked about her — remembering her useful advice and helpful ideas. He had even used her favorite phrase when he told me to keep my head in the game. That was the first time we talked about her. Slow progress.

I open my eyes, staring into the fire now, winded, my shoulders still convulsing. Picturing my dad's wounds prompts another round of frustrated sobs. I need to help him, but I can't. Shit! Looking over at our tent releases another stifled wail. I'm so sorry, Jack! Why didn't I stay with you?

Eventually, my weeping quiets. My aching head slumps to my knees. Please make them okay, I beg silently to the universe. I can't lose anyone else. I just... can't.

When I can finally inhale without shuddering, I check on Jack again. No change. I bring in fresh warming rocks and talk to him quietly. I tell him he needs to heal up and wake up soon, then I tuck the sleeping bag around him.

The never-ending storm continues, and I spend an hour walking larger and larger circles around our camp. I stack firewood for the night and collect baseball bat-sized sticks as weapons. From the edge of the forest, I drag two fallen spruce boughs. I shove the ends of the thick branches into the sand behind the log. The branches' floppy green ends create shelter near the fire. I smooth the sand underneath the boughs, making a flat spot next to the log.

Finally, I pile four large pieces of wood onto the fire and lie down in the sand. The spruce boughs deflect most of the rain, the log shields me from the wind, and the fire warms my front. Bone-tired from the attack, the work, and my cathartic cry session, I sink into the void of sleep.

CHAPTER 30

I wake with a start, lying rigid, digging for clues to where I am. When I register the stormy beach and a flapping tent beyond a dying fire, my stomach knots and it all comes rushing back. A fiery boat. Seared flesh. Cougar teeth. Jack's bloody shin bone. Jack!

I scramble toward the tent, rip open the fly, and scoot into the vestibule. The sun is low on the horizon, so I must have slept all afternoon. I stop moving to quiet the rustling of my rain gear. When I lean forward, I can make out Jack's quick breaths. Thank goodness. His forehead is cool, but not as clammy as before. Under the sleeping bag, his hands and body are at a normal temperature. Good. At least he's not getting worse. That's something.

I pull the cooled warming rocks out of the tent and rotate another batch away from the flames. When I hear a low grumble, I tense, but it's just my stomach. I don't feel like eating, yet my body needs fuel. So I drop the food sack and remove a beef stew, then wander the beach. The tide is lower now and the churning waves left behind sea lettuce bunches. I gather an armful of the translucent, bright green seaweed. At a large tidal pool, where dark purple shadows of mussels wobble below the surface, I crouch to wash the sand off the rubbery leaves. Then I harvest two dozen mussels, the frigid salt water soaking my bandaged hands as I cut through the elastic threads holding each shell to the rocks.

The seaweed and mussels are edibles we typically cook up for our guests to give them a taste of living off the land. Jack and I have plenty of food now and don't need the extra sustenance, but I tuck the shells and leaves into a used zip-top foil bag anyway. Cleaning and cooking nature's gifts will offer me something to do while I try to stay awake through the night.

Back at the fire, I throw my grimy bandages in the fire and examine my hands. It feels good to let the wounds breathe and nothing looks infected. Yet.

With water for my dinner heating, I walk the perimeter of our camp. The dimming light of dusk makes it hard to see, but behind my log, I notice a new row of small shadows in the sand. My heart pounds as I crouch to inspect the ground. Shit.

Beside my footprints are fresh cougar tracks. They run from the edge of the forest, then veer toward our fire. The cougar stopped just ten feet from where I had been sleeping. Double shit. I scour the beach for any signs of the cat, but see nothing. Still, this is not good. Why won't this cat stay away? I'm glad I've already slept. I sure as shit am not closing my eyes tonight. And I better keep the fire blazing. The flames are likely what stopped the cougar from coming into camp this afternoon.

Rattled, I sit on the log by the fire, keeping watch over the entire beach. I cut thin strips of the sea lettuce, then drape it over the hot rocks to dry out. While I wait for the water to heat, I clean the mussels. Getting a good grip on the beard between my thumb and my knife has always been hard. Attempting this task with two missing fingers and open cuts from today's fall proves to be an impossible struggle. I finally use my left hand, which is clumsy but works better.

With the mussels cleaned, I lay them on a flat rock at the fire's edge, to bake in their shells. While I wait, I carefully pour the warmed water into the bag of dry beef stew, taking a whiff of the rich steam. I tuck the sealed bag under my rain jacket, savoring its warmth on my belly. A sudden memory crowds out other thoughts. My mum used to prepare hot water bottles for me on the coldest nights. She would wrap the dusty red, rubber-scented bottle in one of Grosmüti's cross-stitched tea towels. Nothing feels better on a wintry night than being cozy-warm under down covers, with someone rubbing your back until you're asleep. Shit! I hit the fire hard with a stick, sending sparks up into the dimness. I miss my mum. So much.

Then other times, I completely forget she's gone. Like a moment ago, I was deciding how I'd tell her about these huge cougar tracks. I could easily imagine her theories about why the cat was showing itself. When I remember my mum is gone, the dark abyss envelops me again. She's gone. Her voice... gone. Forever. Well, except for the friendly message still on our answering machine, asking people to 'please leave a message after the beep!'. I smack the stick again, watching the orange pricks of light dance up into the dusk. We don't get a lot of phone calls, and since The Last Day, neither my dad nor I have rushed to answer the phone. Whenever the machine picks up, and mum's lost voice fills the kitchen, we stand motionless, honoring her bittersweet echo. We really should update that taped message. But we're not quite ready.

I lay long driftwood pieces into the fire, the ends of them safely out in the sand. I'm hoping to use them as tiki torches around the camp. On the rock, the mussels are opening, signaling they're cooked. I wait for the shells to cool before I pry out the meat. They're not so bad if you grill them over the fire. I sharpen a roasting stick and as each weird little mussel chars, I dip it into the beef stew. The chewy morsels aren't my favorite, but the process evokes memories of easier trips when our family of three guided some beloved guests.

Those guests brought energy to the trip with their smiles and jokes. They had their gear neatly packed ten minutes early every morning, helped with the fire, cared about the wildlife, and showed infinite awe toward every fresh sight we showed them. They asked about the history and learned how to hang food and tarps eagerly, with boundless energy and laughter in the glowing sunshine. Those were great trips. My mum called them contented souls — people who find beauty and joy in everything they do. Just like Jack. The back of my throat closes as I realize she'll never meet him.

Now, in the fading light, I comb the beach, but there's still no sign of wildlife. The seaweed is dry and I peel it off the rocks — it'll be a nutritious distraction to snack on overnight. Finished with the meal, I throw the mussel shells and the foil bag into the fire. As a rule, we don't burn garbage on our trips. But tonight, I don't have the energy to haul down the food sack. And I don't want even the slightest scent of cooking attracting the 'locals' to our camp.

It's a good time to try out my tiki torch idea, so I grab a flaming stick, getting only a few feet before a gust extinguishes it. I smash the stick into the ground — so much for encircling our campsite with fire! A perimeter of light around camp would make me feel safer, but nature has other ideas. I turn away, letting my eyes settle into the dark. Slowly, shapes emerge from the twilight.

Up the beach about fifty feet, I spot a skinny log and plod in that direction. The ocean churned the log smooth, the bark and branches all rubbed off. I wrap my arms around the thicker end of it. Then I stand with a heaving grunt and drag the bulky timber toward camp, counting off the steps to distract from the work. Twenty-seven paces later, I drop the log into the sand.

Now there's definitely enough wood here to keep our fire stoked high overnight. The tasks of the last hour have brought a comforting calm over me. I hoist one end of the log onto the fire, then pick through the woodpile for a good piece to carve. Whittling will help pass the time, and I settle on the sand again with my jackknife. I'm still worried. For my dad. And Jack. But I'm ready to face the night. A few minutes later, the log I added erupts into flames that dance high above me, pushing the ring of darkness farther from our camp.

Chapter 31

I balance a freshly carved spoon on the log behind me, then turn from the flames. My eyes adjust to the gloom, but it's impossible to see beyond the fire's glow. The ocean below me crashes relentlessly, and the wind whips rain against my face, but I can't see anything. No shadows. No silhouettes. Nothing. The moonless night has become an eerily solid black. A shiver runs down my spine.

While warming my hands over the flames, I kick another set of warming rocks into the sand. The cut on my palm feels better than the knuckle on my right hand. I rub the fading scars, but the pain is deep, down inside the bone where massaging doesn't reach. It's time to check on Jack again, and I lug the fresh set of warming rocks with me.

When my groping fingers find Jack's forehead, it's less clammy than last time, and his hands feel warm as I switch out the rocks. Good. The same or better. Not worse. That's good. I lean closer to check his breath, which is hardly audible over the flapping tent fly and nature's commotion outside. But it's there. It's still too fast to be normal, but it's deep, like he's just sleeping. Not like he's passed out. I wonder if he'd wake up if I shook him, but decide immediately there's no point in that. "Get some rest, Jack," I whisper into the darkness. "We've got a big day tomorrow, bud."

Back outside, I stoke the fire by shoving coals under the big log, then add more wood from the pile. I push the big log farther in, watching the new wood blaze. Satisfied, I settle into the sand again. I wonder if Anna is as good with fires as I am. Hopefully, she has kept theirs burning this whole time. She must be exhausted. Like me, she'll be dozing off, then waking up disoriented, trying to figure out where the heck she is. Then she'll remember that her vacation days have turned into a miserable adventure. They must be so worried. My dad and Anna. Anna's not an anxious parent — I could tell that about her. But my mum used to insist she felt an aura when I was hurt or in trouble. Has Anna sensed Jack's distress in the past few hours? I hope not.

I wonder if my dad's being an ass. He can be difficult in the best circumstances, and Anna's definitely not getting the best circumstances. Also, I hope he's been eating. Since The Worst Day, my dad has lost weight. No matter what I cook, he hardly eats. Or sleeps. The light in his room is usually on when I wake up to pee, and I can see him through the cracked door, sitting on the edge of his bed, staring straight ahead. Or swirling a glass of whiskey. Or worse, sobbing silently, head in his hands.

Getting him up, out, and focused is an achievement. Ms. Wells came over a few weeks ago. I don't know what she said, but after her visit, my dad was more together. He had our business brochure updated, returned client calls, and opened up the bookings for the spring and summer. He bought groceries. Vacuumed. I try not to think about whether the boat fire happened because his head wasn't in the game. Is there a connection? Or was it just an accident?

When he did the supply run last week, he seemed better. Not excited exactly, but focused. Competent. Over our canned chili dinner, I had asked him how his trip went. He just lifted his shoulders and said, "Fine. Boat's runnin' good." After another few bites, he'd continued.

"Supply cache was still sealed up." He had furrowed his brow, eyes focused far beyond me. Following a long pause, he asked, "You been up there?"

"To the supply cache? Only the first time, with you, when we dropped it off." He'd just nodded, his spoon scraping the bottom of the Corelle bowl. I had waited for him to continue, watching him swab a bright white slice of WonderBread around the olive blossom print at the bowl's edge. But he hadn't elaborated, just sat. With a weird look on his face.

Recalling that exchange, I'm suddenly certain that my dad left the parcel in the supply cache last week. I glance, undecided, at the tent vestibule, where my pack is sheltered. Should I open the package here, amid a storm? What if it's something fragile? A note or a drawing that gets ruined in the rain? The fire leans over as a wind gust pummels me.

Screw it. I'll open the parcel carefully, sheltered by the tent. My racing thoughts need a distraction from cougar fangs and infected flesh and passed-out friends. I've only known Jack a day, but I'd give anything to have him beside me right now, sharing his upbeat view. His grin would keep this wave of fear from washing over me. Under the tent fly, I peer through the mesh, where Jack's still a silent lump. I gently remove my mum's parcel from the top of my pack and turn so I'm facing the light of the fire.

I take the brown paper package tied up with string... and laugh out loud. That's a line from a song in *The Sound of Music*. The one about favorite things. I shake my head. Too funny. My mum loved that movie. We must have rented it a dozen times together. I'm surprised we never made the connection between that song and the way my mum wraps presents.

Now I pull the parcel out of the zipper bag and untie the butcher twine from the cornflowers. Then I trace my fingertips over the flowing script of my name, remembering the hand that penned it. I shake the box a little, holding it near my ear. There's a muffled scrape of something light sliding around inside.

I flip the package over, carefully peel off the tape, and remove the kraft paper. The box inside is the size of a small novel and navy blue. I stare into the fire, hands clamped around the box, my guts churning and my heart pounding. I swallow.

No use stalling. I slide the lid off the box to reveal a layer of white cotton batting. Underneath is the sparkle of my grandmother's bracelet. So that's where it was! A smile creases my eyes. No wonder I couldn't find it in the house.

In my palm, the gold bracelet glints in the firelight, the thin oval rounds draping elegantly. My frozen fingers struggle to undo the clasp, but after a few attempts, the bracelet is on my wrist. It falls over the top of my hand, and I admire it from all directions in the dancing light. It's beautiful and reminds me of the times I watched my mum get dressed for special occasions. She'd pull on pantyhose, a skirt, and a blouse, then have me clip this bracelet to her wrist as she grinned. My parents didn't go out much, but my mum was always excited about attending a company party or a friend's wedding.

The recent pain-filled memories of her have been crowding out the earlier memories. The ones where she's happy and strong. I pull the batting from the empty box. Underneath the cotton sits an envelope, also with my name written on it. A chill runs up my spine and I shiver involuntarily. Oh boy. The envelope is white, sealed. With my jackknife, I slice it open, careful not to knick the contents.

There are two sheets of thin paper inside, the kind my mum used years ago to handwrite air mail letters on. I flatten the pages and read.

My dear Maia,

I've written this letter a hundred times in my mind. There's a thousand things I have left to say to you. And your dad. But I'm running out of time to say them.

I asked your dad to give you this letter out on the trail. I'm going to imagine you reading this, sitting by a fire on a clear night, under twinkling stars. It makes me smile, to think of your face reflecting flames, breathing fresh air.

Cancer sucks. And I know I can't stay with you two.

But I am:

POSITIVE. I am so confident that you will do well. You're smart, practical, strong. Remind yourself of that when I'm not around to tell you.

PREPARED. I'm ready. I know you're furious with me. I get it. But I need to go.

PATIENT. I have given this fight everything. But it's time to let go. The last thing I want is you guys watching me suffer. No sense in prolonging the inevitable.

I love you Maia-girl. Always will. You're the one in this family with true moxie. Let this bracelet remind you of that. There's grit & spunk & toughness inside you.

Always.

You have so much ahead of you: school, career, friends, lovers, travel. Savour it! Head in the game, girl.

Love M.

I inhale a shaky breath and grip the letter over my heart as the bracelet slips down my arm under my sleeve. My mum's words ring in my ears. I hear her soft voice as I read it again.

Funny. She's not saying anything new. Except the part about me having the true moxie. Moxie has never been my word — it's hers. Always will be. But the rest... it's all stuff I thought I knew. But now I'm sure. Which is good. Nice. I don't know why reading this now makes me feel so much better. It doesn't change anything. She's still dead. I'm still here. My dad's still injured. Jack's still unconscious.

But my mum's words are a boost. Which, again, is weird. They're not exactly happy words. Encouraging. But not happy.

I read the letter one more time, fold the pages and tuck them back in the envelope and the box. Then I drop the box inside the zipper bag and place it all into the safety of my pack.

My mum's last lines shift my thoughts to going away to school. This accident changes things even more. How can I attend school when the only person looking out for my dad now is me? I want to go. I always thought I'd go. But that was with mum pushing me out the door. With her by his side. Now all he has... well... all he has is me.

I move back outside, where I can watch over the whole campsite. The fire paints dancing shadows onto the tent, and I squirm myself lower in the sand, trying to stay out of the rain under the spruce boughs. Brimming with heavy thoughts, I lean my head back on the log, letting the flames warm my front. My eyelids droop, then close. Just for a minute, I think, the wind swirling raindrops around me. I'll rest just for a minute.

Chapter 32

I'm tucked under my down duvet, warm and cozy. The air on my face is raw, so it must be wintertime. I wrap my arms around the hot water bottle, but it's wet and cold. My mum is speaking from far away, but I can't make out the words. Her voice gets louder now, the tone serious. What are you saying? Her speech is a garbled static. Then her face is right over mine, gray-blue eyes flashing with urgency. What do you want, woman? "Wake up, Maia! It's back! Wake up!" My mum's thundering warning rouses me.

My eyes pop open and her voice fades into the wind. I whirl around in a daze, finding nothing but glowing coals and blackness. My heart hammers in my ribs as I feel someone... something... watching me. Leaning forward, I scramble to grab a big burning stick from the fire. I hold the branch in front of me and a gust flickers the flame. I strain to look past the curtain of darkness encircling our camp, spinning to peer in every direction.

And then I see it. Two greenish-white spots gleam from twenty feet beyond the tent. The cougar's eye shine reflects the fire's light back at me. The cat's creeping silhouette looms as dawn lifts the blackness. I lunge closer, aggressively, letting it know I have no fear. I'm beside the tent now, moving between the cougar and Jack. "Get out of here!" I shove the flaming stick at it. "Go back to the woods! You don't belong here!" The words I spit out, roar with hatred. I take another step and stab my fiery torch toward the big cat. It steps back, its head twisted to keep its eyes locked on mine. "Get lost, you asshole! Leave us!" The wind whips my shouts away as I jab at it again. Finally, the cat turns and bounds away, disappearing into the murky morning. A moment later, the gusts pause and a twig snaps up in the woods.

I scan the dark-gray tree line at the top of the beach for movement. The shadows all blend, and I see no sign of the cougar. "Good girl, Maia!" I hear my mum's voice in the wind behind me. "That was kick-ass." Laughter tinges her beautiful voice. I whirl around. Nothing. Of course, there's nothing.

I gaze toward the ocean, where the glow of dawn is building out over the water. Nothing. I close my eyes and drop my chin to my chest with an audible exhale as the glowing fire stick hits the sand.

"You got this, Maia. Go out into the world. Do great things. Meet new people. You're the one in this family with true moxie. Use it." My mum's soft words tangle with the wind, but this time the voice is clearly a memory. A memory I've buried since The Last Day. And suddenly the rest of my mum's brief speech comes flashing back at me. "Your dad isn't a people person," she'd said with a loving chuckle. "He won't change now. And it's not your job to look after him. He loves you too much to let you go. But you will need to go. Promise me? Whatever it takes, you leave this town... find your own way. Okay?" Her words had been a whisper, her thin hand weak in mine, but her blue eyes had pierced with strength.

"I will." I had sobbed beside her. "I promise."

"Good girl." Her reply had been a gasp as she patted my hand. "Good girl."

"I will." I speak into the wind now. "I promise." I set my shoulders, lift my chin high, and study the furious coastline. A strangled sound behind me whirls me away from the shore to scan the tree line. Again, a loud rumble, much closer. Near the tent. It's coming from the tent. Jack! I bound over and whip open the fly, scrambling to get to him.

"Jack?" I try to steady my voice. "Are you okay?" I'm still winded from the showdown with the cat. The tent is dark and only the sleeping bag outline is visible, so I can't tell if his eyes are open. "Jack?" I reach for his forehead, which feels warm and dry. When his head turns toward me and he nuzzles into my hand, my shoulders relax. Then he peels back the sleeping bag, his fingers finding mine.

"What the hell is going on out there?" Jack's slow words are hoarse. Relief glows through me like warm sunshine. Mute, I just pull Jack's hand to my face. I kiss his fingers before pressing them against my cold, wet cheek.

"I'm so glad you're awake."

"How did I get in here?" Jack asks, "The last thing I remember..." He trails off and I feel him looking up at me. "The last thing I remember... is sitting down by the fire."

"You passed out," I say, "so I set up the tent and dragged you in here. Don't move." I tuck his hand back into the sleeping bag. "I'll get the water. And then tell you all about the night we just had." When I return, Jack rolls up onto one elbow, groaning as he moves his leg. He takes a long drink and I pull down the hood of my rain jacket, sitting in the sand under the tent vestibule, retelling the night's adventure. The cougar footprints, the bracelet, and the letter. I even share it was my mum's voice waking me from my dream, warning me the cougar was back. The morning light reveals his wide, dark eyes. But the tilt of his head conveys a gentle curiosity. Not disbelief or ridicule at my insistence that I heard my dead mum.

"I know it wasn't really her," I say. "But I kinda like that my subconscious chose that way to wake me up. All the shouting out there...

the noises that woke you. That was me scaring off the cougar. Again. Just now. Hopefully, it stays away for good. I think it's starting to believe we're not breakfast." I finish with a small smile. Jack looks past me, rubbing the back of his neck and scanning the beach beyond the tent fly where the treetops are dancing and a few seagulls are playing in the wind.

"Jesus." Jack shakes his head. "I was so scared... up on those stairs. When I heard you scream." He sits upright and reaches for my hand again, fingering the gold bracelet. "And when I came around that rock... all I could see was the cougar's back end... and your feet kicking out. Its jaws over your head..." He swallows and drops his eyes to our intertwined fingers. "I thought... I... I dunno what I thought."

"I know... I know." Bright hues of fear and relief and fondness fuse in my heart. Jack pulls me toward him, wincing, but not letting his pain stop him. He cups my chin, his eyes asking permission. Sparkling bolts of fire run down my spine and into my belly.

A warm, rushing tide replaces all sound. This time I lean in to kiss him. His lips are soft and strong. He tastes of sweet cold water and I want more of him, suddenly not caring that there's a city girlfriend. I run my fingers through his thick hair, to his chiseled jaw, over his strong back, and savor all of it. When I move my hand under Jack's shirt, he groans, a low growl from deep in his throat. He leans his forehead on mine, pulling our lips apart.

"You okay?" I whisper with a mischievous grin.

"Damn... Maia. We better stop there." Jack murmurs with a wry smile and a shake of his head.

"You ready to walk out of this wilderness yet?" I give him a quick kiss before sitting back.

"Honestly?" Jack looks fiercely at me. "I'm ready to do anything for you right now."

Chapter 33

Neither of us wants this moment to end. We sit and talk, plan our day, and then imagine what our parents are doing right now. Eventually, I ask Jack about his leg. He grimaces and says, "It'll be okay. It has to be okay." I nod as I hand him his pack and rain jacket from under the tent vestibule, leaving him to get ready.

I trot over to the food sack and lower it from the tree, glancing around me as I work. Daylight makes things feel safer. Though I hope the cougar has given up on us, we need to stay alert. Back at camp, Jack is struggling inside the tent. "Need help with anything?"

"Nope." Jack grunts and I peek in through the tent fly, then step away silently. He's changed his shirt and is adjusting his rain pants over his bandaged shin, his nostrils flared and jaw clenched. My dad used to flinch, watching me battle through my hand rehab exercises. I hated witnesses to my pain.

"Let me know if I can help." I keep my voice light, but my heart is heavy. If it hurts this much to move his leg, how is Jack ever going to walk for two hours? I stoke the fire one last time and set a mug of water in it, then pull two dehydrated meals from the food sack. While I wait, I take a mental inventory of our supplies. With his injury, Jack won't be carrying anything, so we'll leave some stuff behind. Taking the food, water, lighter, first aid kit, and flares is obvious. Leaving without the tent and sleeping bag is risky, but we shouldn't need them again. The ranger's yurt is only a couple of hours from here. It'll take us longer today, with Jack slowing our progress, but we should still easily get there before nightfall. And even if the ranger isn't there, we can sleep inside the yurt.

Jack crawls stiffly out of the tent. I crouch beside him, and he wraps an arm around my neck. He lets out an involuntary grunt as I help him stand. Gingerly, he puts more weight on his injured leg. His jaw tightens and sweat gleams on his temples. Then Jack leans into me, clenching his teeth to take his painful first step. A few more limping hops and we get him to a driftwood log. Jack sits, already breathless, his injured leg half bent in front of him, watching the raindrops splatter across his thighs.

"That was good." I look into his pale face. "You're doing good." I squeeze his shoulder. He looks at me with a wrinkled brow, but nods. I explain my plan for reducing our cargo, and Jack nods again. We agree to bring the sleeping bag and mat, but leave the tent. If we need to, we can build shelter along the trail. With a plan in place, I go reorganize our packs in the tent's shelter.

First, I tuck the lighter into my jacket pocket. Then I stuff the sleeping bag into my pack, roll the mat, and add the food sack and rope. We'll leave behind our clothes. Before packing the first aid kit, I dump two pain tablets into my palm, then drag my pack outside. When I give Jack the pills and water, he takes the medication without a word.

After I strap the flare to my pack, I gaze out over the churning ocean. The northwester is still blowing a gale, huge rollers pounding the beach. It's unlikely we'll see any boats, but we need to be ready to signal, anyway. I take the water off the fire, then mix up the first beef stew packet, handing it to Jack.

"You eat first, when it's ready." I flash him a small smile. "You missed dinner last night."

"What did you eat?" Jack raises his eyebrows at the remnants of sea lettuce dried against the fire rocks. I explain how I distracted myself, supplementing the stew with my foraged meal. He wrinkles his nose. "Was it good?"

"Not my favorite," I say with a wink, passing him a freshly carved spoon. "But it filled the gap. I'll wait for the next batch. I'm not very hungry."

"Liar. You're always hungry." He's right, and I grin back, insisting I can wait for my portion.

While Jack devours his stew and the second mug of water heats, I pull out my knife and walk along the beach. I have an idea. After a few minutes, I find suitable sticks and drag the two weathered branches to Jack. He's watching me curiously through the rain. "Let's cut these for crutches," I say. "Should help you walk with that leg." Jack stands and we measure the sticks. I hack them to size with my saw blade, then work on the tops of the crutches.

Both sticks I chose have a Y forking off one end. Between bites of breakfast, I shorten these top pieces first, then carve off all the poky bits. Back in the tent, I rummage through the pile of clothes we're leaving and pull out two of Anna's base layers. I wrap the shirts around the top of each stick as padding, then tie the sleeves together underneath. Satisfied, I pass the makeshift crutches to Jack.

He props them under his armpits, gripping the sticks partway down with tight fists. He leans into them gently, testing their strength, then takes a lurching step in the sand. "Way better," Jack says. "And not dangerous at all." He jokes and peers across the beach of big, round, ankle-busting rocks. His lopsided grin flashes heat through my belly. I smile back, crumpling my empty foil bag. Jack leans forward, resting on the crutches, watching me. I'm suddenly on my tiptoes, surprising both of us, giving him a soft, long kiss. Even the hammering rain can't dampen the charge between us. Boy, I could do this all day.

"Damn." Jack breathes heavily when I step back. "You do that every hundred yards, and I'll find the energy to walk for days," he says, grinning. I smile back, hoping this journey doesn't take quite that long.

CHAPTER 34

Before we leave, I dismantle the fire, which has burnt down to a big patch of bright red coals in the sand. When I scatter the pieces, they quickly lose their glow in the rain. The flames won't flare up in this downpour, but the fear of wildfire has built a habit of caution in me.

After taking a few steps up the beach, I look back at our camp. The orange nylon of the tent, with our remaining gear inside, is the only hint we've been in this spot. I scan the shoreline behind us, looking for our cougar, but there's nothing. Just rocks and driftwood and sand in the rain. But somehow, I sense the timeless spirit of everyone... everything... that has *ever* been in this spot... lifting me up and pushing me forward. I take a deep breath of the wet wind and turn to follow Jack.

Jack is picking his way across the cobbles. His progress is slow, and it takes careful concentration. But we're moving, and he's doing it on his own. At the beach edge, the trail climbs into the forest, where another steep set of natural stairs carves into the roots and rocks. Jack leans forward on his crutches, peering up the steep trail. "Damn." He glances over his shoulder at me, lips pressed tight. I follow his gaze up the slope. Navigating a regular staircase on crutches is a challenge. Attempting this uneven climb that way would be reckless.

"How about if you sit down?" I picture a way for Jack to climb on his own. The trail is just a single footpath overhung with maidenhair ferns, too narrow for me to help him much. "Could you kinda scootch up backwards?" Jack looks over at me, eyebrows squishing together. I sit on the first root, then twist to place my hands behind me. To mimic Jack's injury, I lift one leg, then push my butt to the next rock with the other leg.

"Might work." Jack nods at my demonstration. We decide I'll go ahead of him, carrying his crutches. There are a few spots where we link arms and I help pull Jack up to the next root. At the steepest section, Jack has to face the slope. The terrain forces him to bear weight on his mauled leg for a few steps. My jaw clenches as pain flashes across his features. But he makes the climb without complaint.

After a quick water break at the top, we progress along the forest trail at a moderate pace. Jack has found a crutching rhythm. This section of trail is uneven, but much easier to navigate than the cobbles down on the beach. I have plenty of time to walk ahead and check the mud depth, directing Jack to the best routes. The wind gusts continue to make the treetops howl, a warning call before showering big drops of water down onto us.

Soon the trail is descending again, a steep approach path to yet another pocket beach. Jack sits down to descend on his butt, handing me his crutches. I lead and am soon standing on a sandy strip of beach. While I wait for Jack, I peer across the gray mist hanging over the waves which crash at the shoreline. The rollers lift and lower dark patches of kelp, where a shaggy black head appears behind a wave.

It's an otter, floating on its back, riding the ocean roller coaster. The furry creature has something white balanced on its belly. It's nibbling at whatever it has in its childlike paws. Its head glances around before it disappears behind another wave. I'm still watching nature's show when Jack struggles onto the beach beside me.

Handing him his crutches, I point at the otter. Jack grins toward the creature. "Cute little buggers," he says. "They were always my favorite animal at the aquarium. We used to go a lot when I was a kid. I could watch the otter tank for hours. That was back when my dad would do things with us." He smiles at the fond memory before his face clouds.

I walk down to the ocean and wave Jack over. His crutches sink deep into the sand. "If we walk down here, it should be easier. The wet sand is firmer." I gesture at the area beyond the waves' reach. We make our way slowly toward another collection of faded buoys, way in the distance, marking the entrance to the next section of forest trail.

When we finally near the trail marker, I point out a perfectly round, two-foot diameter 'window' in the conjoined roots of a pair of spruce trees. "Long ago, when these trees were just seedlings, they grew on top of a fallen tree we call a nurse log." I fall easily back into guide mode. "The seedlings used the nutrients of the nurse log to grow strong. Then, decades ago, the nurse log rotted away, leaving this round window in their roots." Jack stops to take in the view. I walk to the other side of the tree, sit on a driftwood log, and smile through the hole.

"Man, I wish I had a camera." Jack tilts his head and rests his armpits on his crutches. "A beautiful shot," he says, staring through the root at me. "You're beautiful." I stare back at him, motionless, as butterflies stroke my insides. I'm not. Beautiful, that is. But it's nice to have someone say it. Jack picks his way over to me, struggling past a couple of logs. It takes grit for me *not* to jump up and help. But I know Jack needs to do it himself. And I know he's making all this effort for me.

Jack rests on the log beside me, propping his crutches on his good knee and massaging his underarms. Then he puts an arm around my shoulder and pulls me close, leaning my hooded head onto the wet fabric of his chest. "What are you going to tell Liv?" I ask without warning. I hadn't meant to bring her up, but I've been trying to figure out what all this Jack stuff means. I think he feels the same way I do. I hope he does. But I don't really know.

Jack is quiet, watching the rollers break across the beach below us. When he looks down at me, he says, "Two answers. I'm going to take her to grad. It's too late to make other plans. Wouldn't be fair to leave her in a lurch." My heart stops and I pull away. "But after that" — Jack's arm holds me firmly against him — "I'm all yours." I feel the tension release from my body as I sink into his side. "I have no idea how... we live so far apart. But I wanna figure it out. With you." He gently kisses the top of my nose.

I wrap both arms around his middle and huddle into him as my reply. Words don't seem enough, so I look up. He kisses me again, our cold lips saying the rest. Water drips down my forehead from our hoods and a gust pummels us as I pull Jack's spicy scent toward me. He moves his free hand near the chest pocket of my jacket. I'm stunned at how much I ache to feel his fingers on my skin there. I twist closer, shifting against Jack on the log. He gasps and pulls away, cringing.

"Shit!" I just kicked his injured leg with my toe. "I'm sorry!" I say, appalled that I hurt him again. Shit.

"I'm fine." Jack's voice is hoarse, but a smile crosses his ashen face. "I keep forgetting. You make me forget I hurt." He reaches for me. "You didn't do any damage."

We sit, arm in arm, watching nature's wildness for a few more minutes. Finally, I squeeze Jack and stand up. "We should get going," I say, my chest tightening as I think of my dad. "Time's a-wasting."

Chapter 35

While Jack picks his way up the beach toward the bottom of the next trail, I tell him about the dozen different buoys and floats swinging from the spruce tree, hung by the people who've come by this spot. There are deflated faded pink buoys, typically used to mark underwater hazards along this coast. A few are newer vinyl ones in dark blue and yellow, still hard and round. There are also bullet-shaped PVC crab floats in yellow and red, with their ropes threaded through the hole down their center.

The coolest float is a small dark green Japanese glass one, still wrapped in the knotted rope netting used to float their deep-sea fishing nets. "Can you imagine?" I ask. "That glass ball was tied to a fishing net by a fisherman... halfway around the world. Then one day it broke free... floated out into the open ocean, where it was probably trapped in the circular ocean currents... out on the Pacific for years, maybe decades. Then some random storm surge picks it up... lands it on this beach for someone to find. And that person hung it here." Jack laughs at me.

"I love how you get so excited about all this stuff."

"Humans are awesome," I say seriously. "The things we build. The things we figure out. And how we work with nature. It's just amazing."

I think of the huge coastal wind farm and the massive bridges down in the city.

"We are amazing," Jack agrees with a small chuckle, his eyes twinkling at me.

My gaze settles on a float hanging at the bottom of the grouping. It's a yellow styrofoam float my mum had found on her last trip out here. She had hung it carefully, laughing at her contribution to the 'human junk sculpture', as she called it. I stand, waiting until Jack stands beside me, staring down at the yellow float spinning in the gusts.

"She wanted me to go away to school." Jack's brows furrow as he tries to follow my thoughts. "We had a conversation," I say, "my mum and I, on The Last Day. Somehow, I had forgotten... blocked it. But this morning, after reading her letter... this morning, I remembered." My voice trembles. "She insisted I go away to school. She knew I'd have to fight my dad to go. And she made me promise to leave." I look up at Jack, wide-eyed. "I promised." Jack shuffles awkwardly on his crutches and pulls me toward him with one arm as I stifle a sob. I lean into his wet rain jacket for a moment. Then I pull myself together and step back.

"Well, I'm glad." Jack's wearing a sheepish grin. "I'm glad she made you promise. And I'm glad you remembered your promise," he says. "It's selfish. But having you come live in the city would be the best. And your dad will figure things out." Jack's tone is suddenly serious. "Let's go get him some help. You'll figure out how to get away, even if he doesn't want you to go. I know you will." He winks and limps into the brush, up the trail.

The trail parallels the beach, a few feet above the jagged black rock outcrops which jut out into the water. It's not the prettiest section, but Jack can make good time on the level, pine needle-padded trail. He's breathing hard, the exertion of crutching taking a visible toll. I glance behind us, then scan the forest on either side, still concerned the cougar might track us.

Around the corner, as we approach our last climb and final challenge, I stop and drop my pack. I sit on a tall, moss-covered cedar log and pull out the first aid kit. When Jack catches up, he sits beside me with a grunt. I offer him another couple of pain pills and the water bottle. It's been three hours since his last dose, and keeping a lid on pain is better than letting it creep up on you.

"You'll need inspiration." I move Jack's good leg so I can stand in front of him, between his knees. "This last section of trail is hard." I kiss his bottom lip gently. "I wish I could do it for you." Jack puts both arms around me and kisses me back with cold lips. My stomach flips and a warm heat spreads through my belly again. So nice. But I pull away, ever conscious of the minutes ticking by.

"Follow me." The sheen of sweat that's appeared on Jack's blanched brow worries me. But I grab my pack and walk to the base. Jack hobbles up behind me, then peers up into the brush.

"Holy crap!" Jack stares straight up.

"Yeah. I know, right?" It's a wall of dark brown dirt and roots with a few mounds of sword ferns and bright green salal. A gray rope hangs down the steep ascent, ending at our feet. Above us, another rope is visible, tied taut, the end disappearing over the crest.

"What's going on there?" Jack points at the second rope.

"Oh, that's the best part. The ridge is only two feet wide. You basically get to the top, straddle the crest, and rappel straight down the other side on the second rope." I say. "The good news is it takes us to the last beach. The bad news is this climb is gonna hurt." I glance at his leg and then at my palms.

Again, we decide it's best I go first. There's no way for me to help Jack. If I'm ahead of him, I'll be able to help him find good handholds.

After we strap his crutches to the outside of my pack, I take a deep breath and start.

The climb is near vertical, making it difficult for vegetation to grow. The dark brown earth is packed hard, covered in slippery mud. I wrap the rope around one arm and use the exposed roots as handholds as I climb. My hands are instantly filthy, mud cramming into the raw wounds of my palms. I grit my teeth, knowing Jack's in much worse shape than me. When I reach the crest, I carefully sit off to one side, parking my butt in a mossy patch and dangling my feet over the edge toward Jack.

"Go ahead," I call down to Jack. The only sounds are the wind gusts, dripping water drops, and Jack's harsh breathing. He finally pulls himself up beside me, pale and panting. I put a hand over his, saying nothing, as a squirrel somewhere above us chatters its congratulations.

The way down is treacherous, steep, and slick. I wrap the rope around my left arm and hold the tail in my right. I slip down inelegantly and reach the bottom in moments. Jack follows in a similar clumsy fashion, landing on one leg beside me, unable to stifle a loud groan.

"Well, down was easier than up, anyway." He leans even more heavily against the base of the cliff as I unstrap his crutches from my pack. "Any more surprises?" Jack gasps, his eyes shut, grimacing.

"None. I promise. A kilometer of sandy beach and we're at the ranger's yurt." Looking at Jack's blanched face, I'm not sure he'll make it that far.

CHAPTER 36

We emerge from the cover of the forest onto a stunning white sand beach. It stretches in a lazy arc to a tree-covered finger of land, jutting out into the ocean way in the distance. On a sunny day, this beach is a deserted west coast oasis. The frigid water and the scenery both make swimming here breathtaking.

A few hundred meters along the beach, I wash the mud off my hands in a small creek running down the sand from the forest edge. There's a trail of animal tracks moving in the same direction as us. With dread, I examine them, but the prints have claw marks at the tip of each toe pad, confirming it's a gray wolf, not our cougar.

I'm about to point out the tracks to Jack, but his appearance stops the words in my throat. He's staring blankly across the beach, still trying to catch his breath. His cheeks should be bright in the cold, wet wind, but instead, they are a greenish-gray under the bruised half-moons of his under-eye circles.

"Let's keep moving." I stand up beside him. "Just a few more steps now." I coax Jack and he obediently struggles on.

Halfway to the yurt, Jack stops, swaying against his crutches.

"I don't feel too good," he mumbles. Then Jack crumbles against me, collapsing into the sand.

"Jack! Look at me. Jack?" I support his slumped body in a sitting position.

"Sorry," he says, not turning toward me. "I thought... I could... do it..." His eyes scrunch in pain again. I hold Jack's head in my lap and peer through the pounding rain, my pulse racing. There's no trace of anyone. Or anything. The trail marker to the yurt is scarcely visible way down the beach. I could run to see if anyone's there. But the wolf tracks are fresh, and I don't dare leave Jack out here alone. I lay him on the sand and struggle out of my pack, digging for the sleeping bag and mat. I'll just have to drag him.

Jack is barely conscious as I lug him onto his back and into the sleeping bag. I unroll the mat and lay it beside him, dragging first his head, then his feet onto it. Grasping both the sleeping bag and mat low to the ground, I lean back. Slowly, Jack drags along the sand. I try not to notice all the parts of me that burn and ache. Just a few more steps. Then just a few more, I think.

After an eternity, I drop the mat, panting. Wavering drag marks stretch behind us to the tiny outline of my abandoned pack. Over my shoulder, the familiar white dogwood flower logo on the brown park sign is much closer. I grab the mat again with my aching hands and falter backward, trying to avoid rocks. Jack moans as I bump him over a painful obstacle. I kneel, uncovering his head, which has slid down into the sleeping bag.

"We're almost there, bud. How you doin'?"

"Not... too... good." Jack's words are garbled, but I'm thrilled he's still speaking.

"Just a bit further." I kiss his clammy forehead. "You stay awake for me."

"Try." He breathes out a single syllable. I grab the sleeping bag, not sure what he means, and carry on. After another eternity, I pull

Jack against a rocky ledge near the yurt. With renewed energy, I leave Jack, hop up the slope, and sprint down the gravel trail to the yurt. In minutes, I'll be able to call the Coast Guard to get help for my dad. And Jack.

The yurt is tucked beside a stand of trees, sheltering it from the gale. The round sidewalls of the building are made of tan canvas, topped by a shallow cone roof made of a similar fabric. A proper white metal door, built into a wood frame, holds a blue sign reading 'Park Facilitator'. Over the rustic wooden porch, an orange tarp is tacked to a plywood roof on rough-sawn timbers, keeping the rain out.

I run onto the porch beside a beige plastic Adirondack chair and a pile of chopped firewood. Yelling, I pound on the door. Except for a thin line of smoke from the sheet-metal chimney stack, the yurt looks deserted. The window covers are rolled up, but there's no sign of anyone. I yell again. When eventually there's movement from inside, I'm giddy with relief.

A young man in dark green trousers and a short-sleeved beige button-up shirt with shoulder patches opens the door. "Well, hello there!" He wears a broad smile. Then he frowns, taking in the panic on my face. "What's this then?" the ranger asks, as I summon him back to where I've left Jack.

The ranger introduces himself as Craig and I rush him back to the beach, explaining Jack is hurt. Between us, we lug Jack up the trail and into the warmth of the yurt. On the floor, we extract Jack from the grimy sleeping bag. Then we lift him onto a cot against the far side of the yurt. Jack moans as we lay him on the rough gray wool blanket, but is otherwise unresponsive.

The room is cluttered with supplies, and Craig hands me his dripping jacket before attending to Jack. He motions me to hang it on a clothes hanger hooked into the wooden lattice, which supports the skin of the yurt. After I do the same with my jacket, I collapse into the single straight-backed chair.

While Craig unwraps Jack's wound, I explain how the mangy cougar attacked us both. The ranger pauses when I describe the cat, concern in his narrowed eyes. "Tell me everything you remember." He pulls a small notebook from his breast pocket. Craig's pencil scrapes across the waterproof paper as he jots down the details. When he runs out of questions, Craig tells me other hikers have seen a cougar. "No one else has been attacked. But I'll have to get the conservation folks up here. They'll track it and take it out." His words are sad and soft.

Jack's eyes are still closed, but he flinches as Craig pulls the gauze off his wounds. The injury looks much worse now than it did on the beach yesterday. Jack's leg is swollen, and the red skin stretched tight around the oozing punctures.

"I didn't have anything to clean him up with," I say. "All I had was wipes... and ointment." Craig nods and retrieves a huge red canvas first aid kit from under the cot.

"Hey, can I use your radio?" I ask Craig abruptly, looking over at the VHF set up near the door. There hasn't been a moment to explain the bigger reason we're here. But with Jack in good hands, I am again very aware of the passing time.

"Well, let's just see how bad this looks before we decide if we're calling it in," Craig says calmly, misunderstanding the urgency in my voice.

"No, it's not for Jack." Finally, I launch into the story of how we ended up out here together. I explain how our boat burned and sank, and that my dad has been stranded for over two days now, with severe burns. Craig asks a few more questions, then glances over his shoulder at the VHF. When he looks back at me, he's shaking his head.

"This radio's dead." My heart sinks at his words. "This is our first rotation out here, and the battery's not charging. I called it in before it died, and they're bringing a replacement. But with this weather, I'm not sure when they'll get out here... anyway, this radio... it's not working." I stand abruptly. The wooden chair topples as the legs get caught on the uneven plank floor, and I start pacing.

"Shit. Shit! Shit." I ignore Craig's gaze as he rights the chair. I know I'm acting like a crazy woman, but... shit! This was supposed to be our solution. Seriously. A bad battery!? Shit! Shitty useless rangers. Shitty weather. A loud stomp of my foot punctuates every curse word I say and think. Then I sink back into the wooden chair, shaking uncontrollably. I'm so tired. So done. But we're not done. Not yet.

"Listen." Craig limps over to me and places a firm hand on my shoulder. "A group of hikers left here about an hour ago, heading north. Four of them. They have a handheld VHF." As his words sink in, a glimmer of hope rekindles in my aching body.

Chapter 37

"I always ask groups if they have communication." Craig pours a thin stream of hydrogen peroxide into the first of Jack's wounds. "So I know those two couples have a handheld VHF. They were supposed to continue to the south trailhead. But with all this rain, I explained how difficult the mud makes the trail... the sections you guys just came through." I nod my agreement. "The women were already in pretty rough shape. So they backtracked. They'll get their water taxi to do a beach pickup instead, once the weather clears. Let me finish patching up Jack here," the ranger says, "then I'll try to catch them."

"Do you think that's a good idea? You look a little sore yourself." I point at Craig's limp.

"I am sore," Craig says. "I slipped. Yesterday. Getting water from the creek out back. Twisted my knee again. All this mud." He shakes his head and works on Jack's next puncture wound.

"I'll go after them." I'm already pulling on my jacket. "I'll go now." With every passing minute, the other group is getting farther away. Their radio is getting farther away. Our only hope of help.

"I'm not sure that's a good idea. You're exhausted. And hurt." Craig looks down at my palms.

"I'm fine," I say firmly, tucking my hands out of sight in my sleeves. "Jack obviously can't go. And your knee is hurt. My legs are fine. I'll be the fastest. Plus, shouldn't you be here if your supplies arrive?" I appeal to his sense of duty.

"I suppose." Craig finally agrees. I explain I left my pack on the beach and that I could use something to eat. Craig turns to the fold-out table, covered with everything from cooking oil to colorful climbing carabiners. He hands me a small water bottle, then rummages through a cardboard box, pulling out a yellow panic whistle and an energy bar. "When Jack's cleaned up, I'll get your things from the beach." I realize with a chill that my mum's note is in that backpack. There's no time for me to deal with it — I just have to trust Craig will retrieve it.

"I'll be back here in a few hours," I say this with more confidence than I feel, shoving Craig's offerings into my pockets. Then I go to Jack. His face is an awful greenish-white, with dark purple moons under his droopy eyelids. When I touch his cheek, saying his name, Jack's eyes flutter open. He gives me a weak grimace and fumbles for my hand.

"Take my music," Jack whispers hoarsely, reaching for his pocket.

"Jack, no." I protest quietly, confused by the urgency in his voice.

"Take it," he says. "Listen to it. 'Maia's Playlist'." His eyes shut again. "Made it for you."

"I don't get it, Jack." I shake my head. He hasn't touched his iPod in days. "When... when did you make it for me?"

"On the boat... and at the first trailhead beach," he whispers. I watch his fading features, speechless. What... what is he talking about? Jack gives me a weak, sheepish grin and squeezes my hand. "You had me... from the start. Those blue eyes... peeking at me from behind the kayaks." He pushes the iPod into my fist. "From the start."

"I... Jack..." I stand completely still, stunned. Then I wrap my palm around the device and kiss his forehead, thinking back to the boat trip and those first hours on the beach. I had taken all of Jack's actions as hostility and defiance.

"Go find that radio, Maia," Jack whispers hoarsely. "Get help. Make your mum and dad proud." His words are barely audible. "I'm already so proud to know you, Boomdizzle." He pulls me in for another soft kiss. I close my eyes and breathe him in, fingers gripping his cool, damp hair.

"You stay awake." I run my hand along the silky stubble of his clammy cheek. "I'll be back real soon." I look into his too-large pupils, just as they roll back into his head and his lids slide closed.

"Shit! He's out again." I motion Craig over as Jack's head lolls to one side. "Jack? Jack! Can you hear me?" I shake him a little, hoping for a response. But Jack is silent, his shallow gasps the only sound in the small yurt.

"Go," Craig says, pushing past me. "I'll look after him." I nod, stuff the iPod in a pocket, and zip my jacket. "And Maia?" Craig makes me turn. "Call in a mayday, not a pan-pan. For both of them," he says. "Jack needs help right away. Make that clear to the Coast Guard. And from what you've told me, so does your dad." I step out into the driving rain, knowing the ranger is correct.

Chapter 38

The first kilometer of the trail is difficult, but I get into a rhythm, running whenever I can. Before long, I've counted eleven scrambles from pocket beaches, up into the forest, and back down again. I jog past a Medusa-like cedar, a spot we would normally take a break. As I pass, I admire the old giant, its multiple trunks and unruly serpentine branches waving in the wet wind, a raven gliding majestically above it all.

While I hike, images of burnt flesh and cougar bites flash through my aching head. I temper my panic by focusing on my breathing. I'm already at a one-step-to-one-breath tempo. But even without the heavy backpack, my body is protesting this last effort. Boots and rain gear are not running gear. My thighs are burning and I try to gauge how far I've come. I force thoughts to my mum's note and her three words: positive, prepared, patient. Stay positive, you'll get there...

When I stop for a drink, I pull out Jack's iPod. I turn it on and the screen shows one bar of battery. After fumbling with the earbuds, I run my finger around the circular control until I find 'Maia's Playlist'. Then I adjust the volume and continue down onto a cobbly beach. With giant raindrops still pounding my face, I force myself to slow down on the uneven terrain. An injury now would be disastrous for everyone.

Another scramble up onto the forest trail. Maybe 1,600 meters by now? Feels longer, but it's hard to compare the meandering trail distances to the laps of a running track. The energy and... care... in the music Jack's chosen for me, boost my tempo noticeably. Breathe in, breathe out, breathe in and out. Just keep running, just keep running. My back and armpits are soaked with sweat, and my long johns are chafing between my thighs. I'm desperate to remove a layer of clothing but know I'll be cold without it once I reach the other hikers. You're prepared, at least you're a runner...

Maybe 3,000 meters now? It feels like more, way more than seven laps. I'm speed walking across another cobbly beach. Typically, we would break here for a snack with our clients, letting them enjoy the stunning coastline. From here, the tombolo is visible in the distance. It's a thin sandbar, where centuries of storms have moved ocean sediments, leading to a small island.

I suddenly remember chasing Nora across that sandbar on a brilliant, sunny afternoon. Although we didn't know it at that point, it had been mum's last trip. When only a few guests booked, I was allowed to bring a friend along. Nora and I worked hard, but were also given time for fun and silliness. We whispered about the mean girls as we hiked and giggled about the boys we liked late into those starry nights. Back then, I thought Nora and I would be friends forever. Thought we'd go to university or travel the world together. And throughout mum's illness, Nora and her family had been so good. So supportive. Until they weren't.

The last time I talked to Nora was a week after The Last Day. She came over and we sat cross-legged on my bed. I hadn't gone back to school yet. Had seen no one other than my dad. And I was so glad she came. To talk. And cry. And let it all out. But if I could go back... well, I guess I just didn't really know Nora.

Until that day, her family's religion had never affected our friendship. She was like any other kid. A loving and thoughtful friend. But when I shared the details of The Last Day with Nora, her face turned ashen in astonishment.

"You didn't... she didn't?! Oh Maia, no. Life is a gift. From God." Nora's voice had risen. "What your mum did... it's self-murder... a sin." She scooted off the striped duvet and backed toward the bedroom door. "A sin, Maia... a sin... I gotta... I gotta go now." She had scurried out of the house and never spoke to me again.

In a few short days, Jack's friendship has started to fill the hollow Nora left. "Jack," I whisper into the rain now, "please be okay". After another climb, I settle on a stump for a few large gulps of water. The raven shows itself again, this time perched in a fir tree up ahead. Is it following me? I wipe my lips with the back of my hand, then shove the water bottle into my pocket. My fingertips brush against the panic whistle Craig gave me. I had silently rolled my eyes at it, accepting the whistle only because arguing would have wasted valuable time. Now, I gaze across the bay, peering into the open forest along the shore where the trail runs. Where the other hikers have just been. Or maybe still are.

Why not? I shrug and put the whistle to my lips. If the other group hears me, they might come back this way. I remove my earbuds and blow out a slow SOS in Morse code. First three short blasts, then three long, finishing with three more short blasts. When I pull the whistle from my lips, I listen intently but hear nothing other than the wind rushing through the treetops. I catch my breath, then repeat the SOS, blowing out the sequence two more times. Each time I stop to listen. And each time I hear nothing but the raven's caw and the wind's wildness.

After I tuck the whistle away, I turn Jack's music on again. I run along the trail, pushing hard on the easy terrain. The path is scenic and level, winding through an open forest with views of the crashing waves on the coastline below. Not much further, I tell myself. Soon you'll reach the hikers. They must be just around the next bend. When I get to the corner, there's still no sign of the hikers. Be patient, you'll get there...

Another few steps, and the trail branches in two, requiring a decision. The left fork is wide, leading uphill and inland. The right fork is less traveled and leads down to the beach. Now what?

If I take a parallel trail, I risk getting ahead of the other hikers. That would not be good. Just then, a movement on the narrower path catches my eye. It's my raven friend again, staring at me with its black head cocked. It turns, hopping away from me, as the next song croons "Listen to Your Heart" in my ears. Seriously? I can't believe Jack would even have such a sappy song. But it's our family's favorite oldie. And he could not have known that.

The raven. The song. What exactly is the universe trying to tell me? I'm not superstitious, and with the downpour erasing any footprints from the other group, following the big black bird and my heart doesn't seem wrong. As I fall in behind the raven, taking the narrow path on the right, I wonder if I've made another huge mistake.

But then, as I lean into the wind around the next bend, the hikers are below me, across the beach. I stop short, sagging against the tree trunk. They're taking a break, sitting on driftwood logs, but haven't seen me yet. One of them is pointing out toward the waves. Standing, I take a few deep breaths, trying to stop panting. I leave the trail and scramble onto the sharp black boulders edging the beach. Steadying myself with my hands, I make my way over sizeable gaps between rocks until I'm just a few feet from the beach sand. As I hop to the ground, a painful tug on my wrist whirls me around and I watch in horror as my bracelet catches on a jagged rock outcrop, then falls, tinkling against the barnacled rock and landing with a clink. Shit!

I glance over my shoulder. The hikers are still a few hundred meters upwind and haven't noticed me. The narrow gap between the rocks won't fit my hand. When I clamber on top of the rock, the bracelet is visible from above, but still out of reach. Shit. There's no time for this now, so I jam a crooked piece of driftwood into the gap to mark the spot. After I find a radio, I'll figure out how to retrieve my precious bracelet. With a last glance, I turn away, jogging up the beach toward the hikers.

When I reach them, the two Japanese couples chatter words of surprise I don't understand. The small stout woman in red gaiters waves for me to sit down next to her. I say thank you, but remain standing, trying to explain my request. Even with the language barrier, all of them quickly realize something is very wrong. The taller man, Kaito, speaks some English. Soon he's pulling a handheld VHF from his pack, but when he flounders to turn it on, I reach for the unit.

He passes it over and I twist up the volume, then spin the squelch knob until the radio screeches to life. Although I went through the motions of an emergency call when I got my marine radio license, I've never had to do it for real. Now, I punch the channel button until 16 is illuminated, then key the microphone, pausing before I speak.

"Mayday, mayday, mayday." I struggle to keep my words slow and clear. "This is Maia Müller, Maia Müller, Maia Müller." I repeat the call, just like they taught us in the course. "Does anyone hear me? Over." There's other stuff I'm supposed to say in a distress call sequence, but I'm too anxious to know if anyone hears me to do it correctly. There's an agonizing silence, then the radio crackles back.

"This is Coast Guard radio, Coast Guard radio, Coast Guard radio, what is your position? Over," says a calm female voice. I collapse to the sand, relief turning my stomach to jelly. Choking back tears, I answer. A short while later, the kind Coast Guard operator is back. She explains that Search and Rescue from the Canadian Air Force base south of us has been dispatched and will bring help in the next few hours. I bow my head in silent thanks, then look up into the sky through my tears. Above us, the raven glides out of sight as the Japanese women gather around me, tutting and shushing in the universal language of caring concern.

"They're coming." I give them a huge smile, warm tears running down my face as I rub my wrist. "They're coming."

Chapter 39

The hospital doors glide open and I pause on the cracked terrazzo inside, pushing down the bile rising into my throat. I hate this place. Under the buzzing fluorescent lights, I take the echoing concrete staircase two at a time. On the second floor, Sara, the Charge Nurse, sits at the desk of the Burn, Plastics & Trauma unit. She nods a silent greeting, which tells me they've done the dressing change and I'm good to go in. Outside room 214, I wash and dry my hands. Then, from the stainless steel shelves, I unfold a crinkly yellow gown and stuff my arms into the sleeves. After tying it in the back, I snap the thin white elastics of a mask over my ears. I press the nose wire onto my cheeks, then take a long, steadying breath and open the door.

The room is dim, which highlights the multitude of flashing colored lights and illuminated numbers on the machines monitoring my dad. His eyes are closed, and his bandaged hands rest on a pillow over his chest. In sleep, his face holds less of the tension he carries when awake. My mask does nothing to block the stiff scent of antiseptic that permeates the room. Next to the bed, I curl into the chair as quietly as the crinkly gown will let me, then pull my sketchbook from my backpack. He sleeps a lot right now, and they say that's normal. To be expected.

I hate seeing my dad like this. But it's better than those first days in intensive care, when no one could tell me if he'd survive. They sedated him for over a week, while his body fought off the infection that had taken hold after spending three long days in the wilderness. I shudder now, recalling how my throat ached and limbs shook as I sat, hugging my knees, beside him in the sterile room. The idea of becoming an orphan — what a weird word — was a scenario that chilled me. I am not ready to be responsible for myself. Not yet.

Since my dad has been moved to this burn unit, my jumbled thoughts are calming down, and I even cracked a smile yesterday at Sam, the custodian's lame jokes. The team here is more cheerful than in intensive care. They explain what's going on in a way that makes me fairly confident my dad's not dying. They tell us his skin grafts are responding well and he'll be able to move to outpatient treatment soon. Although they haven't specified how many days 'soon' might be. There will be physio and follow-up, but at least he'll be out of this hospital. A shudder runs through me again.

After another long look at my dad's calm, sleeping face, I flip open my sketchbook, escaping into the rhythmic comfort of my pencil drawings. An hour later, my dad is still snoring softly. I forgot my water bottle, so I remove my gown and mask, then walk out into the hallway. Rounding the corner to the water fountain, I almost collide with someone. I start to apologize, jumping aside. As I meet the woman's eyes, I freeze. It's Anna. When I last saw her, she was bent over Jack's gurney, running through the emergency room doors, what feels like a lifetime ago.

A smile blooms across her face as she recognizes me. Without hesitation, Anna wraps her arms around my stiff shoulders. Her hug is long and firm. After a moment, my body melts into hers and I inhale the floral scent of her hair, my eyes closing in comfort.

"How is he?" Anna pulls away, her hands on my shoulders, head tilted and brown eyes blinking with kindness. My mouth is dry and tears well up. I shake my head and push past Anna, bending over the water fountain to buy some time. I have no idea what to say to her.

Thank you? For looking after my dad. Or sorry? For putting her son through so much. And for not returning any of her recent calls. My ears are ringing and I wonder what would happen if I bolted down the hallway, out of this damn place. I'm sure I can outrun her.

I stand up slowly, wiping my mouth, and turn to face Anna.

"Thank you." I look down at Anna's white clogs, my voice barely a whisper. "And I'm sorry." The clogs step toward me and Anna lifts my chin with a soft touch.

"Jack's fine now. I'm fine." Then she leads me to the burn unit's family room at the end of the hall. We settle onto a couch overlooking the city, which glimmers in the sunlight. "Now," Anna says. "Tell me. How's your dad? How are you?" Suddenly I'm talking and crying.

Anna sits with me for an hour, mostly listening, sometimes questioning. When I seem to be talked out, she squeezes my forearm and thanks me for taking care of Jack, for dragging him all that way.

"What you did out there was pretty exceptional, Maia." Anna blinks back tears. "Our family thanks you. Truly." I stare at her blankly, having never thought of it that way.

Then Anna tells me a few stories from her time in the bush with my dad. The accounts are heavily edited, I can tell. Anna wouldn't burden me with gory details that make no difference now. I finger my bracelet, which peeks out from under my sleeve, and I imagine her ordeal.

"Did it help? Having that letter from your mum?" I look up at her, my eyes narrowing. Anna shrugs. "Your dad hoped you'd go to the cache. And Jack told me you did."

"Yeah," I say. "It was good to have her letter... and the bracelet."

Anna seems to know my mum wanted me to go to school and asks what I'm doing in September. I stare at her for a long while, uncomfortable with how much she knows about me.

"You are what your dad and I talked about when things got bad," she says in explanation. When I finally tell her I'm going to technical school, Anna seems pleased. She can tell I'm conflicted about leaving my dad. "He knows you should go to school. He just doesn't know how to tell you." Anna seems very sure of her words and I hope she's right.

Somehow I can't bring myself to ask about Jack, but Anna fills me in as if I prompted her. After he was admitted, they stitched up Jack's wounds, gave him a round of intravenous antibiotics, and discharged him a couple of days later. Good as new. He even went to his graduation. Anna doesn't mention Liv.

But when Anna asks me to call Jack, I shake my head.

"I can't, Anna. Don't ask me that." My stomach churns and my cheeks flush, remembering Jack's touch on my lips, my chest. I'm sure he's forgotten all about me, now that he's back in the city with the big-boobed Liv. I'm a three-day blip in his past. Nope. No way am I calling him.

Chapter 40

Two weeks later, I'm curled up in the chair next to my dad's bed again. He keeps improving, with gowns and masks now no longer required. To pass the time, I've been filling my sketchbook. Today I'm working on a pencil drawing of a raven and am focussed on shading its eye. My pencil pauses and a slow smile builds across my face. Since my dad has been getting better, memories of my days with Jack intrude often, each time flooding my chest with warmth. That is until I imagine the great summer he's having with Liv.

Still, I long to discuss things with Jack. School in September. My dad. A stupid movie I watched last night. Now, my throat closes and I hang my head. It's useless to wish for a return to the past. So I settle for sketching my experience with Jack — the fawn, the distressed Stellar's jay, the boardwalk.

My dad stands across the room in a gray tracksuit he wears all the time now, forcing his fingers through a series of exercises. There's baseball on television and the muffled broadcast seeps out from his pillow speakers. I take a bite of the hamburger I picked up on my way in, then wash it down with a slug of root beer from a white-striped straw.

While I've been in the city, I've stayed with family friends, a couple my parents have known all my life. I sleep on an air mattress in their basement and they feed me breakfast every morning. Then I hop on a bus for the half-hour trip to the hospital, where I spend my days and often nights, too. There's a cot in the corner for me, and hospital rules allow one family member to stay over. And I'm the only family member left. At least in this country.

Across from me, my dad grimaces. The skin grafts of his stiff pinkie finger are covered in fresh white bandages and hardly move. His painful rehab reminds me of my own and I rub my knuckles. I'm absorbed in shading a section of raven feathers when the door clicks open. I don't look up right away, since the nurse isn't here for me. But when my dad clears his throat, and she doesn't say her usual good mornings, I lift my gaze. My whole body stiffens. It's Jack.

My feet uncurl from beneath me as my pencil slips to the floor. I sit back in the chair, staring up at him, my heartbeat now kicking into overdrive. Jack's in jeans, faded gray skate shoes, and a maroon hoodie. One tanned hand grips the door lever. He waves a greeting at my dad, who nods his furrowed forehead, but neither of them speaks. Then Jack scans the small room, locking his gaze on me. God, he looks good. His concerned face breaks into a huge toothy grin, dark eyes sparkling under raised brows. "There you are." Jack says it like he lost me for a minute at the mall. Not like I've been refusing to see him for a month.

I have wondered how I would react if I ever ran into Jack again. My behavior since the rescue has been pretty shitty, so I never expected him to come to me. Anna has visited us a couple of times because she's Anna — a decent human. She keeps asking me to call Jack, insisting he really wants to catch up with me. But I just shake my head and lie. "I don't have anything to say."

I've also wondered how much Jack told Anna about what happened out on the trail. She seems to know all about the action events, but I'm sure Jack never told his mum the rest. Why would he? Then again, Anna's a mother, and most times, mothers know.

Now, in the dim hospital room, Jack's voice unfreezes me. In a single stride, I'm wrapping my arms around his waist, burying my face in his chest with a squeal that surprises everyone, especially me. He smells of spice and detergent. Jack hugs me tight, lifting my feet off the floor. His lips brush my hair as he softly says my name. No more mystery about how I'll react when I see Jack. I fight the urge to kiss him because I'm keenly aware of my dad's presence in the corner, still doing his exercises. Jack must feel the same because he turns to my dad.

"How ya doing, Mr. Müller?" Jack intertwines his fingers with mine, pulling our shoulders together.

"Fifty-fifty." My dad's gruff words respond to Jack while staring at me, his face unreadable. Then a moment later, a crinkle reaches his eyes, and he turns back to Jack. "Take a walk. Take Maia." He juts his chin toward the door, then turns to the baseball game, dismissing us. I pull my hand from Jack's and go to my dad. I wrap my arms around his waist now and press my cheek into his musky sweatshirt.

"I love you, dad," I say, and he grunts in response. Then I grab my backpack, turn to Jack with a shy grin, and lead him out into the hallway.

As soon as we round the corner by the water fountain, I turn to face him. Jack leans me back against the painted cinder block wall, straddles my thighs, and lifts my chin, brushing my lips with his. My eyes close, and I stifle a groan. Why was I avoiding this guy? Good god. The electricity coursing up my spine stuns me, and every inch of my skin tingles.

When the kiss finally ends, I study the drawstring of his hood, not meeting Jack's gaze.

"I'm sorry," I say softly, leaning my forehead onto his chest, not sure which parts I'm apologizing for. The disastrous hike. Or not visiting Jack in the hospital. Or refusing to answer his most recent calls.

When rescue came, they airlifted my dad and Anna out first, then came back for me and Jack. I barely saw him in the chopper. The medics worked to get fluids into him, and Jack was unconscious the entire flight. That day is a blur I'd rather keep blocked out. Then in the following days, with the whole dad-on-death's-door situation, the thought of seeing Jack in a similar state flattened me. So I stayed away.

"I should have come to see you," I say now, looking up at Jack.

"Yes, you should have." He tucks a strand of hair behind my ear, grinning, then kisses me again and grabs my hand.

Outside, we snake our way along the crowded lunch-hour side-walks to a small park in the midst of the hospital grounds. A nurse sits on a concrete bench under a maple tree, eating a sandwich. A young woman in a wheelchair basks in the sun, casts on both legs, listening to music. We pick the bench furthest from the others. Once we're sitting, thighs touching, I zip open my backpack and pull out Jack's iPod.

"This is yours." Wrapping the earbud wires around the small white body, I hand it to him. "Thank you."

"Keep it. My dad bought me another one." Jack pushes the device back into my lap, then points to the gold bracelet peaking out from under my sleeve. "You wear it all the time?"

I nod, then tell him how it got ripped off my wrist just before I made the radio call. As soon as help was on the way, I had been desperate to extract the bracelet from between those barnacled rocks. Kaito and the other Japanese tourists had helped once they understood what I was trying to do. They'd sacrificed a metal fork, bending it into a hook and securing it with first aid tape to a stick. After many attempts, we maneuvered the bracelet from its resting place.

The clasp had been broken, so I clenched it in my fist as I hiked back to the ranger's yurt, exhausted but elated. And then for days, beside my dad's intensive care bed, the bracelet's delicate ovals imprinted into the skin of my palm. Holding it brought my mum's energy to me, her spirit and mine, together willing my dad to survive. Now, since I had the clasp fixed by a jeweler down the road, the bracelet wraps my wrist every day.

Telling him about the bracelet opens a dam and Jack listens intently as stories flood out of me. He asks about the bits he missed after he passed out on the beach. We talk for hours on that bench until the sun disappears behind a building and my stomach rumbles.

"Still always hungry, huh?" Jack grins up at me and I laugh. We head inside and share a quick bite in the hospital cafeteria. Then Jack walks me upstairs, says good night to my dad, and promises to come back in the morning. As the door closes behind Jack, my dad shakes his head and chuckles at my beaming face.

CHAPTER 41

It's a crisp, sunny September morning, two days before classes start. Jack grunts as he places a box onto the bare mattress in my dorm room.

"Is that all of them?" I turn from the tiny closet where I'm unpacking clothes onto painted plywood shelves.

"One more." Jack brushes past me, giving my bicep a squeeze before heading downstairs to his faded red Corolla. He had driven all the way up-island to help me move my stuff here. Our first road trip together.

Once his car was packed with my few boxes, I had been compelled to show Jack the beauty of the area. In sunlight. He'd only seen it at its worst, in a howling rainy gale. On our way down-island, I directed him off the two-lane highway where, at the end of a rough gravel road bordered by mossy tree trunks, we parked to hike beside a large lake, kilometers long. Before reaching the trail, we walked through a bustling camping area, where kids climbed trees, dogs roamed free and adults gathered in circles of lawn chairs, drinking coffee.

Beyond the campsite, the narrow trail hugged the rocky shore, then climbed onto a bluff, giving glimpses of the sparkling lake. Huckleberry bushes lined the path under the massive cedar trees, and sunlight streamed onto the mossy forest floor, releasing the sweet earthy scent of late summer. Jack had been completely at ease, swatting away the cobwebs and laughing when a squirrel suddenly chattered from the underbrush.

The wind picked up on our walk back from the point that afternoon, as a cool thermal rushed down the valley from the foggy coast. We sat on a crunchy, moss-covered ledge, shoulder to shoulder, while glistening windsurf sails danced across the rolling white caps below us. I explained the story of the timber in the distance to Jack — the dark green slopes of untouched old-growth, the silvery gray of recent clear cuts, and the lighter greens of newly planted trees. Colorful patches of working forest connected by granite ribbons of logging road where my dad will soon drive truck.

After the hike, we cooled off with an icy swim at the jumping rocks, then sunned ourselves on the blocky limestone formation that generations of kids have enjoyed. Jack had chuckled as he wrapped a towel around me, conceding that it doesn't *always* rain up here.

When Jack's hatchback wouldn't start at the lake, my doubts about his old car returned. Unworried, he showed me how to pop the hood and hit the starter motor while turning the ignition, using the wooden handle of a small sledgehammer kept under the driver's seat for just that purpose. Once the car started, it ran fine for the three-hour drive and ferry trip back over to the city, just as Jack had promised. He loves that beater, with all its quirks. The peeling paint has that dusty white hue of neglect. When you slam the driver's door, broken glass tinkles inside it, and the radio only works if the heater's on. But it gets him around, which is what matters.

Now I pull the last sweatshirt from the box I'm unpacking and unwrap a photo of our family. The three of us grinning, dad in the middle, his arms holding my mum and me close. We're on the beach where the cougar attack happened, but on a stunning bluebird day. The ocean behind us is glassy and the distant snow-capped mountains of the mainland accentuate the dark-blue cloudless sky. I finger our silhouettes as a smile tweaks my cheeks and my throat closes. Never to be recreated.

After my dad moved from intensive care to the burn unit, I came home from the city for the first time. My dad had put every reminder of my mum away, but I found this family photo in his dresser drawer. The journey back to town for clothes and essentials had been a welcome break from hospital rooms. I watered my mum's barely surviving house plants, then sat in the living room for the first time since The Last Day, and opened the stack of mail. The acceptance letter for this technical school was the last envelope on the pile, and it startled me. Since my dad's hospitalization, I'd been getting through day-to-day, giving no thought to the more distant future. But that letter prompted a whole series of decisions.

Right away, I walked over to Ms. Wells' house with the papers clenched in my fist. Of course, she was happy for me and insisted I accept right away. We filled out the paperwork together and she wrote a check for the entry deposit without flinching.

"I'll figure it out with your dad." She'd brushed off my protests.

I look down at the framed family photo now, my stomach fluttering. You can't be certain about things, I'm finding out, but you can be pretty sure. And I'm pretty sure coming to this school is the right thing. It's definitely the right thing for me. It's not really the right thing for my dad, but he's sorting himself out. His road to full recovery is still long, with more surgeries, splints, and physiotherapy. Back in town, forestry is picking up, and he's been offered a job driving truck. Not his favorite, but something he'll be well enough to do pretty soon. So I'm glad about that.

Of course, we had to cancel the rest of the kayak tours this season. Ms. Wells had helped with that, too. Our clients had been disappointed and concerned, especially the repeat customers who've gotten to know us over the seasons. I'm not sure what Ms. Wells told them, but many of them sent their deposit checks anyway, with notes wishing us well. They shared how much they had been looking forward to their trip and how sorry they were to hear about Maxi's death and our injuries. When you lay it all end to end, our family has had a pretty shit year. By any standard.

When I read my dad some letters that came with our clients' checks, he had laid his head back on the crunchy hospital pillow and sighed. "That's your mother. People person. And I guess they can afford it." He had grumbled under his breath, referring to some of our richest guests. My mum would have told him to take the money and shut up, which is pretty much what he did. Our customers' generosity helped us make ends meet this summer. I'm thankful for that, too.

Jack's footsteps thump up the dorm stairs now, and I watch his tall frame duck into my barren room. He's another thing I can't be certain about. I still don't trust what I have with Jack, especially when we're apart. Away from him, my mind concocts endless scenarios that result in him breaking up with me. Even though he's done nothing to make me think he would.

When Jack came by that first time, I finally asked about Liv. While we shared a sandwich in the hospital cafeteria, he explained she was the only reason he hadn't come sooner. It took Jack that long to make her believe their breakup was for good. "I knew Liv and I were finished. But it took her a while to catch up." Jack spoke with compassion for the hurt he caused her. "And I didn't want to drag you into my mess." Even with this evidence, it's hard for me to trust Jack really chose me.

Trust. The counselor Anna has me seeing says I've got to work on that. Loss in the past doesn't mean you'll keep losing in the future. But that's easier to say than it is to believe. On the other hand, the minute

Jack and I are together, all my doubts disappear. He's great. I mean, really, really great. A light at a time when I desperately need it.

"What can I do next?" Jack dumps the last box beside the others and bounces onto the mattress across from the heavy wood desk. Opposite the door and closet, windows rise above a painted metal heating unit, streaming sunshine across the mottled carpet. Jack hops up and wraps his arms around me from behind, leaning his chin on my shoulder. He reaches past me and picks up the family photo I just placed on the desk.

"You look alike." His gaze shifts between my face and the photo as he holds the frame up beside my head with a grin. It's the first time Jack's seen a picture of my mum. "Especially your smiles. Beautiful."

"Stop it," I say, batting the photo away. He grabs me around the waist with his free arm and kisses me.

"You better get used to me saying that, Maia-girl." He steps back, beaming at me. I'm afraid to get used to it. But I'm going to keep trying.

"Help me pile this stuff in the closet, then you can drop me off at my dad's." I smile, shaking my head, my insides relaxing.

CHAPTER 42

I pull open the glass door and step into the lobby of the burn fund office. The rushing bustle of Main Street silences behind me as the thick door swings closed, and I head past Linda, the receptionist, with a wave and a smile. Bounding up the stairs to the living units, I realize with a start that I waved with my scarred right hand. Huh. That's new — not hiding my injury constantly. Upstairs, the communal kitchen is empty. The other families must be at appointments over at the hospital. They're patients from out-of-town, too, who stay here when they come to the city for follow-up.

Down the hall, I knock lightly on the last door before letting myself in. The room is small, with light streaming through the wall of glass, which leads to a little private deck. My dad is lying on a lounger outside, ball cap over his face, napping in the sunshine. When I pull the sliding glass door open, he lifts the brim of his cap with a bandaged hand. I plop a bag of takeout on the round metal table and settle into a patio chair.

"How was it?" he asks roughly, swinging his feet to the concrete and sitting sideways on the lounger to face me.

"Perfect," I say, unable to suppress a grin. The campus had felt vibrant and exciting. My room might be tiny and spartan, but the windows overlook a patch of forest and I already love everything about it. "You'll have to come by. Next time you're down." He nods, looking down at his hands. My dad wanted to help me move, but carrying things is still a task he needs to avoid. For now. His rugged jaw clenches with frustration. The pace of his recovery is not as fast as he would like.

"What did the plastic surgeon say today?" I open the Chinese food and push a box toward him.

"She's happy." He clamps the fork against his bandaged hand with his thumb, wrestling the noodles. "Says my finger movement is good. Grafts look okay. Wants to do the next surgery in a couple months." I'm glad the doctor is happy with his progress.

"That's good news." I smile at him over my beef and broccoli. "You heading back on the first ferry tomorrow?" I ask, knowing the answer. He nods, turning toward the wail of a siren out on the busy street.

"Be glad to get home. Dunno how folks live here. All this noise." I laugh. We finish our food and I carry the takeout boxes inside to the garbage, where there are two paper coffee cups in the trash. Two...?

"Did Anna come by today?" I ask nonchalantly, pulling bottled waters from the mini-fridge. Dad shrugs, with a tiny sparkle in his eyes.

"Yeah. After her shift," he says, giving no other detail. I hand him a water, glad for whatever is going on between those two. Dad watches me for a moment longer, looking like he wants to say something. I sprawl across the patio chair, taking a deep breath and basking in the warm rays that embrace the city today. "I'm glad you got into that school." My dad speaks eventually, his voice gruff. "I haven't said so. But it's good." He twists the plastic cap off the water with his teeth. "Your mum would be proud. So I'm glad." His voice catches before he takes a drink.

I get up and stand behind him, wrapping my arms over his shoulders, then lean forward to kiss his stubbled cheek. "I love you, dad," I say softly, hugging him harder. Before this summer, I had never said those words. Not to anyone. We weren't that kind of family. But the weeks I spent by dad's hospital bed brought those words to the surface. I'm still so sorry I didn't say them to my mum on The Last Day, but I just hadn't known how. Hadn't had practice. So I had told my dad every day, while he was sedated in intensive care. Every hour. Every chance. I just willed him to hear those three words: I love you. And willed him to come back to me.

Now, my dad says nothing. Just lifts a giant paw to pat mine, leaning his cheek into me.

"I'll call you later," I say. He nods, laying back down on the lounger, shifting the brim of his greasy ball cap back over his eyes. I close the door behind me with a soft click. If he doesn't answer my call tomorrow, a freshly recorded message in my dad's rough tone will declare, "Not here. You know what to do!" I hop down the stairs, grinning. He phoned to tell me the answering machine tape with mum's message is now stored in the filing cabinet, with the rest of her important things. And he sounded proud to take this step forward.

I join the flow of pedestrians out on the busy sidewalk and walk to the corner cafe where I order two lattes, then grab a small table outside to wait. Anna had dragged me here the first time she visited after the rescue. When I was a lot more mixed up... well, a bit more mixed up... than I am now.

I've been hard to help, but Anna's relentless. After our chat on the couch in the burn unit's family room, she took me here for a change of scenery. I had barely finished my coffee when she hauled me back to the hospital, straight into the office of her colleague. Tracy is a counselor there, and she has been great. We talk about all of it. My dad. School. Jack. My mum.

There's a poster on Tracy's wall. Stick-figure faces express the five stages of grief. I've spent a lot of time at the red face, with angry eyes. Sometimes I move from the orange 'bargaining' face to the green 'acceptance' face. And some days I regress. It's a start. Slow progress.

Beyond the bustling sidewalk, I spot Jack plugging the meter for his well-loved Corolla. His bandages have been off for weeks, but below his shorts, the four coin-sized scars on his tanned calf are evident, even from here. I avert my eyes as my chest tightens, then touch the links of my bracelet. Instead of replaying that day on the beach, I picture my mum's letter and her belief in my moxie, like Tracy's been coaching me to do.

Raising my chin and pulling my shoulders back, I get up to wave Jack over, butterfly wings fluttering in my belly. His effect on me is still startling. When he turns, our eyes lock, and he stops in his tracks, a huge grin taking over his features. So help me, that smile! Then, in a few quick steps, he's lifting me off the ground in a massive hug.

Just this morning, Jack drove me to my dad's, but each meeting feels as wonderful as that first day in the hospital. I nuzzle into him, drinking his scent, wrapping my arms around his neck. There's so much ahead of us. I can't wait. For all of it.

NOTE FROM SYLVIA BOURGEOIS: Thank you for going on this adventure with me! If you enjoyed *True Moxie,* please consider telling a friend or posting a short review. It would mean a lot to me. Then, turn the page to read a FREE excerpt from another book in this series, *Here, Now!*

Island Echoes Series

Sylvia's **Island Echoes** novels are stand-alone stories featuring strong women in untraditional roles, celebrating the vibrant setting and industry of the Pacific Northwest, past and present.

Turn the page for a FREE excerpt of *Here, Now*!

HERE, NOW – CHAPTER 1

I've always preferred trees to people. The forest has a predictable rhythm, and doesn't judge or criticize. This afternoon, I will make history as the only woman in America to earn a Master's in Forestry. It's a day of celebration, but first I must survive a luncheon with Mother. Her outdated aspirations for me are simple: a church aisle and vows. But today she'll witness me at a different altar, my academic achievements replacing her traditional dream.

Outside Seattle's Olympic Hotel, an elegant couple ducks into a taxi under the enormous American flags flanking the ornate awning. I duck off the sidewalk and up the marble steps where the doorman pulls open the heavy door. I'm late for lunch with my parents and my new openwork pumps click across the terrazzo floor of the bustling lobby. Two stories above the well-dressed crowd, a 300-pound crystal chandelier sparkles. The room couldn't be farther from nature's hushed clarity, but the echoing grandeur runs a tingle up my spine.

Mother will detest everything about this day: the hateful hotel jazz, the arid academia, and my modern flared heel. I grin down at the gleaming black patent leather, kicking out from under my silky sheath dress with each hurried step. I spent almost four dollars on these shoes, and wearing something I love gives me a surprising satisfaction. Maybe I should have let Mother shop with me, but then I'd be in respectable shoes. I roll my shoulders back, shaking the self-doubt she instills. Today's celebration belongs to me and the Class of 1924. Mother ought to be pleased I didn't just polish my sturdy work boots.

At the tea room I announce myself, and a tuxedoed steward leads me to my parents. Mother nods, remaining seated, then comments on my paleness, eyeing my new shoes with a frown. Predictable, but still so irritating. Father heaves his large frame up, enveloping my small hand in his huge ones, his entire face shining with love, and I beam back. Without his sedate support, I would not have persevered to this graduation. He's gentle and supportive in every way Mother is stiff and severe.

We settle in, Mother's customary monologue beginning with the weather, which she declares to be typically west coast. My father and I murmur responses as she covers the family and neighbourhood news. Meals were so much easier when we were a table of four. Tony always redirected Mother's diatribes with easy humour, and the absence of my little brother's joyful spirit stabs at my stomach even more on special occasions.

Above us, palm fronds rustle in the carved, dark wood second-floor planters. From the corner, the piano player beats out "Maple Leaf Rag", muffling the drone of voices and the tinkling of silver. The upbeat ragtime reminds me of Thomas. He brought me to this hotel's public pre-opening a year ago, where he spun me into a lively foxtrot. It was a lovely night, before all the recent confusion between us. Mother and Father later attended the December opening gala, of course, as did many of Seattle's citizen bond-buyers. The city's older, wealthy crowd helped finance the hotel's ridiculous luxury, and demanded more subdued musical choices.

Mother glares over her shoulder, clucking her tongue and shaking her head. "I wish they wouldn't play this rag — it's indecent." She leans over, squinting at me. "You should get more rest. And stay out of the sun." Her fingers flutter off the table, as if she's going to brush the purple shadows under my eyes. But she deposits her hand back onto the white tablecloth, maintaining distance, and continues. "You know, most girls would kill for your natural dark curls and porcelain complexion. They wouldn't go traipsing in the bush, letting their hair frizz and skin freckle." She sighs, peering at the spots scattered across my nose and cheeks.

"Yes, Mother." Nodding in agreement, I work the tongs to drop a sugar cube into my tea, counting down seconds with a silent exhale. She pivots, sharing news that Alice, the daughter of a country-club friend, has applied for the front desk position at Father's car lot.

"Can you believe? It's so unbecoming for young ladies to work, especially those who needn't." Mother's lips pucker in distaste. Her comment refers to Alice, who works out of boredom, not need. But Mother's words are an attack on my goals, a topic she touches on every time we meet. Under the table, I clench my napkin, gritting my teeth. Next, she gushes about Alice's husband's promotion, which he secured because the woman in that position got married. Her wedded state caused her firing. I raise my eyebrows, unable to restrain my disbelief. My mother's bias against progress and women's independence is infuriating. But she's saved from my response by the returning steward. He places a silver platter in the centre of the table and removes the cloche cover with a great flourish, revealing an enormous selection of tea sandwiches.

The smell of sardines, olives, and pumpernickel wafts over me from the tray and a queasiness fills my throat. I look away from my parents, pretending to admire the architecture, swallowing down the bile. My brain scrambles to find a logical excuse, but the mounting evidence is pointing to just one cause of this daily ailment. I quash these thoughts, unclenching a fist from my crumpled napkin and laying my palm against my lower belly. No. Not today. Tomorrow. I'll think about it tomorrow.

"There's a handsome new fellow working for your father. As manager. His name is Harold." Mother smiles her match-making smile as she expands on Harold's attributes and how well my father's car lot is doing. "He's a Hewitt. Good family. Right, Jim?" My mother looks pointedly at my father, who's been working through the sandwich tray. He swallows a salmon bite, sensing commentary on his never-ending appetite. So he answers amiably.

"Harold's doing a fine job. Fine job." Father nods at both of us, leaning back against the velvet chair. "Going to be the best month since the Great War, June is. A good month." Father smiles and reaches for a tigereye sandwich. "We can thank those speedy new Buick roadsters, we can." Mother expects my father to say more, but when he doesn't, she lists the new engagements her golf friends have reported. So many daughters doing what's expected of them. After detailing the plans for four summer weddings, she dabs her lips with a napkin. Her critical gaze lingers on my hands, where the gritty traces of my beloved spruce seedlings stain my fingernails.

"Honestly, Eva! Your hands. It'll be a wonder if you ever get married. Why won't you wear gloves?" Mother's exasperated question punctuates her list of not-so-subtle critiques of my life. My back stiffens and I start to reply, no longer willing to contain my exasperation. But Father catches my eye, raising a glass of Virginia julep. I clamp my lips shut, drawing in a slow, steady breath. There's nothing to be gained by speaking my truth.

"To Eva. And her education. And her firsts. We wish you well, my girl." Father's toast diffuses the tightness in my chest and we clink our frosted glasses. I move the mint sprig onto my side plate and savour the lemony sweet cider mix. After his first sip, Father shakes his head in disgust. Five years of prohibition and he still can't stomach the fruity replacements respectable establishments are forced to serve.

"Thank you, Father." The lump in my throat surprises me. Mother has showered me in criticism, but Father's acknowledgement saves the tenor of the day, and I'm grateful. My choice of profession has puzzled scholars, colleagues, and friends. They don't understand my connection to the land. Nature is authentic and unpretentious, never imposing norms. It's people who put up barriers where they're not needed. Today, I celebrate the tenacity that got me here. Setting my mother straight can wait for another time.

Here, Now – Chapter 2

Father guides his sparkling new 1924 Buick touring car from downtown Seattle to the lush green grounds of Washington University. This morning's drizzle leaves the cobblestones damp and the gloomy skies match Mother's expression. Once we've parked, the rumbling six-cylinder silenced, I gladly leave my parents and walk to the College of Forestry's stone, ivy-covered building. In the first-floor lobby, my classmates gather, donning black gowns. Our group is small, with only twelve students receiving degrees this year.

The boys pause when I enter, greeting me with wolf whistles. They've only seen me in faded trousers and worn work boots, nothing like this lacy silk sheath. I shake my head, laughing off their brotherly comments on how well I clean up. Already wearing their plain black gowns, they jostle each other in front of the mirror, securing their mortarboards and placing the russet-brown tassels carefully on the right.

I feel Thomas's gaze on me before I turn around. He looks stunning in his gown, the russet hood framing his dark features and bringing out the gold in his hazel eyes. I hate that he makes my heart skip. Today signifies many changes. I can't imagine not seeing Thomas every day. We've been colleagues for years, and other than Millie, he's still my closest friend. But on Monday, he starts work in a downtown office, for his father's lumber business, whereas I have yet to land a job. A heaviness returns to my chest.

"How was it?" Thomas asks, his features softening. He knows I just had lunch at the Olympic Hotel with my parents, and how awful my mother can be. "Looks like you survived." His gaze lingers on my new shoes and sheath dress before his eyes meet mine, sending another buzz beneath my skin. I look away, taking the gown he's holding out for me. The russet hood matches his, since we're the only two from our college graduating with a Master's today.

"Draining," I say. Thomas chuckles at my exasperated tone as I wriggle into the gown and smooth it over my dress. "But the hotel is gorgeous. Ridiculously opulent. And stunning." Thomas hands me my cap, as I tuck stray fronds of my dark, wavy locks behind my ears. The mortarboard is floppy and difficult to place, but soon we agree we're both presentable. Thomas looks at me a little too long, head tilted and his jaw clenched. His soft eyes have lost their laughter, now looking hollow and I feel heat rising up my neck. I wish we could turn back the clock, to change that troublesome night and his subsequent proposal. Before those events a few months ago, there were never awkward silences or pained glances with Thomas.

When one of the boys announces it's time, our jovial group walks toward the indoor pavilion. Thomas keeps pace next to me, but we're both quiet, speaking only when the chatter of our classmates is direct- ed at us. I wonder if Thomas is also considering how a portion of our everyday life is ending today. His camaraderie has been a steady com- fort, and there was a moment I thought I wanted more. He's smart, handsome, and finds my penchant for order amusing. But I need to establish my career before I consider marriage. Without thinking, I press my palm against my middle. Then I wrinkle my nose, burying the heaviness that fills me whenever I relive that day. Straightening, I meet Thomas's gaze again, but he doesn't return my smile.

We enter the pavilion through the back entrance with other excited graduates. A temporary wooden floor covers the dirt of the arena where we sit on folding chairs in rows beside a stage. Our friends and family face us from the stands, usually filled with sports fans. We settle into our class's designated seats and I scan the crowd for my parents. When I catch my father's eye, he grins and nudges Mother. She acknowledges me with a nod but quickly turns back to a woman in a fashionable hat beside her, who's introducing a young man in uniform. As he rises to take mother's hand, she stiffens visibly, clutching her other palm against her breastbone. She sees my brother Tony in that soldier.

Tears prickle as Tony fills my thoughts again. He should be sitting up there with my parents, celebrating my triumph, like he did the summer he taught me to ride his bike. Our birthdays were just a week apart, and I had begged for a bicycle. But it was Tony, the boy, who received one. Even at nine years old, I was discouraged from adventurous, unladylike pursuits. Unwrapping a baby doll with real eyelashes, I stifled the urge to throw it across the room. But Tony saw my defeat and dragged me outside, tackling my frustration.

As a lanky preteen, my brother jogged alongside me with a wide grin, holding the padded leather seat of his shiny blue two-wheeler. I wobbled, fell, and skinned my knees. But Tony cajoled me until I shook it off and got up, gaining confidence under his unwavering encouragement. When I finally balanced and the world around me became a blur of sunlit greenery, his cheer echoed through the quiet neighbourhood. I'll never forget his infectious laugh and the pride on his face as he patted me on the back. If only he were here now. My big brother would support me through this mess I've gotten myself into.

The lights dim and I'm drawn back to today's ceremony. It begins with the valedictorian speech by a fellow I don't recognize. As students from other colleges walk across the stage, I clap absently, mind wandering. My gaze lands on my mother, who's scanning the crowd. A sharp pain stabs my chest. She was so proud of Tony. His quirky grin and endless energy were easy to love. Mother's still trying to understand how she raised such a tomboy. She deserves a daughter who gushes over the latest fashion and delights in whispered gossip. Instead, she got me, who prefers tromping alone through towering cedars in grubby overalls. I wonder how she'll twist today's events into a tale suited for her country-club.

Finally, it's our class's turn and I applaud the boys loudly. Thomas and I are last, and when my name is announced, I carefully cross the stage in the blazing spotlights. As I smile and shake our Dean's hand, accepting my diploma, Thomas's wolf whistle penetrates the roar in my ears. I flash him a grin over my shoulder, but see only the glare of electric lights. Standing tall, I beam at the audience, expanding my lungs to their fullest through a deep, satisfied breath. From the shadows, my father's cheer rises above the rest. Off stage, I pause at the bottom of the steps, feeling dizzy, gripping the stair rail with a trembling hand. Things are moving too quickly. My shoulders curl forward and I try to swallow the ache in my throat.

Behind me, Thomas's name is announced, and I force myself to turn. He smiles and waves at the stands where his mother claps enthusiastically, her heavy diamond bracelet glinting in the faint light. She is impeccably dressed; her feathered cloche hat and luxurious fur stole befitting a woman of her means. I look for Thomas's father, but expect his absence. He'll be at work, managing his lumber empire. Mrs. Clark catches Thomas's eye and blows him a kiss, her intricately beaded dress shimmering and a proud smile filling her face.

He hops down the steps, stopping to offer his elbow with a grin. The gesture loosens the lump in my throat, and I laugh. As he guides me back to our seats, I consider the canyon-sized gap between my mother and Thomas's. Mrs. Clark exudes modern sophistication, whereas Mother, just a few rows away, emanates a deliberate conservatism in her dark hues and modest pearls.

Soon after we take our seats in the folding chairs, the University President makes his final address. As the speech ends, his voice breaks through the fog in my head. He's saying something I've heard before.

"...reach for the stars, but don't forget to recognize opportunities that are right in front of you." The President's loud monotone drones, and beside me Thomas stiffens. He had used the same words the night of his heartfelt proposal, trying to convince me that feeling safe and whole with another person *is* love. His plea then, to see what's right in front of me, was an echo of the President's phrase now. My fists clench in my lap and a surge of sickness hits me, uncontrollable this time. I stand abruptly, pushing past my classmates into the darkened aisle, and stagger toward the back door of the pavilion.

I burst through the heavy doors and into the bright sunlight before I double over, crouch, and heave next to a towering fir. My palm grips the rough bark as tea and sandwich bits hit the grass. I pull a handkerchief from my pocket, dread clenching my gut. Slumping onto the lawn, I lean back against the trunk, eyes closed. This tree is a *Pseudotsuga menziesii*. I repeat the scientific name over and over in my mind. Picturing the quirky genus and species words signals how agitated I am. I've had this habit as long as I can remember, complicated syllables distracting my thoughts from my choking anxiety. *Pseudotsuga menziesii*, I think, slower now, taking another deep breath of the fresh summer air. My head is ringing, but my belly feels better. Then the crunch of gravel makes me squint toward the sky.

Thomas stands a few feet away, his brows narrowing in concern as he moves closer. When he sees the mess in the grass, his lips purse.

"Are you alright? Are you sick?" Thomas kneels beside me, his eyes searching my face. He leans forward, hands inches from me. But I refuse his help with a raised palm.

"Don't. I'm fine. It's nothing."

"You're not fine. Let me—"

"Don't." My voice sounds harsh and I close my eyes again, needing to block out the comprehension flashing across his face. I've been able to read his thoughts for years. And he thinks I'm pregnant.

Get your copy of **Here, Now** *today. Scan the QR code below to go to Sylvia's website. Or search your favourite app or bookstore.*

Thank you for being a reader!

Get a FREE copy of Maia's sketchbook by visiting me at

www.sylviabourgeois.com

About the Author

Sylvia Bourgeois grew up on northern Vancouver Island, in some of British Columbia's most beautiful small communities. Sylvia now lives in Fanny Bay and considers her family, friends, and time outside to be most important to her. When she isn't working her day job or on a boat with her husband, you can find her creating fine foods in her kitchen. She loves to hear from her readers. Visit her at www.sylviabourgeois.com and click now on her Instagram for a colourful glimpse into her life.

BOOKS BY SYLVIA BOURGEOIS

True Moxie

Here, Now

instagram.com/sylviabourgeois/